The Way You Love Me

The Sullivans of Montana,
Book Two

CHERYL BARTON

Published by: Cheryl Barton Publishing, LLC

For permission requests, write to the publisher, addressed to: "Attention: Permissions Coordinator," at the address below.
Cheryl Barton Publishing, LLC
P.O. Box 217
Abingdon, Maryland 21009
www.crbarton.com
Ordering Information:
Quantity sales.
Special discounts of this novel are available on quantity purchases by corporations, associations, and others. For details, contact the publisher at the address above. For orders by U.S. trade bookstores and wholesalers, please contact
prez@crbarton.com
ISBN: 978-1-948950-23-7

Hello Readers,

Thank you so much for staying with me on my writing journey. In 2020, we have all been through a lot. It is my hope that I can bring a bright spot to your lives with a little bit or a whole lot of romance. I have been just as distracted as so many others and haven't been doing as much writing as I would like, but I'm happy to bring you book two of *"The Sullivans of Montana"*, *The Way You Love Me.*

This story is a heartwarming path to an unexpected love. Gizelle Duncan is a woman who has been through a lot with the wrong man and then she meets a cowboy, Perry Sullivan, who sets out to show her what *real* love from a *real* man looks and feels like. His love follows the, from the heart, deep, passionate kind of love you found in book one of the series, *Home for Thanksgiving*, Nick Sullivan and Parker Wingate's forever story.

Come on in, find a quiet place to read, shut out the mayhem happening in the world right now and indulge in some heart pleasing love!

Thank you for allowing me into your life and my stories into your heart. Let's follow the love, together.

Happy Reading,
Cheryl

Prologue

Perry Sullivan pulled his black, six-door, Ford F650 truck into the parking lot of the *Steely Gray*, Bozeman, Montana's most popular and hottest bar and grille in town. He peered out of the truck window at the blue and green neon sign that sat atop the three story, red brick building covered with frozen icicles and remembered times years ago, when he and his brothers would sneak inside, though they weren't old enough to legally be inside of the establishment where alcohol was served like water from faucets. Years later, it was still Bozeman's number one hang out spot, especially with all of the upgrades the new owner, Ivan, made over the past few years, including buying the buildings on both sides of the original location, which now included and end of the block location and using the two levels above the main level as more than just storage space.

The *Steely Gray* now sported a much larger dance floor on the main level and the addition of a second dance floor on the second level. The top floor now included additional dining, not as large of a space as on the first floor, but still, where the first level accommodated twenty or thirty tables, the top floor captured a more intimate setting with tables fifteen or so, tables for two. He added an expanded kitchen and menu options, making this the place to be, especially on a Friday night.

After working all week, people left their jobs in their car rearview mirrors until after the weekend and looked forward to partying and drinking until they cleared their minds of the stressful week they'd just gone through. Unlike them, Perry thought of how his work of running a multi-million-dollar animal, farm and entertainment ranch never stopped on a Friday, but was a seven day a week, twenty-four hours a day job. Despite that, he was finding time to get away from work, even if just for a few hours, to enjoy the atmosphere of beautiful women, beer, food and some of the best live entertainment in the state, not just Bozeman.

As he parked and exited the truck, Perry found himself stepping out into the freezing cold January night, two weeks after the new year had begun. He grabbed his staple black Stetson Men's Diamante 1000X Fur Felt cowboy hat from the passenger seat and slipped it on his head. Zipping up his black leather bomber jacket while making sure no one noticed, he looked around for that familiar silver

Toyota Camry, owned by Gizelle Duncan, the only woman who could get him out every Friday just so that he could encounter her beauty. Over the past few weeks, he'd fallen hard for her and he was enjoying seeing her even if neither one of them admitted that there was an obvious attraction. He could tell that there was something going on in her life that gave him pause about approaching her the way he usually would a woman he was interested in. If he never had patience before, he was a professional at it since meeting Gizelle. She was more than just beautiful to him. Beautiful women came a dime a dozen and he'd encountered them from all walks of life, but Gizelle was different. He didn't only desire her in the way he'd begun settling for with women when he decided to leave his heart of out getting to know them and instead going with satisfying his body's need to be buried deep inside of them. With Gizelle, he saw much more, something he hadn't felt in a long time.

Not seeing her car, he shook off the fact that usually when he arrived, well after most people were already inside and partying, he would see her car and get excited that he'd soon see her inside, hopefully joining him at his favorite table.

Entering the front entrance, he spoke to and greeted the security guys, all who knew him and then walked right in and headed toward the table in the back that he knew would be empty. Being friends with the manager, Cassius Law, someone he's known since their childhood, he knew whatever time he showed up, Cassius wouldn't let anyone sit at the table that had been deemed the Sullivan table, for him and his brothers.

The loud music greeted him along with a larger than usual crowd on the dance floor. All of the tables for dining were filled up and he had no doubt, the other two floors were packed with patrons as well.

He smiled and greeted everyone who waved and called out his name. There weren't too many people in Bozeman or even the surrounding counties or states that didn't know any of the Sullivan clan, especially him as the oldest. All of his brothers, had at one time or another, been at the club. There was Shelton, the next closest to him in age and the family's financial wizard who lived in Bozeman, but not on the ranch where Perry himself lived. Shelton, instead, preferred to live in his downtown condo far from the watchful eye of their parents, Marta and David Sullivan. Shelton was the party animal of their crew and was known for his wild parties and he knew that the family ranch was not the place to carry out his many affairs or entertain with the frequency with which he wanted to, out of respect for their mother.

Next to Shelton was Nicholas or Nick, as they called him. After leaving Bozeman to find himself, he had recently returned home to recover from injuries sustained in a fire in New York where he lived and worked at a local fire station. Thanks to their mother, who none of them second guessed or questioned, Nick recuperated in Bozeman and after meeting the love of his life, Parker Wingate, one of the ranch's veterinarian's, he made the decision to stay in Bozeman and had recently been offered the job of fire chief in Bozeman.

After Nick, there is Dayton, a nationally known, professional race car driver, who didn't make it back to Bozeman as often as their family would like, but when he did, his reputation as a lady's man, like that of his brothers often brought him to the *Steely Gray* where there was never a shortage of women looking to be the next to say she'd experienced the prowess of one of the Sullivan boys. Their mother hated that her sons had a reputation with women that was well known, but she conceded that there was nothing she could do about it and had always demanded that even in their casualness in dealing with women, they still give them the ultimate respect and not walk all over them or treat them like property. None of them ever had and never would.

Pulling up the end of the Sullivan clan was their baby sister, Brielle, who he still prayed hadn't let men like him and his brothers get close to her. He would kill any man who thought that he could use their sister as a play thing. He and his brothers never disrespect women, but they had some stories to tell and any time they looked left or right in a group of women, there was always at least one in the crowd that one of them had bedded. Even knowing that, women still made a play for them and couldn't wait to share that they'd been taken by one of them.

Finally taking his seat, he looked around to see if Gizelle had arrived and perhaps rode with her friend, Heather, a woman she came out with on Fridays. To his surprise and disappointment, he didn't see her anywhere. He knew that meant she wasn't there because if she was, he automatically connected to her aura, he was in-tuned to everything about her, especially her presence. He wondered what happened to her? She never missed a Friday night.

He thought back to a few days ago when he'd called her on the phone and they had talked for hours well into the night. He couldn't remember the last time he'd been that comfortable with a woman where he was able to let down the guard around his heart that had been built up with steel after his last relationship with Veronica that had been heading toward marriage. He thought she was happy knowing not only that they were I love, but that she would have the desires of her heart as his wife. Money was in plenty, but that turned out to not be enough for her.

Veronica hated his life as a rancher, even though he was rich, something he knew was top on her list for a husband. She also wanted a life away from Bozeman and thought that he loved her enough to take his money and run off to the life she wanted someplace else. He did love her, but he loved his family and his life in Bozeman more – a sign that they were not meant to be. His feelings for Gizelle had far surpassed what he felt for Veronica and he hadn't even kissed her, let alone anything else. For him, being this into a woman without any kind of a relationship was a first and he was interested in seeing where it would lead. For the first time, he was willing to follow the pace he wanted her to set if she was as interested in him as he was in her. He wanted more than someone he had casual sex with. The feelings he felt were running deeper than that.

Perry had actually begun to worry as more time went by and she hadn't arrived. His table, though in the back, still gave him a clear view of the front entrance and every time the door opened, he looked toward it to see if Gizelle had arrived. To his disappointment, there were a lot of women, but none were Gizelle. He had been at the table about thirty minutes, and the usual trail of women approached him and flirted or either asked him to dance. Even those he'd had a night or two of sweaty sex came by looking for a repeat. Any other time, he may have taken a few of them up on their offer, but to his own surprise, Gizelle is who he wanted; no other woman would do.

Looking toward the door of the club as it opened again, he stood when he saw Nick enter. He'd called earlier to say he was hoping they could get a beer or two after work and Perry told him where he would be, which was no surprise.

As Nick made his way toward the table, Perry shook his head at the number of women who followed Nick's every move, no doubt contemplating if they'd be able to go home with him later that night. He was the one Sullivan boy that the women had heard about, but had not seen in a long time. Word had gotten out that Nick was in love with Parker, which appeared to make women even more interested in him. Perry greeted him with their usual fist bump followed by a tight hug.

"I see you still got it even as an engaged man," Perry said before sitting back down.

"What? Got what?" Nick asked, sitting in the seat next to him where they could both see all the action around the entire bar.

"You don't even notice it anymore, do you? You're so head over heels in love that you can't even spot women wondering if you'll pick them."

When Nick laughed out loud, Perry joined him as the waitress walked up to their table.

"The usual, Mr. Perry?" she asked.

"Usual? You have a usual? How often do you come here?" Nick joked.

"Don't worry about me. I'm surprised you're out tonight and not keeping Parker pinned in bed. Sandy, bring us six Coronas. We're going to have dinner tonight too, so can you bring back a couple of menus? I feel like a steak tonight!" Perry said.

"That sounds like a winner – Corona and a steak!" Nick added.

As Sandy walked away, Perry glanced at the entrance when the door opened and was let down again when Gizelle didn't walk in.

"So, are you going to tell me about having a regular drink here?" Nick asked. "I didn't realize you hung out here often enough for someone to know what you liked to drink. There must be a woman involved."

Perry started to deny the assumption, but he didn't and he knew there was no need to. He and Nick have always been close, even during the time when he lived in New York. It was him and their father who had flown to the city to check on Nick after finding out about the fire and the fact that he had been injured. They shared a lot over the years and if he could tell anyone about Gizelle, it was him.

"Gizelle."

That was all Perry needed to say and when he spotted Nick shaking his head, there wasn't a need for much more.

"She's beautiful and sexy? How is she in bed?"

He wanted to kick Nick's chair over for making that kind of comment, but he knew what he said was nothing new when it came to banter between them as brothers. Nick couldn't know that what he was feeling for Gizelle was more than that.

"Yes, she's beautiful and sexy and as far as how

she is in bed, I wouldn't know and if I did, I wouldn't tell you."

When he saw Nick's surprised look, Perry was surprised at himself at how overprotective he was of Gizelle and she wasn't even his woman; at least not yet.

"Whoa. What's that about?"

"She's different," Perry admitted.

"She's special?"

"Yeah, she is."

"She's not one of those women you take to your condo and end the night with flowers, a thank you and a big smile on her face?"

"No, not even close. Can you believe all I've done is talked to her, and we've talked a lot, but nothing else?"

"Are you ill? What the hell is your problem? Wait, don't tell me you're in love. Bro, what is the deal?" Nick exclaimed.

"I don't know if I'm in love, but I definitely see her as more than a friend-with-benefit."

Perry watched Nick look around.

"Is she here? I need to meet this woman who has my big brother all hemmed up. You haven't been that way since Veronica, who I'm glad you finally saw the light about."

"She's not here, but she usually is. We don't say we're meeting up or having a date, but we just end up here on Friday nights and we flirt the entire time. We then go our separate ways. I call her, she calls me – we text and we enjoy getting to know each other and I was hoping she would be here tonight, but so far, I haven't seen her. She's usually here before I get here. I guess she made other plans for tonight."

"Damn! Look at you acting like a sad puppy!" Nick laughed.

"Whatever man. I know you're not talking the way Parker speaks and you hang on her *every* word!"

"True. I'm not making fun of you, I swear I'm not. I'm actually saying I understand. Why haven't you made any real moves with Gizelle? What's holding you back?"

Perry leaned closer to not speak too loud as the waitress returned with their beers and menus.

"There is something going on with her and I get the vibe that she's not ready for moving to the next step and I don't mean sex; I mean actually being in a relationship."

"You're ready for that?"

Perry knew what he meant. When his two-year long relationship with Veronica ended six months ago, he told everyone that he had no plans of being that involved with another woman any time soon. He preferred casual relationships with women with an understanding that he wouldn't be making any promises of forever. Somewhere, in getting to know Gizelle, his mindset had changed and he welcomed it.

"With her, I am."

"Why do you think she's not ready?"

"I get a vibe of hesitation on her part. Just when I think we're getting close, I feel her pulling away."

"Maybe something in her past is affecting her when it comes to relationships. You know how that can be. Talk to her and let her know where you are and then ask her out on a real date."

"That's definitely in my plans. I knew you and I were meeting for dinner and drinks tonight, but I was going to see if she wanted to have dinner one night over the weekend. I was planning to approach the idea of she and I seeing each other for more than casually running into each other here at the *Steely Gray*."

"Maybe she's just running late. Let's get our eat on and we'll keep an eye out for her. I can't wait to meet her. I don't know anything about her, but I know how you are with women and if you're into her like I think you are, she's definitely special."

Perry nodded and looked down at his menu. He had spoken to Gizelle the day before and she had been looking forward to her usual Friday night out with her friend who she worked with as a receptionist at a law firm. He wondered what could be keeping her from showing up. Something didn't sit well with him. He couldn't place his finger on it, but he was getting an uneasy feeling and he didn't like it. He was actually worried. If she didn't show up, he would make sure to check on her in case she was ill. The cold winters brought with it the flu and frequent colds.

Shaking off his worry, he placed his order and cracked open his first beer of the night.

"How are the wedding plans going?" Perry asked. It was time to change the subject and enjoy connecting with his brother while forcing himself, as best he could, to not worry about Gizelle. In the back of his mind, he still wondered where she was.

1

Gizelle Duncan sat behind the steering wheel of her beat up silver Toyota Camry, cringing at the incessant banging which seemed to rock the car back and forth due to the strength behind the pounding, first on the window and then on the hood. She couldn't believe this was her life. Horror fused through her body as terror took over every part of her being. She feared for her life and that of her two small children who were in the back in their car seats screaming in fear at the unknown. They were too young to yet understand the kind of rage occurring outside of the car.

At age four, her daughter Carrie struggled with the straps of the seat that kept her in place as she tried to get out and climb in the front seat. Her son, Brody, at age three didn't know what was going on, but his sister's screams seemed to cause his own howls and Gizelle was left wondering what to do next. She felt helpless as their little arms reached out to her and for the moment, she couldn't do anything. They were safer staying in their seats. She wanted to drive off as fast as she could and get as far away as she could, but they were stuck; she couldn't save them from her ex-husband, Clyde Duncan, who would most certainly cause her great harm if he were able to get the car doors opened. She knew what would happen if the banging stopped and he got his hands on her. The harm he would inflict would be worse than any of the beatings she'd taken from him in the past when they had been married. The pounding would change from the car taking the hits to her getting them and she'd had enough of being his punching bag.

Looking out of the driver's side window, she saw the rage that had consumed Clyde which got worse the longer she ignored his demands to let him in. For now, she was too scared to even move and cursed her car again and again for not starting because the combination of the cold and snow that was Bozeman in the winter and a psycho ex-husband who was able to track her down, was deadly. She tried to think of her next move, but the pounding interrupted her ability to think clearly. Each hit to the ratted old Toyota would soon lead to him breaking in and she had to decide what to do and make that decision quickly.

"Open the door, Gizelle!" Clyde hollered over and over. "You know it will be worse for you the longer you make me stand out here in the cold and snow banging on the window of this piece of crap car of yours. Open this door, now!" he yelled at her again.

She jumped every time he hit the car and with hands that shook uncontrollably, she got her wits about her and worked frantically to get the car to start by turning the key but hearing nothing – not even a small attempt of her car trying to start. To say she was stunned that out of the blue, he had shown up in Bozeman, Montana unexpectedly, where she now lived, would be an understatement.

After running away from him and her past life eight months ago, she had a feeling one day she'd look up and see him, but months had gone by without any contact after leaving him in Chicago after their divorce. She thought it was safe to believe that he didn't care that she'd left him, taken their kids and moved to another state, one where he would never suspect she would move to. Bozeman was a beautiful city, but the winters were worse than Chicago and she always complained about how much she hated it there because of the weather.

Her mind raced between wondering how he found her and how he knew where she would be at this very moment. She'd been in contact with the few people she knew in Chicago to inquire about Clyde looking for her and none of them said that he'd contacted them about her whereabouts. She assumed if he would ask anyone, he would have started with the few people he allowed her to be around when they were married and that wasn't a lot of people. She did, at least, think that they were loyal knowing what her life with him had been like. There was no way she was going back to that. She had to get away; she had no other choice. If she opened the door, he would make her regret not only leaving him, divorcing him and taking their kids with her, but for also making him beg for her to open the door. Clyde had too much pride to beg anyone for anything.

Determined, she went between turning the key again and again and pressing her foot over and over on the gas pedal praying it would start. For now, the locks were holding strong, but she knew that wouldn't keep Clyde on the outside of the car for long.

She looked in the rearview mirror as the cries coming from her children grew even louder. Gizelle composed herself, knowing she had to show them calm in order for them to calm down.

"Carrie, Brody, I promise mommy is going to get us away real soon. Everything is going to be okay," she said plastering on a smile strictly for their benefit. Inside, she was screaming as loud as they were. Clyde was scaring them enough and she didn't need to add to it. She wanted to ease their three and four-year-old minds, but it wasn't working. The rage coming from the outside of the car was all they could focus on. She wished she could crawl in the backseat to comfort them and she would as soon as she could get them a safe distance away. She needed him to stop.

"Go *away*, Clyde! Can't you see you're scaring the

children?" she screamed at him without looking out of the side window. She knew from his words what his face looked like. She'd seen it many times before. She kept her eyes focused on the long driveway in front of the she was renting and the road at the end of it that could be her saving grace if she could get to it. If she had her cell phone with her, she would have called the police, but she'd left it inside of the house on the bed where Brody had been playing with it. They were in the car about to head to the store when she realized she needed to go back in and get it. Just as she was about to get back out of the car, Clyde came out of nowhere and scared her. She hadn't noticed the car tracks in the thin layer of snow on her driveway or his car parked on the side of her house. She had been focused on getting the kids in the car and in their seats.

She had started her day happy that she had two days off from work just before the weekend and was planning some fun activities for the kids. They were heading to Walmart to get food and supplies for arts and crafts and then Clyde happened. No matter how much he screamed, she was not going to voluntarily open the door. She knew he meant it when he said how much worse it would be for her if she didn't open the car door, but she didn't care. She didn't care about herself, she cared about the life of her children.

"Do *not* make me angrier, Gizelle. I'm s*erious*! Open this door right now and let me in. This car of yours is not going to start, there is no one around and you can't stay here in this car forever," he shouted.

Gizelle thought she'd finally found some peace even if it was far away from everyone she knew and loved. Still, she'd let her guard down and now she was reliving her life in Bozeman with an abusive man who took his frustrations in dealing with life out on her. She had to get away before he turned his rage onto the kids, something she would never tolerate. Now, she was in a predicament where their safety was at risk. She'd gambled wrong thinking he wouldn't find them. She'd wagered incorrectly when she thought that out of sight meant out of mind for him and he would move on to one of the many other women he was spending time with in and out of bed that he thought she didn't know about. She may not have known about them all, but knowing about even one woman was enough for her.

"Just go away and leave us be. Carrie and Brody don't need to see this kind of fighting between us. As they're getting older, they will remember all of this. Why can't you just leave us *alone*? You never spent time with the kids when we lived together. You said yourself that you never wanted me to have them anyway and I gave you the freedom you said you wanted. Go back to Chicago and leave us alone!" she cried out loud, ignoring the pain in her hands as she hit the steering wheel again and again. Even the horn didn't work or she could draw attention from someone driving on the road beside her house. Nothing seemed to be in her favor.

When she looked out of the window at him again, the sinister look on his face had her physically shaking. He looked like a madman with his eyes bulging out and even with the freezing temperatures outside, she could see that he wasn't fazed by the ice on the window as he snaked his tongue out and licked across the glass. Thinking he was going to punch through it, she prepared herself and waited. What she saw instead was Clyde walking away from the car. He wasn't the smartest tack in the box, but he knew how to scheme. How could she have missed the tire tracks that were so visible now that she was in the car? She was careless after months of being on guard.

Looking through all of the windows of the car, she couldn't see him anywhere because the frost and ice from overnight made seeing out hard beyond a few inches. She could see enough to track Clyde's movements and saw the impression his boots made in the snow. He'd made so many tracks that she didn't know which ones to follow to know where he went. Still, she was afraid to get out of the car. He may not be where she could see him, but there was no doubt that he was still close by. She took the time to try and calm her crying kids in the back of the car.

"Mommy!" Carrie cried out.

"I know, honey. Shhhh," she offered trying to soothe them both. Brody had quieted only because he stuck his thumb in his mouth to self-soothe, a habit he'd stopped once they'd moved to Bozeman. She watched in horror as Carrie tried to get out of her car seat while reaching for the car door.

"I'm scared of daddy and Brody is crying! I wanna get out!" Carrie yelled.

"I know. Mommy is scared too, but we'll get out of here as soon as I can get the car started."

"I want to go in the house, mommy. Why is daddy so scary?" Carrie asked.

"I know he is, but I'm going to get us out of here in just a few minutes. I need to get the car started and we're going to go someplace far away from daddy, okay?"

"Okay, mommy."

"Hold your brother's hand, okay? I need you to be a big girl and help mommy."

"Okay," Carrie said and Gizelle smiled at her when Carrie reached over and took Brody's hand into hers. He continued sucking his thumb, but he appeared to calm instantly from her touch. That gave Gizelle some peace, even if it would be short lived.

Turning back around, she looked through all of the windows again and still, there was no sign of Clyde. She knew he was lurking around and would jump out of his hiding place the minute she tried to get out of the car with the kids to go in the house. She didn't want to play his game. Exhaling, she said a silent prayer and tried once again to start the car and all she got was a bunch of ticking again and again. Crying inwardly, she didn't want the kids to see anything but a smile on her face in order to keep them from freaking out as they did when Clyde first approached the car. Her mind raced to how her life could have gone this wrong when at one time, she was happy and having fun, which had all changed the moment she'd run off with Clyde to Las Vegas and had a quickie wedding after only knowing him a few short weeks. Her family didn't like him, especially because of the seven-year age difference. She liked that he was older, but she quickly learned that older didn't mean more mature. He was a wild, party-hopping, beer-guzzling, life of party kind of guy with a bad boy reputation and she knew that it was that reputation that attracted her to him. Unlike the fun guy she thought she had fallen for, he'd turned into a nightmare.

How could she have been married to a man like him? What had she been thinking? She knew what she had been thinking six years ago when she'd met him at the age of twenty-four at a diner in Chicago where she was an assistant manager and he'd come in with a woman who had more skin than clothes. Even though he was with someone, he spent an hour flirting with her and before he left, he'd openly given her his phone number and told her to call him and he'd take her out to have a fun night. The woman he was with had been pissed off at his blatant disrespect of her, which

Gizelle knew should have been her own sign to stay away from him. The way he'd treated that woman, she should have known that he would eventually treat her the same way.

She didn't listen to anyone who told her to stay clear of Clyde. She was twenty-four and in love. Love no longer lived between them. Instead, she had to flee in order to find peace for her and her children. She didn't want them to suffer the abuse that she'd suffered for far too long. If she had to run again, she would and this time, she would find some place, perhaps Mexico, where he would never find them again. Right now, she needed help or there was no telling what Clyde would have up his sleeve next to terrorize her. Maybe the threat of calling the police would scare him off. She didn't have her phone, but he didn't know that.

Gizelle froze in place when the banging started again, but this time on the other side of the car. She saw Clyde trying to open Carrie's door and then he tried the passenger side door handle.

"You *stupid*...open this door, *right now!*"

Gizelle decided on a plan and faked like she was pulling a phone out of her purse.

"I'm going to call the police if you don't leave us alone."

When she said the word police, Carrie and Brody cried out, knowing they'd heard those words before. They'd lived through the same volatile situation with her when they lived with Clyde. That was the reason she'd packed them up after a judge granted her custody and got as far away from him as she could with the help of her friend, Heather, who lived in Bozeman.

"You can't keep me from my children!"

"Yes, I can. I have a court order that says I have custody and if you don't stop, I swear I will call the police!"

"I don't care about any order and if you call the police, by the time they arrive, they'll find you dead and I'll take my kids. That order is good while you lived in Chicago and not here in this hick town. Open this damn door or I will break the windows and drag you out by your hair. The longer you take, the worse it will be and you know I mean what I say, so open this door!"

Gizelle jumped every time he hit the car window with his fist. She was only steps away from her own house, but leaving the safety of the car meant Clyde would get to them. She needed to get the car moving. Her only resort was to actually call the police, but she had to get away to do that.

"I'm calling them," she screamed back at him.

In the next instant, all hell broke loose. She heard a loud crash and the passenger side window exploded with glass flying everywhere. Before she could react to what was happening, the passenger side door flew open and Clyde flew in. She screamed the moment he reached for her and pulled her by her hair and coat from her seat, across the passenger seat and out into the cold snow where the body slammed to the ground. She struggled against him and knew she was losing the fight as he hollered, kicked and punched at her. As she tried to scramble away, the last thing she remembered was a hard punch to the side of her head and then the world went dark.

2

Perry woke with a plan in mind today and it was to find out why he had not heard from or even seen Gizelle. He'd tried calling her phone and texting her when she didn't show up for her usual Friday night at the *Steely Gray* and when his calls and texts went unanswered for the past four days, his concern grew to extreme worry.

Walking down the three steps that led to his house, he saw his father walking toward him. He stopped just as he was about to get into his truck and waited for his father to reach him at the house he lived in on the Sullivan Ranch. Since the house his parents lived in wasn't too far from his own, he wasn't sure if his father was intentional about visiting him or if he was just walking by toward another part of the private, family side of their ranch. The ranch was gigantic and some who visited often referenced that it was larger than the ranch on an old television show called, *Dallas*. He had looked it up and his family's ranch was twice the size of the ranch on the hit, made-for-television show.

Like the rest of his family, which consisted of his parents, sister and brothers, he owned a house he'd built from the ground up on the Sullivan Ranch, an all-year-round tourist attraction where families could come and ride horses, see lots of other animals and there was even the beginning of an amusement park that they were hoping to expand on over the next couple of years. All of the activities took part on the much-visited public side of the ranch, while family life occurred on this part of the ranch which was guarded by high security fences and a security team in place to keep visitors out of their personal lives.

They were currently preparing to open the amusement park with rides, games and musical entertainment in the next few months so that they would be up and running before the summer rush of visitors to the ranch. Companies even used the famous Sullivan Ranch to host retreats and other large functions which made their ranch one of the most profitable in Montana. There many, many acres of crops and live animals they maintained and they held family events all year long.

Due to the expertise in event planning that his sister proudly boasted with her master's degree in Business, Communications and Public Relations along with a minor in Marketing and Hospitality Management, the ranch was run like a well-oiled machine. He was grateful for parents who made sure each of his brothers and sister held a college degree in something and because of that, their family was successful in business. Even before the idea of an amusement park came about, they had already surpassed one million visitors to the ranch just within the last two years, especially when it came to large parties, weddings and other events that made the Sullivan Ranch stand out amongst all others in the region. Perry loved that his main job on the ranch was its every day operation, which he not only considered a job, but the perfect life for him. He was the perfect example of a black cowboy who loved being on the back of a horse more than he loved riding in a car. He tipped his cowboy hat to his father when he walked up and stopped in front of him.

"Heading off the ranch already this morning?" David asked.

"Hey, Pop! Yeah, I'm going to check on a friend. I haven't heard from her and I'm a little concerned."

Not hearing from Gizelle when he tried to reach her was out of character for her since the first moment they'd met. She'd been reserved and a little standoffish, but if he reached out to her, she always called him back or at a minimum, sent a reply by text. He didn't want to pry, but he felt the need to be a little more overprotective than he would usually be of a woman.

"Friend? What friend? A woman friend?"

"Yes."

"You haven't brought a woman here to the ranch in a long time. Is this someone more than just a regular friend? What concerns you?" David asked as he bundled up tighter against the cold Montana morning.

"I'm not sure, just a feeling. I think I told you a little about Gizelle. She lives about ten miles from the ranch in the old Baxter house."

"That small place with all that land?"

"That's the place. She's been renting it for about six months or so now. She lives there with her two children and in this weather, I want to be sure they're okay with fire wood and things like that. You know how our snow storms can be and though we got *some* snow the last few days, a big storm is coming soon and I want to be sure she's covered."

"You may have mentioned her in passing. You look more worried than just about some simple fire wood, though I see you've stacked lots in the back of your truck. You taking it to her house now?"

Perry didn't want to admit that he was using the fire wood as an excuse to show up at Gizelle's house, something he'd never done before. She was alone in Bozeman, except for a few friends he knew she had. Storms could be brutal and there wasn't much she'd be able to do once a big storm hit and she would be unable to get off of the property to get even the basic necessities.

"Yeah, the last snow storm dropped quite a bit of the white stuff and I'm just looking out for them," he explained.

Perry didn't have to look at his father to know that there would be a confused look on his face. David Sullivan knew when his children weren't being open and honest with him. He didn't pry often, instead, choosing to let his five children sort out their own issues in life. As the oldest, he knew his father didn't grow too concerned when things came to him, but no one has ever seen him concerned about a woman they didn't know much about, but unbeknownst to them, Gizelle was more than just some woman friend.

"Is that it? Just looking out for them? I don't think I've ever seen you this concerned about any woman and I've never seen you hauling this much wood to one, not even that Veronica woman you dated a year or two back. I take it this Gizelle woman is more than just a friend?"

"You've met her, though you may not remember. She brought her kids here before to see the animals on the ranch. She's a gorgeous woman with long curly hair. She's stunningly beautiful," Perry added, now wishing he'd held back the last part. He was giving too much away and that could lead to an even deeper conversation.

Women were not a problem for him and he'd been involved with his share, but none as serious as the one he'd had with Veronica.

"I'm sure I have, but that's not what I'm asking. I'm not talking about a ranch guest. I'm talking about a woman that has your face all wrinkled and creased with worry, son."

Perry exhaled and turned away from his father to close the back of his truck. Besides wood in the back that his father could see, what he couldn't see were the pre-packed boxes of food and supplies he'd asked Sarah Martinez, the woman who was like a second mother to them all and who took care of his family on the ranch, to put together. When he told her he needed some things for a woman and her two small children so that they could fare through the upcoming storm, she'd gone above and beyond and gave him boxes of meat, vegetables, can goods and a ton of pre-cooked meals that Gizelle would only need to heat up. She had also included a box full of toiletries and other things like books, crayons and coloring books, enough to last them months. She didn't even question him when he asked her to do it. That was the woman Sarah was. She had a heart of gold, just like his own mother, Marta. The Sullivans were more than just owners of a large ranch, but they also did a lot for the people of Bozeman, especially when it came to food and other essentials families needed to survive. Knowing he'd stalled enough without answering, Perry inhaled loudly, hating this softer, worried side of himself.

"Yeah, she's a little more than that, at least to me. I know I haven't said much about her, but she means a lot to me, Pop. I think she's got some baggage and I'm trying to not push her, especially with two little kids. I don't know what in her life has made her so skittish and afraid, but I see it. She practically jumps out of her skin if a man asks her to dance or comes up behind her and gets too close. It's not just the usual being cautious or being caught off-guard. It's like she's expecting someone to leap out of the shadows at her. She's always looking around and the smallest things have her shaking nervously. I just want to make sure she and her kids are okay. She's got enough to worry about and I'm sure she doesn't need me hovering."

He wanted to say more and even ask his father how to proceed with a woman whom he felt did not come from a safe background, but he wasn't sure of Gizelle's situation, so he didn't want to speak too much on it.

"But you like her?"

Perry nodded as he turned back around after making sure everything was secure in the back of the truck.

"I do and usually I call or text her and she replies to let me know they're okay, especially when I ask if she needs anything. Lately, she's been on edge and sort of jumpy. I just want to be sure everything is good out at her place. Did you need something before I go?"

"No, I'm good. You know, with the upcoming storm, you could have invited your friend and her children to stay in one of the houses here on the ranch. It's not safe for a woman to be out there on that large piece of land alone with kids. Anything can happen to them," David said.

"I know, but I didn't want to intrude. I'll mention it and if she says no, I'll let her know to reach out to me if she needs anything."

"Have some of the ranch-hands out before and after the storm to make sure there is a path on and off of her property. You know we look out for each other in Bozeman. Your friend may not be used to that, but it's our way out here."

"I hear you, Pop and thanks for that idea. I'll get with Buck when I get back."

Buck Henry had been with the Sullivan Ranch as the head ranch hand and the all-around person who took care of everything, which included being responsible for the security team as well, for twenty-years and if anybody would make sure that Gizelle's property was looked after during a storm, Buck would make sure it got done. The Ranch had ten snow plows and often used them to help the local government with getting snow off the roads.

"Good. When you return, let's talk. I want to set up the meeting to continue the talks about the expansion of the ranch. We have a lot of land and once this winter is over, I want to make sure we can start on some of the new construction and possibly have a small section of it open before the summer rush begins. I know we talked about that and Shelton, our financial wizard, is in full support. He said last year was one of our best years we've ever had as far as visitors and from what he's shown me, the expansion would have us sitting real pretty and you know all the extra visitors to the ranch also bodes well for the city. We want to have something new to bring back repeat visits. Brielle told me that we are already completely booked for events from February, starting with that big Valentine's day shindig she's planning until July when we have the big fourth of July event. Even with the weather in these parts, every weekend and some weekdays are locked in. The small section of the amusement park will be open this year and I want phase two to be open the next year. There is a lot to do. Dayton wants to talk about using his part of the property to build a race track to bring some of those races he participates in to Bozeman. That could mean major revenue for this part of the country and I'd like to hear more about his idea."

Perry smiled thinking of his youngest brother who was traveling the country and with the ranch being his biggest sponsor, the Sullivan name is known all over the world. It helps that the family name is written in big, bold green letters on all of Dayton's cars that he uses for his races.

"Yeah, I talked with him about that before he left after the holiday for his next race. We can patch him in for a video-conference call," Perry said.

"I came by to see what your schedule was like this

week. I have a few other calls I want to get in also and with you running the day-to-day here on the ranch, I need you in on all of them. Shelton has signed on as a partner with an architectural firm and he wants to talk to us about connecting Sullivan Construction up with the firm to handle some of their big projects. There are two large office parks that he wants us in on."

"So, my brother is not only putting his degree in finance to great use, but his minor in structural engineering as well?"

"What can I say, I have kids who see the big picture and are go-getters like their old man!"

Perry patted his father on the shoulder. He was right – he set a great example for greatness.

"I'm already interested. He told me a little about it over dinner a few weeks ago right after he came back from his meeting in Chicago. I understand he wants to build a new office park here in Bozeman with all of the Sullivan head offices under one roof."

"That's what we're meeting about. I'm here for it and I want you and Nick at the table too. Soon, I'm planning to turn it all over to you and Shelton because your mother and I want to start doing a lot of traveling like I promised her. With you kids all grown, it's past time for me to show her how much I appreciate her dealing with me all these years of being wrapped up in this ranch. She deserves all of my attention," he explained.

"I'm happy that you're doing that. Most people

wait until their too old or too ill to really enjoy retirement. Whatever time you need from me, I can make myself available. I've got some surveyors coming in later in the week, but we can set the meetings up before that. Brielle wants a pool added to her property and I have a few guys coming to give me an estimate on that. She's so happy you finally gifted her with her own house here on the ranch for Christmas, yet I still can't figure out why she still spends most nights at your house. She wanted out and in her own house and now that she has it, she loves decorating and fixing it up, but is always at the main house. Go figure," Perry laughed.

"You know your sister and then your mother was going to make me sleep on the couch if I didn't let Brielle have her own house. She said I was discriminating because she's a girl when I let the boys build their houses at twenty-one."

"Well, at least she asked for a house on the ranch and not a condo or a house in the city!"

"That's true. I guess I'm glad I came to my senses before that conversation came up. She's my baby and at least this way, we can keep an eye on her. The world is crazy and I'm not sure she's ready for it," David explained.

"Trust me, she's ready. The fellas and I have made sure of that and anyone who knows us and knows she's our baby sister had better watch out. We don't play when it comes to her," Perry added.

"I know each of you have her back and that's why I'm good with retiring and spending time away from the ranch traveling with your mother. I know she'll be fine, but if you hear of any talk about her wanting a place off the ranch, talk her out of it or she'll find me and her mother moving in with her!"

"I hear you. I'll stop by the house when I get back and have mom work out some times this week and makes some calls. Does that work?"

"That'll work and no rush. I can tell by the look on your face that you're in a hurry to get going to check on your friend. I'm going to check in on Nick before I make my rounds on the ranch this morning. He's really been spending a lot of time at the fire station in his role as the new fire chief and we haven't seen a lot of him lately. I saw his truck come on the ranch late last night. I want to know if he wants in on any of the meetings. He may be taking a backseat to ranch leadership, but he should be kept in the loop with all that's going on, especially with the expansion. We'll need his input on fire code standards. I'm sure he's up by now and probably trying to rush back off the ranch."

Perry faked a laughed when he thought about his father checking on Nick knowing that most likely, Nick was still being held captive by his lady love, Parker. They all loved Parker and it was her love that has kept Nick in Bozeman and not on his way back to New York. Parker had moved in with Nick into his house on the ranch and the way they were often seen all over each other, he already knew what was going on behind closed door and if his father decided to barge in on them, he would either get an eyeful or see the end result of the smile from here to the far east coast that Nick would be sporting when he opened the door.

"I wouldn't bother my brother just yet. He and Parker are still in bed. I talked to him briefly last night and you may want to give him a few hours. He's working three days straight and came on the ranch last night to get in his quality time with Parker before his three days on."

"Hours? He's the new firehouse chief and according to him, he needs to always be up and over there getting that place in order or is that excuse so that when he has free time and we see him, he can spend it all with Parker? It's good to have him back home for good, huh?"

Nick had moved to New York some years ago after life got too stressful with old memories for him on the ranch where his childhood sweetheart died in his arms after a horse-riding accident. He had gone to New York to run away from his life, but Bozeman wasn't a place to run away from. It was a place to come home to.

"I'm glad he's back and his timing was perfect for taking over the job as chief. I haven't seen him this happy since before he left for New York years ago.

Parker is good for him," Perry said.

"Yes, she is. I know your mother couldn't be happier. I hope your friend is okay. I won't keep you. Call me when you get back to the ranch," David said and walked away.

Perry nodded and checked one last time to be sure he had enough firewood and hopped in his truck. Before pulling off, he tried calling Gizelle again and this time, unlike the others, her phone went straight to voicemail. Now, he knew something was wrong. This was now the fourth day since he'd seen or talked to her and his worry amped up a few levels. Turning his truck around, he headed off of the ranch, waving at a few of the ranch hands who were putting up the new ranch signage at the entrance. He usually went the speed limit, but today, something told him he needed to go a little faster as his thoughts turned to when he'd first met her and became enthralled by everything about her.

He'd met the beautiful Gizelle Duncan one evening in town when he'd let his brother, Shelton, talk him into going out to the *Steely Gray* to get a break from working so hard. Shelton was the money man for their family who did a great job of keeping the ranch in the black for years and because of his financial savvy, they were venturing into other businesses and the fact that they were prospering was because Shelton knew numbers.

On that night out, they were having a good time

drinking and flirting with the ladies and then his eyes locked on Gizelle and he never took them off of her for the rest of the night. He'd seen beautiful women, but none like Gizelle. He watched her and one of her friends dance and have fun all while shooting down one man after another who asked them to dance. Shelton teased him when he saw his focus had been on Gizelle and dared him to make a move. There was something about Gizelle just from looking at her that told him she was a woman he needed to meet. He knew that Shelton believed his interest was about the physical and the action that could take place with her, but he knew different; Gizelle was different.

As the night went on, he figured he'd ask her to dance and add himself to the long list of men she turned down. Getting up the nerve, he walked over to her table, introduced himself, tipped his hat to her and asked her if she would like to dance. He waited for the rejection he'd seen her toss out all night, but then she took the hand he'd extended out to her and she joined him on the dance floor. For the rest of the night, they danced to fast and slow songs and he'd stayed out much later than he'd originally planned. The last thing he wanted to do was leave and be without her in his arms. Following dancing and as her friend flirted about the bar, he sat and got to know Gizelle better. He quickly got the vibe that she wasn't looking to be involved with anyone, especially with two small children at home. He respected that and told her that he hoped they could be friends. From that day forward, they'd become good friends, connecting at the bar, having drinks and a few times, even dinner. She told him she only hung out on Friday nights because she had a sitter and she devoted her Saturday nights to doing fun things with her children, something he respected and admired. She'd recently let him meet them when he invited them to the ranch to check out the animals. Carrie and Brody grew as fond of him as he had of them.

Picking up the speed, he was more determined than ever to get to them to make sure they were okay. There was a nagging feeling that everything wasn't okay, but he had to get to the house to find out for sure.

3

Gizelle woke, startled for the third day. At least now, she and the kids were alone and Clyde was gone. For the first two days after he dragged her from the car and into the house and then he grabbed the kids from the backseat, he'd pretty much held them captive in her house. They day that he'd knocked her out cold, she finally came to and found herself inside of the house, she immediately scrambled to get to Carrie and Brody who were sitting on the sofa with Clyde looking terrified, pretty much stoic as if they were afraid to move. Standing on legs that hurt from being dragged across the ground outside and the floor inside, she moved with determination and ran to them where they gripped her neck so tight, she had to struggle to breathe. Ignoring Clyde's presence, she held them tight and did her best to reassure and quiet their tears. Clyde looked at her briefly, but didn't say a word. His face said all she needed to know. She stayed on her knees on the floor in front of the kids until both fell asleep in her arms, just like that.

From that moment until he'd finally left the day

before, she and the kids lived in terror of him being in the house. She'd tried to find her phone and realized Clyde must have found it and gotten rid of it or hid it from her. She did her best to remain calm to not anger him more. Brody had soiled himself that first day, afraid to even speak a word. She had to beg Clyde to let her clean him up. He finally relented and allowed her to give both kids a bath where he stood watch at the door as if she would disappear out of the bathroom window that even the kids may not be small enough to fit through. Her plan hadn't been to get away anymore, but to keep them safe where they were.

Turning over on the mattress where she and the kids had slept since Clyde left, she looked toward the bedroom door where she'd propped a wooden chair against the door handle and moved the large, Maplewood dresser and bedframe to keep anyone from getting inside the room. She was happy that the bedroom had its own bathroom and that she'd always kept snacks and water in her bedroom closet to keep from running up and down the stairs when the kids wanted snacks. Even moving slightly, she felt her body shaking with fright that Clyde may still return. He threatened that he would and if she was gone, he would find them again. She was too terrified to move from the room. This was the safest she'd felt in a long time.

Days of enduring his anger and she didn't know

what to do. She no longer saw a way to escape him.

"Mommy?"

Now in her bedroom with the door locked, she heard Carrie call her name and pulled both kids closer to her and soothed them back to sleep. She didn't know what time of day it was, but figured it was early morning because of the direction of the sun. In the morning, it beamed through her bedroom window and later in the day, the sun would shine bright on the back of the house. The weather was frightening cold, but the sun was just coming up over the horizon as heat from it flooded the room.

With Carrie and Brody now back to sleep, she had to figure out what her next move would be. She couldn't stay in the house and in the bedroom forever. She also knew that there was a possibility that the rest of the house was a mess. She'd heard Clyde throwing things around and destroying her house before he finally told her he was leaving, but would return and that there would be hell to pay if he came back and she wasn't there with his kids. If she could think of someplace to go, she may risk his warning and try to leave even if she had to walk with both kids in her arms. She was desperate and the beating she took from him after he dragged her into the house, she knew would not be limited to just her. He would soon be mad enough to strike out at the kids, something she saw in his eyes the first night when Brody kept crying for her and Clyde screamed at him like a crazed lunatic. He'd complained about how she treats Brody like a baby, telling her she needed to let Brody 'man-up'. She thought it ridiculous when he was only three years old. Still, she didn't fight with him to keep him from striking her again.

Getting up, she went to the window, looked out and saw no sign of Clyde's car or any car tracks down to her house. If she could just get the kids dressed, she would try to get out and maybe run to a house nearby for help.

Her thoughts turned to Perry and wondered if he noticed her absence on Friday night at the *Steely Gray* where she and Heather had taken to going to every Friday night. Since the moment she'd first laid eyes on him one Friday night, she'd never missed another one. Before that, she occasionally went out with Heather and then her eyes landed on the six-foot tall gorgeous specimen of a man.

Perry was beyond handsome and to see him in his cowboy hat did all kind of salacious things to her psyche and her body. She'd never come across a man who emitted so much sexuality and self-confidence and what she enjoyed was his focus on her. She'd heard stories about the Sullivan boys, especially Perry who the ladies seemed to love, but at the same time, were disappointed that his attention to them didn't go far beyond the bedroom, though none complained. His walk was the sexiest she had ever seen. She watched the slight curve to his legs and when he saw her, he would wink, tip his cowboy hat and her heart would melt. If there was ever such a thing as love at first sight, she had experienced it that first night. At this point, they were friends and that was fine with her. She'd rushed into a relationship with Clyde and though they were night and day when it came to personalities, her marriage had left her scared of going into something else.

She thought of Perry now because he was the only person she could think to get to when it came to getting away from Clyde. What really surprised her was the fact that Heather had not come out to the house to check on her. They were supposed to connect on Friday, even though she was off, to go to their usual spot. She'd had a babysitter lined up, but not one word from Heather. Even if she had called to see if they were still on, she wouldn't have received a response and would have hoped that would have brought Heather out to check on her.

No one was coming for her and the kids. It had been three or four days now, she'd lost count, and not one person was curious as to why she had not been seen or heard from. Her job would not have come calling because she was scheduled to be off until Tuesday, which she believed would be tomorrow. Thinking of the car, with the window broken out, the inside would be freezing, but if she could get it to start, she would go to the nearest house or if she had to walk, she would leave the car behind.

Clyde had taken her keys, but she had another set for the car and for the house which were in the closet.

Turning back to the kids who were dressed in thick, wool pajamas, she wondered if she could leave the room long enough to grab warm clothes for them from the room they shared across the hall from her room. Once Clyde had left, she'd barricaded them all in her room. If she had to, she would wrap them up in warm blankets and just bolt and take her chances against the cold weather. The closest house was a little less than a mile away. She could make it on foot.

Standing from the bed, she walked into the bathroom to check her face and arms. The moment she saw that one side of her face was bruised, she began to cry. She could still see Clyde's hand print around her neck and several scrapes and cuts along her hands and arms. She looked down and saw that the scrapes on her legs where her pants had torn when Clyde dragged her had begun to heal, but with the lightness of her skin, large, red bruises had formed. Her hair was a mess, but that was something she could fix. Grabbing a ponytail holder, she cried through brushing her hair and securing it on top of her head. She grabbed a washcloth and wiped her face and replaced the bandages over her scarred hand and fingers. She was a mess and was thankful Carrie and Brody were asleep to not hear and see her cries.

"Perry," she whispered.

Gizelle knew it wasn't his place to rescue her from

her messy life and lately, she'd been up and down with her reactions to him, especially when he flirted with her. She didn't know how to respond when everything and everyone frightened her. She wanted to be free to engage with him, but in the back of her mind, there was the fear of the unknown and Clyde had done that to her. She knew Perry was different and he was interested in her. Would he still be interested if he knew of the drama that followed her to Bozeman? Had he been wondering what happened to her? Perhaps, he assumed she decided to do something different on Friday. After all, there was a lot to do in Bozeman. Maybe he thought that she'd gone out on a date with someone else even though he hadn't asked her out, she could tell they were getting close to that. She feared what her response would be because she didn't want to seem overzealous and like other women, she wasn't the most experienced with satisfying the needs of a man. She'd heard women talk about being with him and she felt like her limited experience wouldn't be enough to hold his interest.

Perry turned all heads when he walked into a room and the number of women who flirted with him, even when the two of them were talking, was an endless stream. Still, when they connected on Friday nights, he graciously declined all attempts at other women to flirt with him and he focused his attention on her. She would give anything for that attention right now.

Leaving the bathroom, she checked on the kids and then walked into her closet and grabbed a blue sweatsuit and a thick white crewneck shirt. She pulled out her beige winter boots and prepared to find her way out. She couldn't stay in the house. It was significantly colder, no doubt from a broken window or two that she'd heard Clyde breaking before he told her he would return and take her and the kids back with him to Chicago. Thankfully, she'd had enough blankets to make sure they were warm.

After dressing, she walked back into the bedroom and grabbed blankets to wrap the kids in. She saw their boots near the bedroom door and remembered their hats, coats and gloves were near the front door downstairs. It was time to go.

Just as she reached the mattress to wake them, she heard what sounded like a car or truck coming down her driveway. Her first thought was that Clyde would be back and he would be angry that she barricaded the door. Checking everything that she'd applied to keep the door from opening, she scuttered back to the mattress and pulled Carrie and Brody into her arms and waited. She looked around the room for anything she could use as a weapon and remembered the poker from the fireplace in her room. She was determined that Clyde would not touch her again, in any way. Moving quickly, she grabbed it and looked at the curved, pointed end. If she had to keep Clyde from getting to her again, she was going to make sure it was his last attempt.

Going back to the kids, she pulled them close, locked her eyes on the bedroom door and she prepared for what was next. She was tired of being a victim.

4

Arriving at Gizelle's house, Perry could see that a car had been in and out during the storm. Though light, the tracks could still be seen. He could see that it hadn't been her car because it was still covered in ice and it wasn't facing the direction of the tracks he saw. Using the plow on the front of his truck, he made a clear path to her car before getting out. When he walked around to the passenger side, he stopped in his tracks at seeing the broken window. He looked toward the house and saw what looked like boot footprints, larger than Gizelle's would have been, coming from the house and leading around to the side. He followed those prints where they seemed to disappear to where a car looks to have been parked. Had someone broken into her car and driven off, leaving it like that? Where was Gizelle? Where were her kids?

Being cautious, he pulled out his phone and dialed her cell phone again and as with other calls, her phone went straight to her voicemail. He left a message anyway as he kept his eyes on any movement around her house.

"Gizelle, it's Perry calling again. I'm at your house and worried. Your car has been broken into and I don't know if you're in the house or someplace else. Please call me so that I know you're okay."

Hanging up, he walked back toward the front door and noticed something was odd about the way the door looked. For starters, with the brisk cold, her front door was slightly ajar and then upon closer examination, it looked like it had been forced open and just pushed toward being closed, but not making it. There were scratch marks as if someone had used something to pry the door open. His senses were on high alert. Making the decision that he wasn't leaving until he saw what was on the other side of the door, he entered the house cautiously.

He looked around for a light switch while keeping his eyes keen to any movement. When his hand encountered a switch, he flipped it on and his heart practically leaped out of his chest when he saw the pure devastation in the living room. He had never been inside of her house, but knew that she would not live in the kind of destruction he encountered.

Someone had broken up a lot of the furniture and it was scattered all over the floor. He saw that a window was broken and the pieces of glass were scattered about on the floor. He kept his cool and continued walking through the house, reaching for his cell phone as he walked. He called his best friend who was also the Sheriff of Bozeman, Marcus Coley. He was happy when Marcus answered on the first ring.

"Marcus, I'm at Gizelle Duncan's house, old man Baxter's place and it looks like someone broke in and destroyed the place. I mean, it's *really* bad," he said hurriedly while also keeping his voice down. He didn't know who or what was in the house with him. He thought of going back to his truck to grab his rifle, but his first thought was on where Gizelle was.

"Where are Gizelle and her kids? Are they okay?" Marcus asked.

Everyone in town knew of Gizelle and loved her two bubbly kids. She often brought them with her to the law firm where she worked and they could often be spotted at the library checking out books. He also knew that they loved the local diner where the best cheeseburgers and crispy French fries were served. Gizelle spoke of taking them there once a week when weather permitted.

"I don't know. Right now, I don't see them, but something went down here and it can't be good."

Perry moved slowly throughout the first floor of the house. He assumed if Gizelle was home, she'd hear him moving about. Looking into the kitchen, he saw a sink full of dishes and old food sat on the table and counter, most of it uneaten.

"Perry, get out of there and wait outside for me.

I'm on my way."

Perry could hear the siren in Marcus' truck turn on and knew that his friend would speed like a bat out of hell to get to him. There was no doubt he heard the desperate tone in his voice.

Against Marcus' wishes, he took the stairs up, to the second floor and kept his eyes and ears on any movement. Hearing none, he kept moving, keeping his back to the side wall.

"I can't do that. They may be in here someplace hurt. You know we don't have this kind of random crime happening in Bozeman, but when we do, it could be deadly with her living here alone. Everybody knows everybody, but you never know. Get here as fast as you can and if someone is still in here, you'll need to bring an ambulance with you because I'm pounding away until I don't detect any breathing, especially if she and the kids have been hurt."

Perry heard Marcus' loud exhale of displeasure, followed by one expletive after another.

"Dammit Perry, I'm on my way! I'll be there in two or three minutes!" Marcus yelled.

"Do that and in the meantime, I'm going to look around for them."

Perry hung up and continued up the stairs. He took them quietly, but still in a hurry. He didn't know if whoever did the damage was still in the house or not, so he proceed cautiously and could hear his own heart beating ferociously in his chest.

When he reached the top landing, he noticed all the doors were open except for one. Walking quietly, he looked inside of the rooms with the opened doors and saw that those rooms were also a wreck as if someone picked up furniture and tossed it about, breaking it up in the process. One of the rooms had bunk beds and the step to the top bunk was broken into pieces. The dresser drawers had been pulled out and clothes were strewn about everywhere. Someone was enraged when they went through Gizelle's house tearing things up. Walking up to the one door that was closed, he tried the handle and it was locked. Placing his ear to the door, he could hear the whimpers of the children and his heart raced. He started to break through, but didn't know what he'd find on the other side. Was an intruder in there with them? He leaned close to the door and took his chance on asking.

"Gizelle, it's Perry. Are you in there? Gizelle?" he yelled louder, but in a calm voice to not frighten the children.

He heard movement and after hearing what sounded like someone moving furniture from in front of the door, it opened and on the other side stood Gizelle whose face was stained with tears and clinging to her were Carrie and Brody, who like her, looked like they had been traumatized by whatever occurred. He immediately pulled them all into his embrace and silently said a thank you that they were okay. When Gizelle screamed, the piercing cry ripped him to shreds and he held her closer. He looked to his left and to his right where Carrie was holding one of her legs in a death grip while Brody did the same on the other. He smiled hoping to reassure them that he was there to help.

"I'm so glad to see you," Gizelle said right before she began crying uncontrollably again, which caused the kids to start crying as well.

He tried to quiet them all. With Gizelle holding tight to him, he placed his hands on top of each child's head and caressed them softly, hoping the soft touch would calm them.

"It's okay. I'm here now and you're going to be okay. What happened here? What happened to your house? Are you hurt?" he asked, throwing question after question in her direction while trying to check out the room to make sure no one else was there.

Gizelle wiped her eyes and looked to the kids who were terrified and then back up at him. When she held on to him as if her life depended on hit, he let her. Whatever she needed, he was there.

"It was Clyde, my ex-husband. He did this to the house. I ran with the kids into my room and locked the door when he finally left late last night. I was too shaken to leave the room afraid that he was outside or someplace else in the house. He threatened that he would return and hurt me if I was gone. I decided to barricade us in the room and hoped that he wouldn't get in if he got back. I didn't know if he was going to come back and do more damage."

"What? Your ex-husband did this to your house? How long ago did this happen?"

Perry was fiercely angry, but tried not to show it. He knew that Gizelle and the kids had already experienced an angry man.

Before she could answer, he heard the sirens of several police cars pulling up outside.

"I don't know; it's all a blur. The days ran together. We've been in here for a long time, three or four days; I think. Is today Monday?"

Perry was startled. She didn't even know what day it was.

"Yes, it's Monday. You've been here since Thursday or Friday?" he asked.

"Friday. He showed up Friday and it's been terrible since then."

"Are you sure he's not still here anywhere?"

"I don't know. I heard him drive off last night. I looked out of the window and saw him struggling to drive away in the snow. I just couldn't move and every time I did, the kids would scream so I sat still. I grabbed the blankets from my bed and covered us up in the corner and waited. I don't know what I was waiting for, but we waited."

He was relieved they were okay, but he was on fire at what her ex-husband could have done to her if she hadn't locked herself in the room with her kids.

"I know you said you had an ex-husband, but you

didn't tell me he was violent. You said he lived in Chicago or something like that."

"He does, but he came to Bozeman saying he wanted us back with him. I could tell he was drunk and enraged."

"Did he hit you or the kids? Harm you in any way?"

He saw her look to the kids who were listening and without speaking she turned her face around and Perry saw the large bruise on the side of her face which looked like a large hand print. Never had he been as angry as he was at the moment seeing her face bruised and the kids scared. He then looked further down and saw a large handprint around her neck. He tried to control his anger and almost lost it if they hadn't been joined in the house.

"Perry!" Marcus screamed.

"Upstairs!"

"What the hell happened here?" Marcus asked coming up to them with additional officers in tow, all with their weapons drawn.

When Perry saw them, he gestured for them to lower them because of the kids.

"I need to get them out of here and to someplace warm and safe," he said to Marcus.

He then turned to Gizelle, lifting her face up to his.

"Get what you and the kids need. You're not coming back here. You're coming to the ranch with me."

"Perry, I can't drag you and your family into this. Clyde will come back and he will tear up this town until he finds me and the kids if we're not here."

"He can try getting on the ranch if he wants to, but I guarantee you he won't get far. I can't leave you and your kids here and besides, everything in this house is broken up. You can't stay here. The ranch is the safest place for you right now. Look at Brody and Carrie. They can't stay here, so please come with me," he pleaded.

"I need to grab some things for them," she said.

"You do that and for now, let me take the kids and you get what you need. Grab me some blankets I can put around them and get them in my truck to get them warm. Are their car seats in your car?"

"Yes."

"What about shoes, coats and gloves?"

"If they are still here, they would be near the front door. I'll just grab a few things for me and them."

"I'll have Nora help you get some things together," Marcus added as he joined them in the room.

Perry knew Nora and saw her on the stairs. Marcus was keen to knowing that he may need a female officer to help out.

When Gizelle tried to move away, the kids, who had grabbed onto her legs tighter started to cry. He waited and let her soothe them before heading out.

"Hey, look at me," she said. "You know Mr. Perry

who has the horses, goats, cows and pigs you liked when we visited his ranch. You loved all the animals and he was really nice. He even had hot dogs and potato chips with us. Remember him? He lives on that great big ranch where you had fun and ate too much ice cream. You like him, remember? He's going to walk with you downstairs while mommy gets us some clothes so that we can go back to his ranch. You will get to see the animals again. Go with him and I will be right behind you, okay?" she asked, hoping she was reassuring them.

Perry looked down as both kids looked up at him and even though he was furious, he forced a bright smile to calm the kids down. Surprising him, Carrie reached her arms up at him and he picked her up in his arm. He knew she was still scared when she gripped his neck tightly with her arms and laid her head on his shoulder. Brody placed his hand in Perry's and when he put his thumb in his mouth, Perry picked him up too and turned and walked toward the steps. Marcus grabbed the blankets from Gizelle and wrapped them around the children.

"Hurry, Gizelle," Perry said behind him.

"Okay," she said as Nora helped her pull some clothes out of the closet.

Perry walked down the stairs with Marcus behind him.

"Who did this? Does she know?" Marcus asked after giving his team orders to check everything and every room of the house.

"Her ex-husband, Clyde."

"What? Her ex-husband did this? What the hell?" Marcus asked.

Perry shook his head yes.

"If I get my hands on him!" he shouted and then calmed himself, remembering he had the kids with him.

"I need to talk to her while this is all fresh in her head," Marcus said. "I need to get some men out looking for this clown," he added.

"Can you do it at the ranch? Let me get them settled and away from here as quickly as possible first. I don't think you'll get much out of her until she's able to see this place in the rearview mirror."

He smiled when Marcus nodded his agreement.

"You got it. I agree with getting her away from here first. Is she hurt?"

"Yes, but I don't know to what extent. I'm going to see if she wants to go to the hospital to have her and the kids checked out. If not, we have doctors on the ranch."

"It's a good thing you came by. What made you do that?" Marcus asked walking outside with him and opening the truck door to allow him to sit the kids inside until he could grab their car seats from Gizelle's car.

"Did you see the broken window on the car? Why would he do that? I'm guessing she may have been in the car when he accosted her. That bastard better hope he doesn't run into me! I came by because I had been trying to reach her and she wasn't responding. Usually, if I called her, she may not always answer or call me back right away, but she always responded. I wasn't getting any kind of a response so I decided to come check on them after we had that snow two days ago. I wanted to be sure they were okay and had enough fire wood and this is what I found – her car window broken out and her and the kids barricaded in a room."

He tried to keep his voice down and not scare the kids.

"You showed up just in time."

"No, I didn't. If I had shown up just in time, he'd be dead and this would be a totally different situation," Perry replied fiercely.

"I hear you and I understand. As your friend, I say I would be with you, but as the law, I have to tell you to pull it back and not get yourself in any trouble. Let me handle this. You know I've got your back and finding this guy will be a priority."

Perry raced around and started his truck up to get the heat pumping. Closing the door, he walked to Gizelle's car and Marcus helped him free the seats from the back.

They looked around to the land that surrounded the house as well as the road that ran along the side of her house. They were both thinking the same thing –

that Clyde could be watching them from a vantage point. Perry didn't care. He wanted Clyde to see him and come for him. Every time he thought of the magnitude of the fear on Gizelle's face and that of her kids, his own anger rose higher. When he opened the back door of his truck to put the seats in, he looked to the second row of seats and saw that the kids had already fallen asleep as they warmed. He put the seat on the back row as Marcus did the same on the other side.

"We need to get her car to the ranch. I'll have the glass fixed and get it looked at to see if he damaged it in other ways, like in a way to keep her from leaving."

Perry looked up just as Gizelle exited the house followed by Nora. They both carried two large, full duffle bags in their arms. He raced over to take the bags and loaded them in the back of his truck. He then moved to shift Brody and Carrie to the car seats without waking them and covered them back up with the blankets. After helping Gizelle inside of his truck, he turned to her as she fastened her seat belt.

"Do you and the kids need to go to a hospital first? I'm looking at your face and neck and you should get checked out. Did he hurt you in any other ways?" Perry asked with Nora standing right behind him. Keeping his eyes locked with hers, he wanted to relay to her in his eyes what he was asking.

"No, he didn't touch me other than where he hit me and marks from him dragging me from the car and into the house."

"I wondered about the car. He did that?"

"Yes, and dragged me across the seat and knocked me out. I don't remember anything else until I woke up later and saw the scratches and scrapes and felt the bruises when I moved around."

When she began to cry again, he stopped asking questions which caused her to relive what happened.

"Hospital?"

"No, I'm good and he never touched the kids. They are just frightened. I just want to get someplace where I can hold them in my arms," she whispered.

"We're heading straight to the ranch," he said.

When Gizelle leaned her head back and closed her eyes, he hoped that she would quickly find sleep like the kids and know that she was safe from this point forward.

Closing the door, he turned back to Marcus who had given more instructions to his team.

"All good here?" Marcus asked.

"Yeah. We're heading straight for the ranch. I'll send some of my men over to secure the place up. Can you leave one of your men here until some of the ranch hands get here?"

"Of course. They'll be here assessing the scene for a while and getting pictures. I'll be by the ranch shortly. Get them to safety and we'll talk when I get there."

Perry nodded his head and walked around to the

other side of his truck and got in. He was thankful when he saw that Gizelle had fallen asleep. He put the truck in drive and headed home. He couldn't help but think of what had gone on in the past four days and tried to not let his imagination wonder too far. He would soon get the story from Gizelle. He hadn't told her yet, but he had fallen hard for her and he felt overpowered by the amount of love he felt for them. What he was feeling wasn't casual and seeing them hurt and terrified, he knew that in his car with him was his family, he loved them and no one messed with those he loved; no one. He looked to all three of them as he drove off and knew that taking them to his ranch, he would keep them safe or he would die trying.

5

Marta Sullivan walked into her office after finally finding the paperwork on the expansion of not only the entertainment side of the ranch, but also the school that had opened a year ago on the ranch. She loved Sullivan Ranch. It meant everything to her family, a place built from hard work and a lot of love over the years. Her heart was with the school they were able to open and operate, not only for the children of those who worked on the ranch, and there were hundreds, but also for anyone in Bozeman who had a desire for their children to get a good education. They had twelve school buses that picked kids up from all around Bozeman and she was looking forward to adding more grades with the construction of the building that would hold the upper-level school grades.

The school had opened beginning with grades pre-kindergarten up to the fifth grade. They were now expanding to add a middle school by the end of the year and then the upper school early in the fall. The excitement over the growth had become infectious not just on the ranch, but all over Bozeman. She was expecting Perry back any minute to talk about the many ways they planned on expanding and she would be ready with additional ideas. She looked up when the front door to the house she shared with her husband, David, opened and he came in shaking off snow and complaining about the cold. She didn't know why he did that considering they lived in a place where snow was as normal as breathing.

"Whew, it sure is cold out today," David said, removing his overcoat.

"It's cold every day and you say that every single day. Is Perry with you?"

"No, he's not back yet. I don't know how long he's going to be. He left to check on a friend. Shelton's on his way in. I told him you wanted to talk to him this morning before he hopped into a busy day of meetings in town."

"I'm surprised he found time to come onto the ranch today. He hardly ever spends any time at his house here, instead preferring to stay at his condo in the city and since he built that office building where he run Sullivan Enterprises, he's hardly ever here other than for work purposes. I know he loves that place downtown, but with Nick back, I love having everyone on the ranch. The snow storm coming up is going to hit us hard in a few days. It would be nice if he conducted his business here on the ranch."

"That's why he coming to the ranch today. He said something about warming up his house and spending a few days in it. I checked on Nick too. He's coming over in a little while."

"I can't tell you how happy I am to have Nick back here. I've missed him for a long time. Seeing him for holidays, when he didn't give an excuse for not showing up, was great, but now I get to see him all the time."

"I know you have and it's good to know he's staying because he wants to and not out of some guilt trip or warning of more hurt you would try and lay on him. Don't think that I forgot that you threatened me and Perry with hurt, harm and danger if we didn't get Nick back to this ranch after his accident in New York. I think they were more afraid for me than for themselves," David joked, hugging Marta tight and kissing her on the neck and as usual, she swooned at his affection and was already thinking about continuing later that night when they were alone.

When she waved him off, he laughed even harder.

"I would have laid a million guilt trips and hurt each of you if that's what it would take to get him home, at least more often. Now, I don't have to because he's home for good and I couldn't be happier. I need to call him and find out if he wants a special lunch to take with him to the firehouse. I have Sarah making a big pot of spaghetti for all of the firefighters at the station house. I'll need you to get someone to take that and some fresh baked rolls to them later today if Nick leaves before it's ready. There are also two pies and a chocolate cake she baked for them last night and yes, the one I saw that you already cut a slice out of."

"I couldn't help it. That cake was smelling some kind of good."

"You know I like to send a big meal over to them at least once a month. I've been doing that for years. I may add an extra day now that my son is there all the time."

"Will there be some left over for me?"

Everyone loved Sarah's cooking, especially her homemade baked bread. She had been with them since the oldest of their kids was running around in diapers. She was one of the family and cooked the best meals.

"Yes, I told her to make enough for you to have for a few days."

"You take such good care of me," David said, coming up behind her again and planting soft kisses across the back of her neck.

"Get a room," Sarah said entering the room.

"If I could get my husband to slow down a bit, we'd be in our room and you wouldn't have to see our public displays," Marta joked.

"Hmph, I'm used to them after all these years I've been around. The two of you still act like you're newlyweds, even after five children."

"And it's still as hot!" Marta declared.

"Yes, it is and the only reason I keep my hands to myself is because you're here," David quipped as Sarah laughed at their antics.

After one last kiss, Marta saw David look down at the plans scattered all over her home office desk.

"I know what you're going to say," she said before he could comment.

"Sweetheart, you're going to drive yourself crazy over those plans. I told you we have it covered. We have months before the end of this school year and even longer before the next one begins. Everything is on schedule for the school construction and we already have all the permits we will need."

"I know. I want everything to be perfect," she said.

"You've already exceeded your own expectations and yet you're still worried."

"I know. I don't want you to think I don't have faith in you because I do. I'm thinking too hard about this. I need to start working on getting more teachers in place while Perry and Shelton focus on the expansion and the cost."

"You know our boys would never let you down. As soon as Perry is back and Shelton comes in, give them all of this. We need to have several meetings this week and they'll need these plans, too. We're going to go over everything for the school and for the amusement park. I need to get some plans out of my truck before they get here and we can add them to your stack. Did Brielle stay here last night? I need to talk to her about the possibility of adding an unscheduled event to the calendar for later this month."

Marta opened her mouth to argue, but didn't. She has learned over the years to just go with the flow. She knew that their spunky and very opinionated daughter would have something to say about a last-minute change to the schedule for the month.

"David, you are going to drive your daughter crazy. No, she stayed at her house last night, but she was here late. You came in really late and she was already gone. She's going to go crazy if you want her to add anything else to the planning and event schedule for January. The event hall has been booked up for months since back in the summer, even this weekend after the snow storm. What's going on?"

"I have a friend from New York who would like to fly in some of his business associates from around the country for two days of meetings. He had been planning on a Colorado location, but said he thought about the ranch and hoped we could squeeze him in. He'll use his jet to fly everyone in, so Brielle won't need to make any kind of flight arrangements and they plan to stay in some of the cottages on the ranch and I already told him we'd work it out. I remember asking her about the number of empty cabins as we begin renovating them before the summer and she mentioned we had guests in most of them, but that some were still vacant and could be used. I know she'll be upset, but she's good at working out last minute details like this."

"I'll let you tell her about it so that she can scream at you directly. I'm sure it will eventually be fine, but you know our youngest likes to throw a fit, just because. I think she's over at the school today. She was planning on helping with the Martin Luther King holiday program the kids are having today. Sarah sent over desserts this morning and last I heard, Brielle was already there. I meant to ask you about her pool?"

Marta thought she'd toss that out there after Brielle asked her to put in her bid of support with him.

"You too? Pool? Perry mentioned it this morning. Who builds a pool in the winter? Besides, we have three indoor pools, one here at the house, an Olympic size one at on-property gym and the one at the onsite hotel. Why does she need a special one at her house?" he asked.

"She likes to invite her friends to the ranch and I'm sure now that she has her own house, she'll be having them over for parties and events this summer and she wants to be ready. She's been begging for three years for that house and now that she has it, you should expect a list of additions. She's a girl and a very spoiled one thanks to her father and brothers!" Marta declared.

"She's my baby girl and I'm supposed to spoil her.

Maybe I can keep her from being angry with me about the last-minute event if I agree to the pool."

"I already agreed to the pool and so did Perry, so you're late," Marta laughed.

"And you say I spoil her. I'll stop by the school. You sure you haven't heard from Perry? I was expecting to see him back on the ranch by now."

"No, nothing. Are you worried about something?" she asked.

"Not really. He seemed concerned about a friend and I was wondering how it went."

"A friend? A woman?" she asked and immediately regretted asking.

"Don't start," David warned.

"Start what? I merely asked a simple question."

"Baby, there are no simple questions when it comes to you. Yes, a woman and no, I don't think it's anything serious."

"I was hoping he'd find someone serious after that catastrophe of a relationship he had with Veronica. I didn't like her," Marta admitted.

"I know you didn't, honey and you made that quite clear to Perry, though I'm glad you played it off in her presence."

"Well, I didn't want to be rude and I wanted Perry to see for himself that she wasn't the one for him."

"You can't pick who your children fall in love with."

"I know, but Perry loves hard and I want it to be

the right woman."

"That and you want grandchildren," David joked.

"Well, there is that. You would think with all these kids, someone would be married with children by now."

"Nick is well on his way and I hear that he and Parker want kids right away."

"Oh, I can't tell you how excited I am about that. I'm looking forward to their June wedding."

"You have one son getting married, so leave Perry in peace and don't push him. He enjoys being a bachelor."

"I know. I've heard the stories. Thank goodness, they aren't bad."

"They're men and there will be stories. There have always been stories about our sons. Give him time, he'll find love. I believe they all will. I'm going to head out. If you see Perry, tell him to come find me."

Marta nodded and went back behind her desk and sat down. Even if her husband warned her to not get involved in their children's personal lives, a reminder he gives to her often, she still wondered about this woman Perry was concerned about.

6

David walked toward the door of his house and grabbed his coat just as his cell phone rang. He smiled when he saw Perry's number knowing he'd just been thinking about him.

"Hey, Perry. Are you back on the ranch? I was just talking about you to your mother. I told her you stepped off the ranch for a bit. If you're calling to see if I'm here, I'm at the house. Come on over and we can talk then," he said.

"Pop, this can't wait until then. I'm not back at the ranch yet, but I'm on my way and I'm not alone. I told you I was going to check on Gizelle and it's not good. In fact, it's worse than I thought."

David stopped moving as if not moving would help him hear better.

"Talk to me, son. What's going on?"

"Well, I went to her house to check on her and the kids and things were crazy."

"Yes, you did. This is the woman I think you're a

bit smitten with."

"Well, right now I'm trying to protect her. I got to her house and there was mayhem. She has an ex-husband who frightened her and her children and totally destroyed the house, the furniture and attacked her. She and the kids were huddled up in one of the bedrooms scared and cold because the door had been left ajar and he broke out one of the windows on the first floor. He'd terrorized them for days."

"Ajar? In this weather? What's going on?" David asked, now pacing in place.

"Pop, she has a hand print bruise on her face and one on her neck. He hit her and I don't know what else he may have done."

David could hear him panting and he tried to focus on the words, though Perry was whispering.

"What!" David exclaimed loudly. When he turned around after his outburst, he saw the startled look on Marta's face as she moved swiftly toward him with a questionable look on her face. He held out his hand to halt her knowing she was about to ask him what was wrong. For now, he could hear the anger and rapidity in Perry's voice and his son needed him.

"Yeah, he hit her, Pop and I found her alone and afraid. They had been there for days like that."

"Where is this guy and what do you need? Did he hurt the kids too?"

"No, just Gizelle. The kids are scared, cold and tired, but I think they're fine."

"Where are you now?"

"I'm on my way to the ranch and I'm bringing them with me. Pop, I knew something was wrong and I should have come earlier to check on them when I couldn't reach her. Something nudged at me for the past two days and I should have checked on her before today. Now, look what happened," Perry said angrily.

"Son, this isn't your fault. No man should ever treat a woman and his kids that way and he should never have laid a hand on her. How is she holding up?"

"Pretty good. We are about ten minutes way. I have them here with me in the truck and they're asleep."

David was fuming. What man hits a woman? Not a real one!

"Did you call Marcus?"

"Yes. He's still at the house with other officers taking stock of everything. He's going to meet us at the ranch soon to talk to Gizelle about what happened."

"Shouldn't she go to the hospital?"

"Pop, I tried to get her to go and she doesn't want to. She said she's fine."

David could hear the frustration through the phone.

"Okay, don't get too worked up. We'll have the doctor here on the ranch take a look at her."

"That's what I thought, too, which is why I didn't

push back on her not going to the hospital. She's so scared right now, I just want to get her and the kids someplace safe."

"Where is this guy who hurt her?"

"Marcus has men out looking for him, but from what Gizelle has told me so far, this guy will know that and is probably out of the state by now. I'm sure he's long gone and for his sake, he'd better be," Perry declared.

"Don't you do anything crazy. Let Marcus handle it. In the meantime, what do you need?"

"Is mom there?"

"Yes, she is," David said, waving for Marta to now come closer.

"This guy is crazy, Pop. I have to keep them safe."

"You already know bringing them to the ranch is the safest place to be. I will get extra guys at the entrance immediately."

"I appreciate it, Pop. Listen, can we send some guys over to fix the door and windows at the house and perhaps try and salvage what can be salvaged from the wreck at her house as far as her furniture? She's renting it from old man Baxter and he'll need to know what happened. I didn't see how bad it was until I got inside. I would have stayed behind to fix it up some, but I wanted to get them out of there."

"You did right and I'm getting guys to her house right now. You said the Baxter place, right?"

"Yeah, and I don't think Clyde is going to show

back up, but tell the guys to be on the lookout, just in case."

"Of course. This guy could try coming back if he wants to while Buck, Sam, John and Horace are there," David said boldly. He knew that no one ever messed with the men who worked on the ranch.

"Enough said," Perry laughed slightly. "No one messes with those linebacker-looking ranch hands," he added.

"Exactly. I need my cell to get these guys moving, so hang up and call your mother on the house phone. She's here and about to blow a gasket only hearing my end of the conversation. Drive carefully and we'll talk more when you get here. Don't worry about a thing. We Sullivans protect what's ours and before you get all crazy over my comment, I already know how you feel about that little woman and one day, I hope you share your feelings with her if you haven't already. She needs to know that there are men out here who are the complete opposite of the fool who hurt her. Call me when you arrive. I have a few things to check up on and to get the guys in motion."

David hung up the phone and grabbed his coat.

"What in the world is going on? What was that about?" Marta questioned.

"I know you only heard my end. I suggest you get to your phone because Perry is about to call and tell you everything. Right now, he has things he needs me to do for him and I don't have time to run this all down to you. We're expecting guests, a woman and her two young children."

Marta was about to ask more questions when the phone on her desk rang. She turned and ran to it before Sarah picked it up and he took that breather to make the calls he needed as he walked out of the house and down the three wooden steps as he dialed Buck's direct line first.

"Buck, I need you to get me four extra guys at the entrance to the ranch with weapons and have a group make a pass around the fencing to be sure there are no breaches. I'm only talking about the private, family side, not the side where all of the activities happen. I don't want our guests on alert as if something is wrong. I don't want anyone on this side of the ranch that's not personally cleared by me, the kids or my wife. Family and staff only. All visitors must be checked and rechecked and all trucks not only looked at around the outside, but open the trailers and look inside also. None should have any unaccounted for personnel."

David knew Buck wouldn't ask a lot of questions. The reason why he had hired Buck and kept him on for the past twenty years as the main overseer of the ranch was because all Buck needed to do was hear the seriousness in his voice to know that he needed to take action with as little questions as possible.

"I'm on it, boss," Buck answered.

"Great. Once you're done getting them in place, I

THE WAY YOU LOVE ME: The Sullivans of Montana

need you, Sam, John and Horace to go board up a house that belongs to a friend of Perry's and see what else you can do to fix it up. Someone caused some damage. Marcus and his team are there and can give you the background. I want to be sure it's closed up and no one can get inside. It's the Baxter place."

"On that, too, Boss."

"Be careful when you get there. The guy who destroyed it is a crazy fool who likes to beat up on women and he isn't operating on all cylinders. Any man who would put his hands on a woman doesn't even care about himself. Call Marcus if you see anyone suspicious lurking."

"This guy hit a woman? I want him to come lurking while I'm there. He'll think twice before he raises his hand to another woman, that's for sure," Buck said.

"Stand in line, buddy. We're all in line behind Perry with that one and right now, I've got to keep my son out of jail. I could hear from his tone that he'd like to run up on this guy. Don't make me worry about you, too, but you know we take care of our own when we need to," David said, meaning every word.

"You got that right. It would be best if this guy found another country to go to because if he stays around these parts and we come up against him, he will regret the day."

"Marcus and his team will catch up to him, but for now, we're keeping her and her kids safe here on the ranch."

"Understood. I got it covered. Do you think four extra guys is enough at the main entrance? I'll also send some guys to the two back entrances as well," Buck offered.

"I'm sure that'll be fine. No one would dare come onto this ranch, but this guy doesn't know about us, so he may be crazy enough to try."

"He won't leave in one piece if he does."

"That's for sure!"

David hung up the phone and quickly ran back in the house to grab his weapon. He didn't make a habit of wearing it around the ranch because he had enough security on the premises to handle any issues, but he didn't know the full story of what was going on and until he did, he would rather be safe than sorry. He walked into the house and stopped briefly as he listened to his wife talking a mile a minute.

"I can't believe he actually hit her. Do I need to have one of our doctors come take a look at her or maybe ask Parker to come by? Okay, I understand. Get them here safe. Do they have clothes or are they coming with what they're wearing? I can have someone go out to get whatever they need. Okay, so I'll talk with her when she gets here. Bring them straight to the house. I'll have some soup and sandwiches made up and I'll have two rooms here at the house fixed up for them. Don't worry about a thing. Your father and I have our assignments and we're taking care of things on this end. I'll call your sister and brothers and have them come lend a hand, too. Okay, see you then."

David walked closer to her as she exhaled and sat down behind her desk to gather herself.

"Are you okay?" he asked.

"I will be once Perry gets Gizelle and her kids here on the ranch. I'm angry over what he just told me. That woman and her kids must be scared out of their minds. I'm going to get Brielle's old room together for Gizelle. Her daughter and son can sleep in the spare room across the hall from her, unless they want to stay close to their mother. Brielle's old bed is large enough for all three of them. If those kids saw what her ex-husband did to her, they are probably clinging closely to her. I just want to hug them all," she said somberly. "Those babies are only three and four years old. I want to strangle this guy," she said.

David was agreeing with her sentiment and knew where his wife's mind was going. Her own experience in her family with an abusive man had to be on her mind.

"I know, but right now, we have things to do. The good thing is they're okay and Perry went on instinct when he went to check on them or there is no telling how long they would have been closed up in that house, terrified. This guy could have even come back and done even more damage. Let's look to what we can do and not to what has happened."

Marta looked up at him with tears in her eyes and David knew he was right. She was thinking about her sister, Jean. He walked over to her and took her by the hand to console her.

"Don't do that, babe. I know where your mind is going and though there was nothing we could do to fix Jean's situation, we can make sure Gizelle and her family are safe."

"I know, I know," she gasped. "I need to call our kids and get them moving."

"Do that."

He watched his wife gather her composure as she picked up the phone to call Brielle, Shelton and Nick, she also called for Sarah and gave her instructions on getting the rooms ready as well as something for them to eat. He stood and watched in awe as his wife of over forty years went into mother-bear mode, even for Gizelle who wasn't one of her children. She knew if Gizelle meant something to Perry, that was all she needed to know.

According to Perry, they were cold and hungry, but not for long. It wasn't even that this woman and her children were clearly special to Perry because he knew that she would go into action for anyone in need, but hearing what happened to Gizelle brought up old memories for her and a soft spot when it came to abused women.

"I'm going to get my gun and head out. Call me if you need me or I'll see you when Perry gets here,"

David said walking over to the gun room and pulled out his key to open the padlocked door. Behind that first door, he keyed in his passcode to open the bank like vault where he had a massive gun collection.

Getting what he needed, David walked out of the house after locking his gun room back up. As he knew Marta was thinking of her sister, he thought about Jean Thompson as well and remembered the beautiful woman and her big bright smile during happier times in her life before her husband, who had been abusing her for years, took her life. The thought of her made him think of his niece and nephew, Khloe and Kenneth, the two children Jean had left behind who were raised by another one of Marta's sisters, Rose-Marie. He made a mental note to check on them. He knew they were all coming to the ranch for the wedding coming up in June, but perhaps, he could find a way to get the family together before then. For now, he needed to deal with the issue at hand and focus his attention on how he can help his son protect Gizelle and her kids from an abusive man. Jean hadn't been as lucky, but he wouldn't let history repeat itself with Gizelle.

7

Parker rolled over and landed smack up against Nick who moaned and pulled her even closer. She planted a soft kiss on his bare chest as she tried to get even closer. If she could stay like this, naked in bed with Nick, she would sign up immediately. If it wasn't for their lives outside of the house they shared on the ranch, she would do just that. Leaning up, this time she kissed him on the lips and smiled when he smiled back at her, though his eyes were still closed.

"Your kisses are why we're still in this bed at this hour," Nick crooned against her neck.

She started to reply when she felt his lips capture hers in a kiss deeper and more possessive than the one she'd given him. Her body tingled as she knew it would because any attention from him always excited her.

"Mmm, I hope there is more," she uttered softly against his lips which were still intimately close to hers.

"All the time, baby."

Parker smiled brighter when he finally opened his eyes and locked onto hers.

"You know, we should be ashamed of ourselves. It's the middle of the day and we're still in bed."

"No one cares and they all know what we're doing, so we may as well live up to their imaginations," he said, snuggling her neck and kissing every piece of exposed skin his lips could find. His hand traveled down the length of her exposed hip as he then moved it around to grasp the lusciousness that was her behind causing her to slide close enough to feel his excitement rise. She loved how Nick felt all over her body, making up for nights when she had to sleep alone because he had to be at the fire station house.

"All this sexing we're doing is crazy. I think we should abstain until after the wedding," she said. When Nick's body stiffen, she pinched his chest so that he'd know she was joking. She was already questioning her idea of abstaining. Now that she's had him and had him a lot, how could she give it up for a few months until the wedding.

"Hell no, and don't speak of it again. I love making love to you every chance I get and I really love how it feels to be inside of your body. If you make me wait, then I'm going to put you over my shoulder and run to find a justice of the peace to marry us today!"

"My sister would kill me if we did that. She's looking forward to my big day. I have a lot of planning to do."

"Yes, you do and while you do that and knowing it's probably going to be stressful, you'll need me to be your stress reliever," Nick crooned and to prove his point, he moved his hips in her direction, allowing her to feel how just the thought of making love to her had his body harden, especially his erection which had already, once again, come to life after their third round of morning lovemaking.

Parker tried to speak, but the words were lost in her throat the minute he felt him long and hard against her soft body.

"Okay, okay, I see what you mean, but I can't stay in this bed with you all day today. I have things to do. I promised Brielle I would help her with setting up for a party that's taking place tomorrow evening since I'm off for a few days. I still want to check on a mare who'll be giving birth in a few days."

"What? How did she know you were off today?"

Parker bit her bottom lip trying to figure out how to tell him she had let that cat out of the bag the night before.

"I'm sorry, baby. She was talking about the party and I assumed you would be at the station house later today and tomorrow especially with the storm coming up in a few days. I know you have a lot of planning to do in case of any emergencies. I didn't know that you had a few days off. I told her I could help her out. Brielle and I have gotten pretty close and I like that we're friends. I haven't really had that since moving to Bozeman, other than my sister. I thought it would be something fun to help out with. I told her I was off and free if she needed help. I had no idea your plan was to keep me in bed all day and night. We need to come up for air."

She tried to move to get out of the bed when Nick pulled her back to him.

"We don't have to get up right this minute. Look at me!" Nick said and moved the blanket so that she could see what she had felt moments ago under the blanket. His nakedness stirred her body to life.

"You know I love your obscene sex drive, but I need to hit the bathroom while I can still walk straight," she joked as she finally slid out of the bed.

"Hey, don't blame me. This last round with all the acrobatics was *your* doing and yours alone. I was here to go along with the ride. I must say you have great balance!" Nick joked.

Parker picked up a pillow that had landed on the floor next to the bed and threw it at him.

"Oh, really? You enjoyed it though, didn't you?" She reached for and put on t-shirt Nick had on the night before and slipped it over her naked body.

"I did and don't cover up. Come right back so that we can pick right back up. You can't let me walk around in this state all day. Help me before you go help my sister. Take pity on your soon-to-be husband.

Walking back over to the bed, she placed a hot,

tantalizing kiss on his lips. When she tried to stand, Nick held on to her head and made love to her mouth, making sure she had plans to come back and finish, knowing what would be waiting for her.

"I got you, baby."

"You know, we need to talk about our life after the wedding."

"What?"

"Are we going to stay on the ranch or do you want a house off the ranch?"

Standing to her full height, she looked over at him.

"Off the ranch? I assumed we would live on the ranch. I love this house and there is room to expand when we decide to have kids. Besides, you'll be at the station house a lot and I want to be around the family here on the ranch. I want our kids to grow up here."

"I was hoping you would want to stay on the ranch. You may not know this but I have a large portion of the property that I own that I haven't done anything with. Dayton is the only one thinking about building something major on his portion of the property. He's planning on a professional size race track to host some of the races that he travels around the world to take part in. Shelton already lives off the ranch in his condo, but he has a place here on the ranch and he hasn't done anything with his largest part of the property either. Perry and Brielle haven't spoken of any plans either. I think Perry is going to start a smaller version of this ranch and call it his own, but who knows when. He's really wrapped up in helping my father expand this ranch for now. We could build another, larger house on my property and think of what else we want to do with it, only if you want to. We'd still be here on the ranch, but not walking distance. My part of the land is at the far end, only minutes from the main driveway. What do you think?"

Parker hadn't thought about it. She knew that Nick liked when he lived away from Bozeman in New York and of all of his siblings, he was the most private, so it didn't surprise her that he may want a life separate from the ranch. Hearing him, it sounded like he had already thought through the idea of staying and wanted her opinion since they were building a life together. She loved working on the ranch and everything about it. She sat on the edge if the bed and faced him.

"Nick, I love the ranch. I will be your wife and anyplace you want to be, I will be with you. As long as we are together, I don't care where we live."

"Are you sure? I know you're thinking that I may have wanted to move away from the ranch since I once lived in New York City."

"I didn't know what you were thinking, but I assumed we would talk about it at some point."

"I know and like you, I want to live here on the ranch. Being at the firehouse a lot, I would feel much better if you were here close to the family, too."

"Good, then we're on the same page. When you're ready to build something new, I'm all in with you. Now that we've decided on where we're going to live, I'll be back in a few minutes to take care of what's been poking me since our last round," she joked and ran off.

As soon as the door shut, Nick relaxed back onto the bed just as his cell phone interrupted the silence.

"Perry! What's up, bro? If you're calling about taking me with you to check out those new horses, I now have the time since Parker committed her day off today to Brielle."

Instead of getting an immediate response, Nick felt the intense moment of silence and he sat straight up on the side of the bed; something was wrong. He waited.

"No, that's not it. I have a situation," Perry said.

Nick felt tension building up in his back at the painful tone of his brother's voice. It wasn't often that Perry sounded vulnerable, but he heard it now and it troubled him. Perry's voice actually sounded strained.

"What's going on?" he asked keeping his voice as calm as possible until he heard what the problem was.

"I need you. I'm on my way to the ranch with Gizelle and her kids and you're the only person in this world who can keep me from dropping them off and going back off the ranch to find this clown who put his hands on her."

"Wait, what? Someone laid hands on Gizelle, that woman I think you're a little bit in love with? What's going on?"

As he listened to Perry tell him what happened, Nick got out of bed and grabbed a pair of boxers from the dresser drawer before going into his closet for a pair of jeans and a shirt. He was still moving about when Parker came out of the bathroom.

"Perry, he did what? He hit her? Is she okay? What about the kids? Did he hurt them? Is she alright? Okay, where are you?" Nick asked as he looked around for his books. He didn't spot them until he turned around and Parker stood with them in her hands. He leaned down and kissed her sweetly, loving that they were so in sync. "You're almost here? Okay, I'm heading to the house right now. What do you need, brother?"

Parker didn't know what was going on or what Perry was saying on the other end of the phone, but whatever it was had to be serious. Nick was practically out of breath in his effort to get dressed.

"Nick?" she asked.

He leaned over and kissed her again and smiled while mouthing to her that he would explain.

"Parker? Yeah, she's here. You need her, too?" he asked. "Okay, she's getting dressed, too and we'll meet you at the house. Under no circumstance are you to leave back off of the ranch. Stay and wait for me before you do something crazy. As you said, I'm the only one who can talk you down off the ledge. You already said Gizelle and the kids were fine and bringing them to the ranch was a great idea. No one will get to them here and if they try, they won't get beyond Buck and his guys at the gate. Parker and I are on our way."

No words were needed between him and Parker as they got dressed together. She knew there was a need and like him, the family was everything. All someone had to do was put out the signal and everyone geared up.

**

"I have everything covered. There are fresh linens on the beds and soup is cooking right now. There's also plenty of spaghetti or anything else they may want to eat. It will only take me minutes to whip something else up. It's been a long time since I've had little kids in the house or cooked for any," Sarah said.

"I'm sure whatever we have will be fine. Be prepared to run hot baths and Perry said Gizelle gathered clothes for them before they left, but who knows what that is," Marta said as they moved about. Every couple of minutes, she would go to the upstairs window to look out to see if Perry had arrived.

"Whatever they don't have, we can check with the stores on the ranch or I'll send someone into town to get anything they need."

"Thank you, Sarah. Is the doctor on the way?"

"Yes. I put in that call for you. Luckily, she was

already on the ranch checking in with the nurse's suite at the school. She's on her way here to the house right now."

"Good. I got a text just now from Parker that she's on her way with Nick. Perry or David must have called them. Can you believe this guy hit her? Perry told me there is an imprint of this man's hand on her face. What kind of monster hits a woman?"

"Monster is the right word."

Sarah knew what Marta was thinking and knew what was coming next.

"This made me think of Jean. Anytime I hear of a domestic situation, I think of my baby sister. My mother never got over losing her."

Sarah had been around almost twenty years ago when the youngest of Marta's sisters, Jean, was killed by her husband in a domestic abuse situation. He had killed her and took her away from her two beautiful babies, Austin and Ariel, who needed her.

"I knew this situation would take you back to that one. You don't talk about Jean often, but something like this was bound to bring up what happened to her. I know you talk to her kids all the time."

Sarah talked as she moved from room to room on the upper level of the house making sure the ladies who kept the cabin rooms cleaned that she'd asked to get two rooms ready with clean linen were moving with a swiftness.

"I talk to them several times a week. Both are in

college and doing well. They'll be here for the Nick's wedding this summer. I still remember that dreadful day as if it happened yesterday. Jean never told any of us about the torture she'd been living through. My mother was already upset that Jean at twenty, had moved out and in with that man and even though he was beating her almost daily, she still married him. It wasn't until after he'd killed her and we were given her personal things that I found her journal where she'd detailed every heinous thing he'd done to her. He killed my baby sister and buried her body in the mountains as if she wasn't a person. He had been beating her and none of us knew it. She hid that abuse from us all and we were busy living our own lives to even notice what she was going through."

Sarah walked over to Marta and held her hand tightly.

"There was no way for you to know if she didn't tell you or let you into her life."

"The only way I've survived is knowing he's behind bars and will be there for the rest of his life, if I have anything to do with it. He killed her because she was going to tell the police that she saw him doing something with an underage girl. He was a pig and my sister did not deserve to die. There is never a reason to put your hands on a woman or anyone for that matter. When Perry told me this man had hit this woman, Gizelle, images of my sister flashed across my eyes."

"She'll be looked at as soon as she gets here. What

about the children? I assume because they didn't go to the hospital that the kids are okay?"

"Perry said only Gizelle was hurt and that the kids were scared and cold, but that's it, which is a blessing. Still, we don't know what the kids have seen and those images will always be a part of their memories."

"Well, they're family now and we'll do what we can to replace those bad memories with good ones. I don't know how long they'll be here, but we'll take good care of them," Sarah said and checked around to be sure they were ready for their guests.

"They can stay as long as they want. I have a feeling this isn't just a regular friend of Perry's, though he didn't say otherwise. I know my son and he wears his heart on his sleeve. I could hear in his voice how deeply he cares for this woman. I hope that man is many, many miles away because that's the only way Perry won't end up in jail for killing him. I don't want that for him. I hope Marcus finds him soon."

"Perry is passionate and if this is a woman he truly cares deeply for, that man had best stay far away. Are you going to be okay if I go down and finish in the kitchen? I want to have everything ready for them the minute they arrive. I'm sure the family will all be around later and I want to plan something big for dinner."

"I'm going to be fine."

Sarah and Marta jumped together, startled when they heard what sounded like Perry's truck pulling up to the house. Racing to the window, Sarah confirmed for her that Perry had arrived.

"It's them," she said.

Without any further words being exchanged, they rushed down the stairs and straight to the front door.

8

After pulling his car to a stop in the circular driveway of his parents' eight-bedroom, eleven-bathroom home, Perry hopped out of his truck and walked around to the other side. He was happy when he opened the back door to find the kids still fast asleep. Looking to the front, Gizelle was also still asleep.

Reaching to undo Carrie's car seat strap as easily as he could without waking her, he turned when the front door of the house opened and out walked his mother followed by Sarah. He saw their ready for action faces and looked to them for direction. Just when he was about to speak, Brielle came running up after jumping out of her silver BMW truck which she had pulled up behind his truck. He then saw Nick and Parker running toward the house to help. He loved that he could always count on them. He looked to Brielle first and then at the kids. He didn't need to tell her what he needed. She moved toward him quickly.

"Parker and I will get the kids," she said moving

around him to get Carrie while Parker opened the other door and reached for Brody. He heard Gizelle coming awake in the front seat and he moved to help her out gently when heard her grunt most likely from the pain of her bruises. As Sarah walked over to help her, he went to the bed of his truck and grabbed the bags she brought from the house. Nick rushed to help him and when he stopped for a second to take in what was happening, he realized Gizelle hadn't said anything and seeing people rushing around may be a bit overwhelming.

"Everyone, this is Gizelle Duncan and those are her children, Carrie and Brody."

He smiled when his mother descended the steps and pulled Gizelle into a slight hug, without being overwhelming. She hugged her tighter when Gizelle began to cry and wrapped her arms tightly around her. He knew what one of his mother's hugs felt like and that it would be exactly what Gizelle needed.

"You're okay, dear. You're going to be fine and so will the children. You can call me Marta and this is my husband David."

Perry turned as his father walked up.

"Gizelle, this is my brother, Nick, Sarah, who takes care of us all, my sister Brielle and this is Nick's fiancé, Parker."

After introducing her to everyone, he exhaled when she gave a little wave.

"Hello," she said softly.

"It's nice to meet you, Gizelle," Brielle said as she held Carrie in her arms while Parker walked with Brody toward the front door. "My mom has beds prepared for them and since they're still asleep, Parker and I are going to lay them down in one of the bedrooms. Is that okay with you?" she asked.

"Yes, and thank you."

Gizelle looked behind her in the direction of the main gate that they'd come through. It wasn't visible from this far onto the ranch, but Perry saw her eyes follow back down the road from the house. He moved closer to her when he saw where her eyes had focused.

"I don't want you to worry about anything. You and your children are safe here on the ranch. No one gets on without scrutiny and no visitors at all. Come on inside where it's nice and warm," Marta said, taking her hand.

"You're very kind," Gizelle said.

Marta looked at her when she winced as they walked.

"Are you okay? Perry told me about your face, but are you hurt anyplace else?"

"My back hurts a little. I think I've been so anxious that I didn't notice it until now."

"Don't worry. There is a doctor on the ranch today and she's on her way over to check out you and the kids," Marta said as they ascended the stairs that led into the house.

"Perry mentioned that a doctor would be here.

Thank you for that. Thank you for everything," Gizelle said crying again, trying to hold the tears back.

"You cry all you want and need to. We're here for you. There is food if you're hungry and a hot bath and bed if you want it. I'm sure Brielle has already tucked the kids in and you'll want to be close to them. Is there anything I can get for you?"

Before Gizelle could respond, David, Perry, Nick and Sarah entered the sitting room where they ended up once inside the house.

"Are you okay?" Perry asked.

"I am, thanks to you and your family."

When Parker appeared behind Nick, Gizelle looked her way.

"The children are still asleep. Neither woke as we laid them down. We only took off their coats and shoes and left them in their pajamas. We did cover them in plenty of warm blankets," Parker said.

"Nick, go turn up the heat on that level," Marta instructed.

"Thank you. They'll probably sleep for quite a while. They were very tired and barely slept over the past few days. They did sleep all night last night, but they woke up several times."

"You were there for a day in that room?" David asked. "Perry told us some of what went down."

"We were in the house for about four days I think, since Friday just before dark. We were there the last night and the day by ourselves until Perry found us. I was afraid to come out. I didn't know where Clyde was, if he was still at the house somewhere or he had left and possibly would come back if I tried to leave. He never did and by the time Perry got there, I was too afraid to move. The kids wouldn't let me move without them and I had no idea what to do. He took my phone and I could hear him breaking things. I've never been so scared in my life."

"You're safe now," Perry said taking her hand. "Why don't you go with my mom and get yourself warm and settled in while I get your car moved to one of the garages. I can hear the tow truck pulling up outside. Is there anyone I should call for you? Your job?" he asked.

"Actually, I'd like to call them if I can borrow a phone."

"There's a phone in my office. Let's take care of that while we wait on the doctor," Marta said.

"Okay, but can I get a minute with Perry, please?" she asked.

The room emptied out, leaving her standing in front of Perry, looking up into his face. With him well over six feet tall, she had to lean back a little from her stance at five-foot six, in order to see his face. While she and the kids were huddled up in her house, she kept thinking about him, wondering if he was concerned not hearing from her. Since the day they'd met months ago, they rarely went more than a few days without a call or a text, mostly texts. It had been a few days since they talked and she had silently prayed that he would sense something was wrong and come for her, which he did.

"Let's sit down," Perry said.

Gizelle sat down beside him on the brown leather sectional.

"Thank you for coming," she said quietly.

"I didn't hear from you and you weren't returning my calls or texts. I felt like something was wrong. In case it wasn't, I had gathered a bunch of fire wood as an excuse to be at your house," he said smiling, feeling like a huge weight had been lifted now that he had her and the kids safely on the ranch.

"You didn't need an excuse to come by the house."

"I wasn't sure. I was worried, which is why I showed up and I'm glad I listened to my sixth sense."

"So am I. Do you think your sheriff friend has any information on Clyde?"

"Probably not or he would have come by here or called by now. He's on his way though. He needs to talk to you while everything is still fresh on your mind."

"I think it will always be fresh on my mind."

"Don't worry about that. We need to get you and the kids settled in, warmed up with some bowls of Sarah's homemade soup. If there is anything you need, let me know."

"I don't know how to thank you. I know this is a bit much for you to get involved in."

"It's not and don't think that way."

Gizelle laughed a little.

"I guess if we were leading to anything one day other than just being friends, that's over with now, huh? I'm sure you don't need this kind of drama in your life. I really thought after I'd left, filed for divorce and for custody of the kids and didn't hear anything from him, that he'd just let me go. I should have known better because of how possessive he is."

Perry took both of her hands in his.

"There's no doubt that I've been interested in you, but held back because I know you were trying to get your own life in order and I didn't want to get in the way. Just so you know, nothing has changed when it comes to my interest in you. We're going at your pace and we still will. Right now, protecting the three of you is my priority, but have no doubt, sweetheart, I still plan on there being a me and you. For now, focus on you and the kids settling in and we'll have plenty of time to talk about us. I am going to check-in with Marcus to see what's going on. If you need me, use any phone around here to call me. I'm going to deal with your car first and then you and I can work on getting you a new cell phone. You need to have one. Are you okay for now?"

"I am, thanks to you. I need to call my job and tell them what's going on and then I'll check on the kids. They will be out for a while, but when they get up, they'll need to be able to see me."

"Good idea."

Perry stood and pulled her up with him, bringing her into a tight embrace.

"Thank you, Perry. Thank you for coming for me."

"I'm glad you're okay and I would do it a million more times."

As they moved apart, Perry watched her as she joined his mother who gave her the house phone to call her job. Turning, he walked through the front door and closed it behind him, finding his father and Nick standing on the porch talking.

"How is she?" David asked.

"She's going to be fine. I think once she gets some rest, she'll relax more. She's worried about her children, as any mother would. I swear, I want to kill this guy. Did you get a look at that huge bruise on her face?"

He finally let go of the frustration he'd been holding in since arriving on the ranch. His heavy footsteps across the wooden porch vibrated in the air as he paced around, letting go of the negative energy that flowed through him.

"Son, I can see how riled up you are and I need you to pull it back."

"Look at her car?" Perry said pointing to the tow truck that had driven up. He waved to Tomas, the driver who he'd known for years.

"He did that?" Nick asked.

"Yeah, he did. Tomas, take it around to the

garage," Perry yelled to him and they watched as he backed up and took the car around to the back of the house where there were eight garages. He'd get someone to fix Gizelle's car later.

"Did you see her neck?" he declared loudly.

"I did and I know it's painful to think about, but for now, let it go and focus on what she needs. I'm sure she doesn't need you thinking about revenge or running out of here to hunt Clyde down. That's not the answer," David offered.

Perry huffed in anger.

"Pop is right, bro. Gizelle needs your support of her current situation, not your anger in support of what happened. There is time to focus on that another time. I see the doc walking this way," Nick said.

"I'm good. I'm pissed, but I'm focused on what's important right now."

Perry inhaled the cold winter air and turned to greet the doctor.

"Doctor Boyle!" David said cheerfully.

"It's Amanda and I'm fine. I was at the school and got a call that there was someone you wanted me to check over? Hey Perry, Nick," she added.

"Hey, Doc. Yes, she's here. Her name is Gizelle, a friend of mine," Perry explained.

"Is she hurt bad?"

"I'm not sure how bad. She's inside with my mom and she has two kids who are sleeping upstairs."

"Are the kids hurt?"

"No, I don't think so, but Gizelle can fill you in with more," Perry said.

"Why aren't they at the hospital?"

"I couldn't get her to go and the kids were terrified enough. Gizelle said they hadn't been harmed and she was afraid that if we took her to the hospital and they separated her from the kids to fix her up, they would go ballistic not seeing her. I convinced her to come here because I knew we could call you to help. I'm glad you were already here on the ranch."

"Okay, you did right. Take me to them," she said.

Perry opened the front door of the house and entered behind her.

"Marta!" Amanda exclaimed and went into what she knew would be a warm, welcoming hug.

"Amanda, it's always good to see you. We have a patient for you. She went upstairs to check on her children. I'll take you up while the guys stay down here," Marta said the moment she saw Perry move in the direction of the stairs.

Knowing the message behind his mother's words, Perry followed David and Nick into the kitchen, giving the doctor time alone with Gizelle. Brielle came down the steps into the kitchen from the back stairs and joined them.

"Before you grill me, the kids are fine and still sleeping. I went back up to check on them one last time and Parker is in with mom, Gizelle and Dr. Boyle. This is really something, huh?" she asked.

"It sure is," Nick said as they sat around the kitchen table while Sarah stirred one pot after another on the stove. "I know we're all concerned about Gizelle, but you know mom is also thinking about her sister, aunt Jean. I abhor any man who puts his hands on a woman or child in a violent or unwelcomed way."

"I'm with you on that, brother," Perry said. "Gizelle has told me some about her life before she moved to Montana, but she left out the part about how abusive Clyde was to her."

"So, are you and Gizelle dating and how have you been able to keep that a secret?" Brielle asked.

"No, we're not really dating and it's not that I don't want to get closer to her. Right now, we're friends, but in being completely open and honest with you, this situation showed me how short life is and how quickly things can happen and that the most important thing to me right now is their safety. She's an incredible woman and my heart hurts knowing I couldn't protect her from him. I was keeping my distance, but not anymore. I will hurt anything and anyone who tries to hurt her or her kids. I just hope I don't have to," Perry added.

"Son, I don't want to see you get into any trouble. Let Marcus and his team handle this and you focus on making them feel at home here. They are welcomed to stay as long as they like."

"Thanks, Pop. I don't want to tell her what to do, but I'm hoping I can convince her to not go back to that house and to stay here on the ranch. I think she saw this as a temporary situation in the heat of the moment, but I can't let them go back to that house without me being there with them."

"There is plenty of room here at the house for her and the kids or they can move into one of the vacant cabins we have here on the ranch. There is plenty of room either way," David said.

"I'm thinking of letting them move into my house here on the ranch and I'll take one of the smaller cabins. My place has plenty of room and it's the closest to the main house here. I don't know, I just want them safe."

"Bro, you don't have to figure this out today. For now, we're all going to pitch in to help her," Nick said.

"Yes, we are," Marta said joining them.

"Where is she?" Perry asked jumping up and looking around and not seeing Gizelle.

"Amanda and Parker are still examining her. I asked again if she wanted to go to the hospital to get checked out and she was about to breakdown, so Amanda is doing the exam here. I gave them some privacy and though she said the kids were uninjured, Amanda wants to give them a quick checkup too. They're still sleeping in Brielle's old room, but she'll get them up when Amanda is ready to check them over."

"Hey! What's everyone doing gathering in the kitchen like a town meeting?" Shelton said entering the kitchen, unaware of the activities around the day. "Why are there so many men at the entrance and some have rifles in plain sight?" he added.

"Oh, you've missed a lot. I left you a voicemail. Have a seat and we'll bring you up to date," David said.

Perry kept his eyes on the stairs and waited for any chance he could get to check in on Gizelle.

9

The day had been long and Gizelle was more than grateful for Perry and his family. No one has ever cared for her as much as they had in one day. After arriving on the ranch, the doctor had checked her over and though she was bruised in several places, nothing was severe enough that warranted a trip to the hospital and she was thankful for that. Carrie and Brody were fine, as she expected, but they woke a few hours after their arrival on the ranch and didn't see her and as she sat in the family room at the house with Perry and his parents, the moment they heard the children crying, she got up to run to them, but Perry beat her to them by a mile when he took the steps two at a time. As soon as they reached the bedroom, both kids looked around confused until they saw her and reached out their arms to her. After getting them calmed down, she was able to get them hot baths and in their favorite pajamas which she was glad she thought to bring along. They then had soup and sandwiches that Sarah had prepared, which they devoured.

Proving that children are easily acclimated to any new environment, within an hour of eating, they were laughing and playing with Perry as they watched their favorite cartoons in the large media room off of the kitchen.

As people came and went from the house throughout the rest of the day, she was reminded that Clyde was still out there someplace. The sheriff had come by that evening after she arrived and then had come back later to give her an update, which wasn't a whole lot.

So far, they had not been able to locate Clyde, but law enforcement was on the lookout for him. Her house had been secured, thanks to the men Perry's father had sent to fix it up and the owner had been contacted and was sympathetic. Since he knew the Sullivans and knew they were good people, he told her to not worry about the house and to let him know if she was planning to move back in. He would waive her rent for two months while she figured her situation out. The thought of going back to the house terrified her. She felt vulnerable in the out of the way house.

When she'd first moved into it, she thought it was a safe place and a safe distance from Clyde. For now, she felt safer than she had in a long time, but that would end when she had to return to her life, something that frightened her. For now, she enjoyed the quiet time with Perry and the kids. She'd been at his parents' house for almost a week and Perry came by every day and in the evening when he stopped by, he stayed until she prepared to give the kids baths and got them ready for bed. Tonight, the house was quiet with his father out taking care of things around the ranch while Marta took some time to herself in her reading room in another part of the house. Sarah had left for home after preparing dinner. That left her, Perry and the kids alone around the fireplace watching television. Not long after dinner, Carrie and Brody had fallen asleep, one in her arms and the other laid across her lap. She and Perry talked about what happened. She knew it was time to tell him everything.

"Your family is amazing."

"Yes, they are and I love them like crazy."

"I've never had a big family like yours. It was always me and my mother. She didn't have the best relationship with her family and I didn't know them very well, though they lived in Chicago. They were estranged after my mother ran off with some band and then met my father at a casino on an Indian reservation. Once he died within a few years of my birth, my mother had to go back to Chicago and I never knew my father's family. I thought Clyde was my escape when I met him after my mother passed away and I had to fend for myself."

"Has he always been violent toward you?"

"No, not at first. The first year was fine and we were happy or so I thought. Then he started drinking and doing drugs, hanging out with some unsavory friends and as time went by and I had kids, I didn't want what he was turning into around them. We fought all the time and then what started out as arguments started escalating to physical abuse. I left when it got really bad and he screamed at Brody, pulling him hard by his arm one day and all I could think was his abuse would shift from me to the kids and it was then that I knew it was time to leave."

"How did you end up in Montana?"

"You remember my friend Heather?"

"Yeah, I remember her. She is who you would come to the *Steely Gray* with, right?"

"Yes. Well, I've known her since my days back in Chicago. We remained friends when she moved here to be with some guy a few years back, right after I'd had Brody. We stayed in touch and when I shared with her that I needed a place to start over, she suggested I come here and she would help me with the kids. I figured it was far enough away and though I'd never in my wildest dreams think that I'd be living in Montana, I fell in love with the place. The kids and I stayed with her for about three months since she was again single. The guy she came here to be with had moved on to someone else. With money I had saved up and the job I was able to get at the law firm as a receptionist, I was able to rent the small house we moved into. For the first time in my life, I felt like I was living my life on my terms and then little things started happening."

"Things like what?"

"Well, in the past three weeks, I would leave work and I would have a flat tire out of nowhere. When the mechanic looked at it, he said the tire had been slashed. I was pulled over by one of the deputies one day because the lights on the back of my car were broken out. I know I didn't bump into anything and he said it was possible some kids may have done it. There were times that I felt like someone was following me, but I couldn't confirm it. It was just a feeling I got. Lately, with the new snow, after picking the kids up from daycare, I would see car tracks leading to my house and footprints around the property. I called the property manager and it wasn't him."

"Did you tell anyone about all of this?"

"No. I just thought it was kids or something. I never thought it was Clyde. After the divorce was granted, he never reached out to me by phone, email, nothing. Because our situation was domestic battery, I assumed he didn't want to make a fuss about anything and my lawyer told me he had signed the divorce papers and didn't fight custody of the kids. I thought I was free and that he wanted to be free of us. I was so wrong," she murmured.

"You couldn't have known and I don't care what happens in life, there is never a reason for abuse of any kind. You're safe now."

The idea of being safe from Clyde sounded good, but she was afraid to live in a world where she imagined danger didn't exist off of the ranch when she knew that wasn't reality.

"For now, but what happens when we go back home? I'm going to have to leave Montana to get away from him."

"No, no, no. No more running and you don't have to go back to the cabin. You and the kids can stay right here on the ranch until you figure things out. You can keep your job and the kids will be safe here. I can have someone looking out for you when you leave the ranch. You can put the kids in daycare here on the ranch, so you know they will be safe. At least stay until he's captured."

"Your parents don't want me and two little kids taking up their space. I feel like I'm intruding, though they've been extremely kind. I appreciate everything you and your family are doing for us knowing you don't have to."

"Yes, I do. I feel the need to protect you, Carrie and Brody and that's what I intend to do. My parents have no problem with you being here and as far as these two, my parents are going to eat them up. As you know, they don't have any grandchildren, though my mother drops hints all the time," he laughed.

"Did you see how Carrie followed your mom around all day?"

"She's already in love with my mom like every person in the world who meets her does. You'll be fine and you can stay as long as you want."

"Your parents said the same thing. I feel like we're going to be in the way and all this drama could be brought to the ranch and I don't want that. I don't want Clyde bringing any hurt or harm to your family."

"Don't worry about my family. Trust me when I tell you we can take care of us and between us and the staff around here, no one will get to any of us without going through them first."

"I saw those guys. Where did you recruit them from, the military?"

"You would think so. We employ hundreds of loyal staff and we're all like family. Don't think you're in the way or that you're bringing any harm here. Clyde does not want the Sullivans in his life. He may like to hit on women, but if he tries anything here, he will never raise his hand to anyone else again. Besides, there is no way for him to know you're here. It's not like we've been dating or anything that would link us," Perry said and then regretted his words. He didn't want to bring up a conversation about the two of them. It wasn't the time or place for that. "Sorry about that," he said.

"Perry, it's okay. It's not that I haven't thought

about it over the past several months and then you said earlier this week that you were feeling the same way about me and that you still did. I don't know what we've been waiting on. It's like we've both been dancing around our attraction to each other."

"I like you, Gizelle, that's no secret, but I've kept my distance and I'll keep doing that because my only concern is keeping you safe. Whatever will happen with us, I believe will happen. I don't want you to think that you being here on the ranch is my way of taking advantage of that and getting close to you. I've wanted to do that for some time, but first, I want you to feel comfortable and get your wits about yourself back. I can wait."

Gizelle didn't have to hear the words to know that Perry was an incredible man. She knew that from the moment she'd met him. She could have thought that about him and then realized differently if they'd gotten involved like she did with Clyde, but she knew in her heart that the man she was looking at was the kind of man that all women wanted and she was no exception.

"I appreciate that. I like you too and I've wondered what was going on between us. I thought maybe you weren't interested besides being friends."

"Sweetheart, you have no idea how much I'm interested in being more than friends. We can talk about that another time. For now, stay on the ranch as long as you like. I was actually thinking about a different arrangement if you plan to stick around a while. If you want more privacy, you and the kids can move into my house and I can move into one of the smaller cabins. My house has much more space with several bedrooms and is already fully furnished. It could use a woman's touch to give it a softer feel and we can move some furniture and things in for the kids so that they feel comfortable. Like I said, the kids will be fine in daycare here on the ranch. We have three different class rooms for three and four year old children and they will love it."

"Did I tell you that your mother said there was an opening at the school for an additional administrator and if I wanted the job, even temporarily, she offered it to me. We talked about me going back to work and she didn't want me to worry about my safety while also knowing that I need to get back to some normalcy."

"That's a great idea. You'd be working where the kids are every day. Are you thinking about taking the job?"

"I am going to take it. I've been thinking about it all day. Tomorrow, I'm going to tell your mother that I accept. Everyone is going above and beyond for us and I can't figure out how to say thank you enough."

"One thing you will find about my family is that this is who we are and we are happily helping you out. You're special to me and that automatically makes you special to them. I like the idea of you being on the ranch and I can see you more often."

"I'd like that a lot."

"We will keep them safe."

"I have no doubt about that. I heard your dad talking earlier with his men about the measures he wants in place. This place is like Fort Knox."

"That it is. He's ramping up security, but believe me, this ranch was safer than a military base even before you arrived. Everything precious to my dad is on this ranch, starting with the family and safety is always the priority."

"So, there are two separate parts to the Sullivan Ranch? What side did I visit with the kids?"

"Yes, there are. When you visited, you were on the entertainment side of the ranch which is open to the public for a fee based on what they want to visit. There is the zoo, the petting farm, horse riding and so much more. You only saw the animals and one day soon, I'll take you on a tour of the entire facility. Then there is the family side where we all have houses and live and so does a lot of the staff. The ranch is humungous, but still manageable. There is no entrance to this part of the ranch that's open to the public. This place is guarded around the clock and we've never had an issue here. Any issues have always happened off the ranch, so I'm pretty certain you'll be safe here. What do you think?"

Gizelle smiled as she moved Brody from her arms to the seat beside her where he squirmed, but fell right back to sleep. She turned as much as she could with Carrie on her lap and faced him.

"I think you are an incredible man, unlike any I've ever met before. You care when you don't have to. I feel safe with you and I already told you that I like you."

"The feeling is mutual. There will be a time to explore that, at least I hope so."

"So do I. For now, yes, I'd like to stay on the ranch. I love Mr. Baxter's little house we were in, but it's not safe right now and I appreciate your hospitality."

When Perry took her hands in his, she'd never felt more safe or more comfortable.

"Do you think you'd like to move into my house? If so, I can stay at the main house here or, like I mentioned, I could also have my things moved to one of the cabins and we can get you and the kids settled in a few days. My mother will love the chance to furnish rooms for Carrie and Brody. Be ready for her to take over," he joked.

"I'm okay with that. My kids have never had grandparents and already, your parents have told them to call them Gigi and Pop Pop."

"And so, it begins," Perry laughed. "They already have my parents eating out of the palm of their hands. They're going to spoil your kids."

"I saw them laughing and smiling today as if nothing had happened earlier in the week and as long as your parents don't mind, I love it."

"They don't mind at all. It's getting late and I need to start getting my things packed up so that my mom can have a crew at the house to see what needs to be done to get you moved in. For now, enjoy being here at the house where Sarah cooks the most delicious food and there is plenty of space for the kids to run around and play. I'm glad you're safe and the Dr. Boyle said the bruises will heal soon. I can barely see any sign of them already."

"I'm glad it wasn't worse. I've never seen him so angry. Clyde really had the look of a monster on his face."

"You won't have to worry about that here."

Perry stood to leave.

"Thanks for looking being you," Gizelle said standing and following behind him to the door.

"Do you need me to help you get the kids upstairs?"

"No. I'm going to sit with them here for a little while longer. This room is relaxing, warm and inviting and I want to enjoy it a little more. Are you sure you have to leave right now?"

"I want to check in with Marcus and with the staff and then spend some time looking over some work for meetings I have over the next couple of days. We had some heavy snow yesterday and after one, I typically do a check of buildings on the property. I'll stop by first thing in the morning. What are you planning to do?"

"Get the kids enrolled in daycare is my priority for tomorrow and spend some time talking to your mother about some things."

"I was thinking of stopping by here to have lunch with you."

Gizelle knew her inner excitement showed on her face.

"I would love that."

"Since you're going to take the job here on the ranch, are you going to call your current boss to let him know your plans?"

"I will after I speak to your mother."

"A lot is happening and it's happening pretty fast. Take some time to yourself. You deserve that."

"I will."

"Say, have you spoken to your friend, Heather?"

Gizelle didn't want to tell him about the cryptic conversation between her and Heather. She needed to think through the awkward conversation before she shared the strange chat.

"I talked to her yesterday. I called the law firm and gave her my new phone number."

"She's a good friend, huh?"

"I have a few other friends here, but she's been good to us."

"Did she not wonder where you were for four days? I know you're close," Perry asked.

As soon as he said the words, that idea came to

her mind again.

"I did wonder about that and I asked her when I called her. She said that she knew I was off for a few days and wanted some quiet time with the kids. When I didn't call her to say I would be meeting her at the *Steely Gray* that night, she assumed I was staying in with the kids."

"Let me know if you want her name added to the visitor's list or anyone else. No one is allowed on this side of the ranch without prior approval from someone in the family, so think about that."

"I will."

Without thinking, Gizelle moved to wrap her arms around Perry and held on tight. She leaned further into him the moment his arms pulled her close to him. They stood like that for several minutes with neither of them saying a word.

She knew that this is what it should feel like between a man and a woman. There should never be any harm. His arms felt perfect and she looked forward to the direction their friendship would take when they were both ready; when the time was right.

10

"It's been three weeks, Marcus and there's been no sighting of Clyde?" Perry asked.

"Sorry, but nothing. This guy is ghost. I don't think he's in Montana any longer, but we won't be caught sleeping just in case he is. We have all eyes out for this guy. How are Gizelle and her kids doing? I'm going to stop by the ranch this week to check on them. I stopped by the law firm that she listed as her employer and they told me she's not working there anymore. Is everything okay?"

"They're doing good. Carrie and Brody have settled in nicely on the ranch and they go to the daycare here and are loving it. Sometimes, at the end of the day, my mother picks them up and takes them to the house with her where she lets them help her and Sarah bake cookies, the highlight of their day. Gizelle is now working on the ranch at the daycare. She was going to go back to work at the law firm, but when my mom offered her a job, she decided to take that. With the expansion of the school to add the upper grades, my mom was already looking to increase the staff for the school and the daycare and so she added a position for Gizelle at the daycare center and she's already thinking of moving her over to the elementary school to run the main office. I thought she would do it temporarily to give herself something to do, but when mom asked if she wanted to keep the job permanently, she said yes and gave her notice at the law firm."

"Hey, all that sounds great. What about the house? I have been going by her house and having others keep an eye on it and there have been no signs of her moving back in yet, though I see it's been fixed up."

"Yeah, well, she and the kids have moved into my house here on the ranch."

"What? It's like that?" Marcus asked.

"No, it's not – at least not right now. I've been staying at the main house, but I'm going to move, temporarily, into one of the cabins on the grounds. Right now, it's easy being at the house and it's right up the road here on the ranch from my house. I like being this close if she needs me. My mother has completely transformed my house into a home for Gizelle and her kids. She feels safe on the ranch and after what happened, there was no way my mother was going to let her move back there as long as Clyde was still on the loose and I wasn't going to let them move back to that house without me, so here on the ranch was the best place."

"Dude, you love that house."

"Of course I do, but you should have seen the kids the second day after they woke up there once we got them moved in. Brielle had brought toys and movies and they were playing and laughing like the misery that Clyde brought had never happened. I don't want to move them out. The house she was living in will stay boarded up for now, but she's planning on letting Mr. Baxter know that she's not planning on moving back. Even if she leaves the ranch, she's thinking about getting a smaller place that's around more people and definitely one with an alarm system and possibly a garage if she can afford it."

"Dude, I have never known you to be like this when it comes to a woman. I don't even have to ask if she's having any troubles. If she does, I know you've got it covered. She's lucky to have you."

"I'm the lucky one. Gizelle is special to me and I've been enjoying spending time with her and her kids these past few weeks. I want them to feel like this ranch is home and even though no one can get on the ranch because of the tight security, my house is the most secure and when I explained the security system to her, I saw relief come over her as if she knew she could finally get a good night's sleep without the worry of Clyde showing up."

"Man, I've known you a long time and your heart

is all in with Gizelle. I could tell that even before that stuff happened at her house. We've been out enough times hanging with the fellas and when the subject of Gizelle came up, you would light up like a Christmas tree. She's special."

"That she is, but we're taking things slow. Right now, the focus has been on keeping them safe while you and your team look out for Clyde."

"Well, the safest place for her to be is definitely on the ranch. Do you know that Buck actually called your father the other day when I came to the ranch to make sure it was okay to let me on? That was a first, but definitely not a problem. I understand the extra security."

"Yeah, Buck does not play when it comes to the safety on the ranch. Dad mentioned that and told him to add you to the list of people to let through without checking. You should be good when you come by again."

"I'll be by sometime tomorrow. We've had a rash of break-ins and my team has been busy. Tell Gizelle I said hello."

"I will. I've just finished my last meeting of the day on the expansion and thought I would go by the school to check on her. I'll tell her you'll be by tomorrow to update her."

"I'll see you then," Marcus said and hung up.

Perry moved around the cabin he decided to finally start living in and giving his parents back their privacy in their house. He was too old to be living at home when there were plenty of other places to live on the ranch. He decided on the two-bedroom cabin closest to Gizelle. It was already furnished with a bed and other pieces of furniture, which was enough for him. His only necessity was a bed that he could crash on after his long work days.

As he looked throughout the cabin to take note of what else he would need after moving his clothes in, he thought back over the three weeks that Gizelle had been on the ranch and how much time they were able to spend together. He loved that they were getting the chance to get to know each other more and he loved when the kids saw him, they ran and grabbed onto him for a hug. Recently, he'd gotten accustomed to visiting them at the end of a busy work day either to share dinner with them or just sit and watch television as Carrie and Brody told him how much they loved their school. He was happy that they were happy and that he could be a part of their day. Today, he was hoping for something a little bit more. All of their time had been spent on the ranch, but tonight he was hoping he and Gizelle could go on an actual date, off of the ranch. He knew she didn't care to leave the ranch, still afraid of Clyde being out there somewhere, but he hoped she would trust him to keep her safe.

After taking one last look around, he locked the cabin up and walked the short distance back to the main house to give his mother an update on the expansion and to ask if she would be open to watching Carrie and Brody for a few hours. He already knew the answer, but still, he wanted to ask. He wanted to have something in place for the kids if Gizelle said yes to going out with him. As he got closer to the house, his mother came out on the front porch and waved.

"You're here! I was thinking about you. Proposals have begun coming in and Shelton wants to sit down with you and your father and decide who will get the contract as the subcontractor on the project coming up in the Spring."

"Yeah, Shelton called me about an hour ago and I told him I have some time, but to let me take a look at the proposals first and then we can talk. Can you email me everything and I'll take a look?"

"Come on inside and I'll email them now. How are things?"

Perry followed her and knew she was asking about Gizelle and the kids.

"Things are good. I'm actually headed to the school to talk to Gizelle. I was thinking of seeing if she'd like to have dinner and maybe take in a movie with me off the ranch. I want her to be safe, but she also needs to get off the ranch some."

"She's still afraid of the unknown, but with you by her side out for an evening, she'll be fine and I'm sure she'll love it. Gizelle is a major asset to the staff. She's even come up with some ideas for generating donations to the school, starting with the law firm she worked for. She reached out to them and they've not only agreed to donate computers to the current and new school, but they also want to have staff at the firm come on board as tutors. That started things rolling and so far, we've had six other companies offering the same service. I really like her."

"I know you do, mom."

"You like her, too."

He looked her way and then looked back down at the papers in front of him that he was fake reading.

"Is that so? You know this?" he asked without looking her way.

"You know how long I've loved your father? I know love when I see it and you and Gizelle need to stop acting like you're not a little bit in love with each other. You spend all of your down time with them and Nick and Shelton already told me they've tried to get you to go out with them a few times over the past few weeks and you don't even bother to make up an excuse; you just say no, you're going to check on Gizelle instead. I see what's going on even if you don't want to openly say it."

"There is no getting anything past you, huh?" he asked.

"You know I want all of my children in happy, healthy relationships and I think Gizelle is perfect for you and those kids love you."

"They love you and Pop, too."

"True and they are preparing me to be a

grandmother."

Perry caught the sly look she gave him before she cut her eyes away and like him, faked like she was reading something on her desk.

"If you say so. You need to talk to Nick and Parker. I hear she wants a house full of kids and Nick said he wanted as many as she did. You'll hear the sound of more little feet around here within a year of them getting married I'm sure."

"I sure hope so. It's good to see my boys finally settling down and yes, I mean you as well as Nick. Now, Shelton and Dayton are another story. I think there isn't a woman in the world that can tame either one of them."

"You have no idea, mom."

"I know your father has shielded me for years from the antics of my wild sons."

"Yeah, it was best you didn't know, but Pop kept us in line as much as he could."

"If nothing else, I know he taught you that though it's all fun and games with one woman after another, you knew to not set out to hurt any of them physically or emotionally and that's all I could ask."

"You're right about that. We would never, ever hurt a woman and even though we spent a lot of time with a lot of women, I'll say it like that, we were always respectful or we would have to deal with David's wrath and then he threatened to clue you in if we didn't listen to him and none of us wanted that."

"Ah, the threat of Marta Sullivan works every time," she joked.

"Yes, every time."

"My sons are the best parts of their dad. The woman each of you find that you love and want to make a life with will be the luckiest woman alive."

Perry paused before continuing. When his mother looked his way, he held her glance. "I really like her. She's unlike any woman I've ever met. She wasn't trying too hard to impress me and she didn't dress like she was shopping for a one-night stand and believe it or not, she had heard about the Sullivan boys and wasn't infatuated with that either. You know your sons have a reputation with the ladies which is no secret around Bozeman and other surrounding towns and cities."

"Yes, I know and luckily, I haven't heard anything crass or disrespectful. I know that women have thrown themselves at all of you since you were teenagers and even back then, some of the grown women would make comments about you which I had to shoot down and threaten them with bodily harm if they laid a hand on any of my sons."

"We heard about that," he laughed.

"I'm sure you did. A few times, your father had to hold me back from laying hands on a few older women who thought they would get a sample of my sons, from what I've heard it called."

"Look at you, the boxer!"

"Yeah, well, believe me, this nature of protection you feel toward Gizelle is bred from my protection of all of you. It's who we are and though I'm sad about what Gizelle went through, I'm glad she has you to lean on in her time of need."

"I'm hoping it's not just that."

"I know it's not. Gizelle is not the kind of woman to only want to need a man because she needs to have one. She's capable of taking care of herself. It's more than that and I want you to be open to being ready for more. You're the oldest and of all of my children, you love the hardest, though you don't do it casually. You are a lot like your father and men as kind, warm, loving and caring as he is are rare, but you've got that gene. Gizelle has been through a lot, but on the other side of all that misery is a woman who still wants to be loved by a good man. She hasn't had that, but I believe she sees it in you. Let her know I'll pick the kids up, okay?"

"Well, I haven't actually asked her out on this date yet. I'm just coming from my last meeting of the day and I stopped by the cabin that's closest to my house and decided to move in there. I'm going to head over to the school before she gets off to see if she wants to go out tonight and if so, I'll call you about picking up the kids. If she wants to wait, I'll let you know when. Luckily, there isn't a forecast of snow this week, so if she wants to postpone our date, we can do that."

"I'm glad about that. Usually, when we get past

one snow storm, another is close behind."

"It's actually kind of warm today."

"Well, you had better get going. I'm going to be interviewing a few potential new teachers for the next school year and I want to be done in time to pick the kids up because I know Gizelle is going to say yes. She's been waiting on you to ask her out for the past three weeks and probably longer. When she's here, she's always talking about you and how she looks forward to you stopping by after work. Every time someone comes in the door, she'll look toward it with excitement until she sees it's not you. Both of you are in love and it's obvious to everyone, but the two of you. Get out of here so that I can make some plans for me and the kids tonight. I want to get snacks and movies lined up. Your father bought them sleeping bags that they can use in the family room when they're here. He saw it on some movie he was watching with them last week. You worry about me spoiling them, but he's got me beat."

Perry stood to leave.

"That's my cue before you start talking about grandkids again. Thanks for watching them tonight."

"Anytime. Have a good time and don't worry about them. We'll get them to daycare in the morning in case you want to do a late movie. Watch your back out there."

"I will. I know that Clyde is still out there and I'm watching for him and so is Marcus. I'll talk to you later."

Leaving the house and walking over to the school, he hoped Gizelle's night was open for time with him. His mother was right, he was in love with her and that love grew with each passing day. He wouldn't hit Gizelle with the pressure of sharing that he was in love with her just yet, but he wanted nothing more than to spend an evening with just the two of them. Though others believe that Clyde was probably back in Chicago by now, he felt differently, but one fool doesn't stop the progression of life. Normalcy was needed which included giving Gizelle a real chance to know him as more than just a casual friend and see that not all men were like her ex-husband.

11

Perry pulled up to the restaurant and exited his brand new dark green Ford Mustang, a car he'd bought months ago, but hardly ever drove. Tonight, was a special night and having Gizelle in the passenger seat looking more beautiful than he had ever seen any woman, turned this into the perfect evening to get it on the road. As he came around to the passenger side, he handed a large tip to the valet and opened her door, marveling at her exquisiteness.

"Can I say again that you look gorgeous tonight. I don't think I've ever seen you in red which is definitely your color."

When Gizelle stepped out of the car with one pristine, toned leg at a time, his body reacted with a desire so fierce, he hoped he could get through the night without foaming at the mouth and embarrassing himself. The sexy black leather boots that rode all the way up to her knees added to her delectable look. The red form fitting, wool dress and black leather jacket had his attention the moment he showed up at the house to pick her up and she opened to door to his knock. For a few seconds, he'd lost the ability to speak after seeing her. Her hair was down around her shoulders on one side and pinned up on the other. Never had he seen a woman more lovely.

"Thank you. This is a dress I've had forever and never found an opportunity to wear. I grabbed everything I could from my closet and when your men who fixed up the house brought the rest of what I'd left there, this dress was in those bags and I thought it would be perfect for a night out with you."

"I'm glad you chose tonight and that you chose me to wear it with. I am the luckiest man in the world," he said taking her hand and escorting her inside of the restaurant.

Perry was glad he was able to get a reservation. He didn't just pick any restaurant in Bozeman, but he chose the most popular fine-dining experience, a place that usually required reservations days, oftentimes weeks in advance. Knowing the owner personally helped make getting in for the evening a possibility.

"This place is beautiful. I've heard of it and I understand there is usually a waiting list that can expand days and sometimes week just to get a reservation. How long ago did you plan this night?"

"I know Saul, the owner and when I initially called when you agreed to go out with me, I was told there was a table available two weeks from now. I thought about going someplace else, but I really wanted to bring you here. The food and ambiance are the best around. I sent a text to Saul and he told me to come on through and he would make sure a table was available for me."

Gizelle looked up at him and smiled.

"I like that you know people."

"Anything for you," Perry said removing his hat, taking her by the hand and planting a sweet kiss on the back of it. He was going all out for her tonight.

He turned to the hostess who cheerfully greeted them.

"Hello, my name is Perry Sullivan and I have a reservation for two," he said.

"Yes, Mr. Sullivan. I was told you would be arriving soon and to promptly seat you. Please follow me."

He looked around and true to what he'd heard, the place was packed with patrons. He'd been a patron himself a few times in the past when he met with major business clients who liked to be wined and dined at the best establishments.

"Big crowd tonight," Perry said to the hostess as she sat them at a table that overlooked the beautiful Bozeman mountains, a sight that was picture perfect for a romantic dinner.

"It's like this most nights. Mr. Saul is thinking of opening another location to accommodate more guests. I hope this table is satisfactory? Mr. Saul told me to make sure we seated you at our most popular table and it gives you more privacy than any other."

"I'll have to thank him when I see him. Is he still here?"

"Yes. I'll let him know you're here. I'm sure he'd like to stop by your table to say hello," she said. "Your server will be right over and please, enjoy your evening."

"She's right. This has to be the most popular table. Look at the view of the mountains. The many gorgeous views are one of the reasons I love Montana. I haven't traveled to a lot of places in my life, but being here and seeing the mountains every day and night take my breath away," Gizelle said.

Perry had an answer about the outside view, but it was the view in front of him that he admired the most.

"The view is perfect."

When her eyes turned to his, there was no doubt she figured out the double entendre, making a reference more to her than the one outside of the large bay window. When she blushed and looked down and then back at him to capture his eyes, he fell in love again and again. How could a man not love a woman so sweet and peaceful; so beautiful a specimen that knowing the mere thought of having her in his life would make him whole? Words of love were on the tip of his tongue every time he saw her, but he hadn't yet revealed his feelings. Slow and patient had to be the names of the game if he was going to be able to let her come to her own realization that what he was feeling for her was true and not like her past experience. His plan was to show her how he felt and not only tell her with words that any man could utter.

"Thank you."

"You're beautiful when you blush."

"Whenever I'm around you, I feel like I'm always blushing. You make me feel so beautiful."

"I'm glad to hear that, but one thing I do know is that you were beautiful before I met you. I'm sad if you haven't always felt that way, but you will from now on – *that's* a fact. Thanks for agreeing to dinner tonight. I've wanted to ask you out on an actual date for a long time."

He saw her about to say something and then she stopped herself. He didn't push, but waited to see if she would be open with him.

"I feel good being out with you, but I feel like I should be careful with what I say in order to not embarrass myself."

"No eggshells, Gizelle. No tiptoeing around anything. Good or bad, be free expressing yourself around me. You won't find any judgement here. I'm a big boy and can handle it all."

"I was going to say something not as open as your admission and I changed my mind."

Before she could finish, their waiter arrived. Patient as ever, he would wait.

"Good evening. I'm Nigel and I'll be taking care of

you this evening. Can I start your evening out with a drink?"

"Are you okay if I order us some champagne?" Perry asked Gizelle.

"Champagne sounds wonderful."

Perry looked at the menu and selected a bottle of his favorite, *Dom Perignon Champagne Cuvee.*

"I'll bring that right over and give you some time to look over the menu," Nigel said before walking away.

Again alone, Perry turned his full attention to Gizelle.

"You were saying?"

He wanted to pick back up where their conversation was about to lull due to her shyness.

"I want to say something, but I don't want to seem too forward."

"Say whatever is on your mind. You can always be honest with me about anything."

"Okay. I like you Perry. I like you a lot and in case you didn't notice it, when you showed up at the school today, I was pleasantly surprised and very happy to see you. I know we see each other all the time since I've been staying at your house on the ranch and let me just say, I love that house and thank you for letting the kids and I stay there. They love their rooms. It's going to be hard leaving one day. It's the first time they have had separate rooms. I thought it would be hard, but they sleep good at night and so do I. Who knew there was a bed shaped as a race car that had rails so that Brody wouldn't fall out?"

"My brother, Dayton, sent that bed when he heard about all that has been going on. My mother told him about the kids and that she was going to decorate the rooms for them. He also sent the Cinderella bed ensemble for Carrie."

"He hasn't even met us and he did that?"

"It's the Sullivan way!" Perry said proudly.

"We're going to miss it when the day comes where we have to leave the ranch and go back to our lives."

The idea of them leaving unsettled him.

"We are not talking about you leaving and I hope that's not what you want to talk about. You know you can stay as long as you want, no pressure about anything."

"Thanks, and no, I'm not talking about leaving and I never feel any pressure. Your family and the staff at the ranch are wonderful. A girl could get accustomed to life on the ranch."

"Again, something else that's good to know."

"All of this because of my drama. Should I be this happy? Am I allowed to be this happy when this is all a part of your life?"

"What happened wasn't your fault and I've been interested in you since the moment we met. Nothing has changed that and I was trying to give you space. I know you were focused on your job and Carrie and Brody. I also know that being in Bozeman, you've heard of the reputation of the Sullivan boys and that's not how I wanted you to see me. I enjoy having you as a part of my life, not just the things you may have heard about me or what I've done for you lately. I'm more than that and so are you. I've been known to serial date, but there has always been an open and honest understanding of the casual nature of my involvement with women. When I met you, I didn't want that with you and so I tried to take my time and show you the genuine me."

Gizelle smiled at him, easing his mind.

"I've heard a lot about you and your brothers and your conquests and there's nothing wrong with it. You are a very handsome man and from the Stetson you wear on your head to the cowboy boots on your feet, you exude virility in your own ruggedly, good-looking way and there isn't a woman on this planet who wouldn't find that appealing and sexy."

"Wow! When you tell it, you really tell it!"

He was often complimented by women but hearing it coming from Gizelle made it sound extra special.

"Was that too much?"

"Never too much and I hope I'm not doing too much with my next move because I've been thinking about doing this for a very, very long time."

"Your next move?"

"Let's just say that as much as I love that shiny, pink lip gloss that's covering your scrumptious lips that you probably took time deciding which shade would go best with your dress, I think I'm about to mess it up a little."

"O-okay, yes," Gizelle stuttered out.

Perry could see how nervous she was and when he reached over and slid his hand along her neck and moved her closer to him, he could feel her heart racing through the pulse on her neck.

Without any further words and keeping his eyes locked securely on hers, Perry leaned to his left, with his eyes going between taking in Gizelle's full, gorgeous lips, to the dark pools of her eyes, the color of black coal, looking back at him like a dark, mysterious dream, he moved and kissed her lips sweetly, taking in the feel of their softness.

"Sweet," he said softly pulling back right before leaning back in for more.

This time he allowed his lips to linger on hers, giving her a chance to sample more of him as he did her. Neither of them cared that they were in a public restaurant or considered who may be watching them because in the moment, there was only the two of them. To him, the kiss had just the right amount of heat and spice laced with an intoxicating zest as he tested the waters of their obvious attraction to each other. The air crackled around them as his stomach lurched with anticipation of how he could really love her mouth if they were in a more private place.

Their lips caressed each other with a searing heat

that enveloped the moment into a life-long memory.

As Gizelle lean further toward him, giving as much as she was getting and unbeknownst to anyone else but them, sparks flew all around their heads as they fed their desire for each other. When he thought to pull back and give them a chance to breathe, Gizelle's lips opened slowly and with opportunity came the chance to deepen the kiss.

Parting his lips along with hers, Perry searched her mouth with his tongue, dueling with hers while kicking himself for taking this too long to taste her.

Gizelle was dizzy. Her head was spinning as Perry's lips outlined the shape of her mouth. She wanted to leap into his lap to get as close to him as she could, but she knew now wasn't the time and so she focused on the feel of him and allowed him to feel her want, her desire for him the same way she was enjoying the passion he was showering her with. This, she knew, is how a man kisses a woman.

"Wow!" Gizelle said when they pulled apart.

Perry watched her and it seemed like she was moving in slow motion when she reached up and rubbed her lips where his had just been as if she had to convince herself that the kiss had actually happened and was as hot and potent as he felt it had been. By the look on her face, she was feeling it deep inside just as he had.

"I've been missing out on that all this time?" Perry said and quickly kissed her lips one last time softly before sitting back in his chair. He was one swift move away from lifting her into his lap and forgetting they were in a restaurant.

"You felt that, right?"

"I felt that and then something else that is best left to another time and place. It's a good thing the champagne is on its way because I need cooling off!" he laughed. "Thank you for that. I really needed to kiss you. I've been dying to do it for months," he admitted.

"I wish you had."

He took her hand and held it.

"I won't hesitate again," he said, searching her eyes.

Perry loved what he saw there. He knew a lot could be garnered from looking into the eyes of someone you cared about and he saw longing staring back at him, the exact same feelings that were emanating from him.

"I'm happy to hear that."

When Gizelle looked down at the menu, he did the same knowing that they were both thinking about what the steamy kiss between them meant. For him, it meant that he'd found the woman of his dreams and he was never letting go.

"Any idea what you want to eat?" he asked.

"I'm thinking about the stuffed fish of the day with wild rice and asparagus. What about you?"

"I'm going to have the stuffed chicken with mixed

vegetables and roasted potatoes."

The waiter returned with their champagne and he ordered for them. With that out of the way, they now had time to just talk. He wanted to be an open book.

"So, I met your family except for Dayton, who I can't wait to meet and thank for his generosity. Where is he?"

"He's out of the country in Canada. Usually, his races are here in the United States and we try to attend some to show our support. Over the past few years, he's gotten into international races and sits at the top of the champion's list. He'll be home in a few months for Nick's wedding coming up in June."

"I love weddings. They remind me of the hope of everlasting love."

"Would you marry again?"

"I look forward to it. My marriage was tragic, but it hasn't soured me on love and marriage. I want to get married again and have more children. Carrie and Brody gave me a new lease on life. What about you? You've always been single. Is that because you don't want to be married?"

"I look forward to getting married and having children one day with the right woman. Before you ask, I'm not speaking of some mysteriously, unknown woman. I'm not speaking of anyone in particular at this point in my life, but I will say that you intrigue me and my interest in you is not casual or temporary. I'm hoping enough time has gone by and that you're ready for something more than friendship with me; I know I am with you. I want to know how you feel about that."

When she looked at him quizzically, he wondered what was running through her mind. Good thoughts, he hoped. He told her no tiptoeing and that was meant for him too.

"I've been ready and I don't want what happened to put a damper on anything. I've felt us growing closer, especially over the past few weeks. I'm not blind to the attraction between us. I don't know what my future holds, but I hope it involves you and me together."

Perry exhaled loudly as a sigh of relief slipped across his lips. He was hoping her past wouldn't keep her from seeing the potential for a real relationship not built on intimidation, but on love and respect.

Pouring them both a glass of champagne, he lifted his glass toward her.

"Let's toast to us and to the present as well as the future."

"The present and the future," Gizelle repeated. "It's looking brighter even in the darkness of the night. Thank you for showing me that I don't have to continue living in the past. I see my future is already looking up," she added.

"Well, if I have anything to do with it, your future is looking bright."

"I've been in the dark for so long, I look forward to the light."

"Tell me about your life and family. I want to know everything about you."

If this was a beginning for them, Perry wanted it to start off right. When she smiled and began telling him about her childhood, he didn't feign interest but was all in.

**

Clyde pulled his old blue Chevy Tahoe off of the main road and onto a dirt and gravel covered path, not stopping even though there was no light to see where he was going. The night was so dark that when he looked down at his hands, he couldn't see them and could barely see the outline. As he drove along, he hoped he could see enough to keep from running into a tree or any other barrier that could damage his truck.

Because he was where he shouldn't be, he had to drive with his lights off to make sure he wasn't spotted. He wasn't chancing anyone coming up on him especially when he knew he was thought to have left Bozeman. He wasn't going anywhere without his kids or without getting his hands on Gizelle. She defied him and left the house. He got angrier when he spotted cops and some other men boarding up her house. By now, his plan was for them to be on their way back to Chicago. He had already given her enough time away from him and his friends made a fool out of him pointing fingers and calling him soft for letting a woman get the best of him. He would never allow it again.

From what he was able to find out, she and the kids were holed up at this place called the Sullivan Ranch. For days, he'd tried to find out how to get on that ranch to get what belonged to him. The day before, he'd driven back and forth down the long road where the ranch was and what he discovered was that it spanned well over ten miles. From the road, there was no way to get on the ranch without being seen. That was what he could see during the day and so tonight, he decided to come back to find a vulnerable point without being seen – hoping that the cover of darkness would keep him from being detected, especially by any cops. Whoever was hiding her from him didn't know what he was capable of, but Gizelle did and when he got his hands on her, she wouldn't think of running from him ever again. It was clear that she didn't take his threat seriously when he told her not to leave the house, yet when he returned, she was gone and so were his kids. He had to go into hiding because there was now a warrant out for his arrest. They had to know by now what he had done to her to get her back in line the way a woman was supposed to obey her husband, divorced or not. She was his and would always be his.

Parking his truck behind a bunch of trees where it could not be seen from the main road, he stepped out and saw the edge of the ranch property a few yards away. What he didn't expected when he decided to try and find her was that the ranch would have barriers so high that there was no way to get over them without some kind of ladder. If he could find just one point of entry, he knew he could find her.

In the dark, there was no light on his side of the property barrier. He could see that there was plenty of light available on the ranch, but he had to get on that side. He thought about bringing a ladder, but warning signs around the perimeter warned of impenetrable alarms and with the size of the ranch, he doubted if that was a fake warning just to keep people out. Still, he was hoping to find a way in and a way to get his children. If he got them, he knew Gizelle would soon follow. If he knew anything, it was that she loved those kids and what he hated most was that she loved them more than she loved him.

As he walked along the edge of the property along the barrier that didn't even have an opening for him to see inside, his anger grew. He was tired of Gizelle being defiant. What she didn't know was that he wasn't planning on leaving Bozeman without her. He didn't like women getting the best of him and if he had to, he would show her once and for all the consequences of walking away from him.

"I'm coming for you, Gizelle," Clyde said out loud with no one around to hear. Pushing forward, he walked with determined steps in the pitch black of the night allowing his fury to fuel his steps. He was done playing games with her.

12

As they drove toward the ranch after dinner, Gizelle swayed in her seat, listening to music and thinking about how much better and relaxed she was feeling. A lot had happened in a few weeks, but today had been the better of all of those days.

Sitting across from Perry at dinner, she'd not only learned a lot about him, she discovered something new about her interaction when it came to a man. What she found was that for far too long, she'd settled for how Clyde treated her and accepted it as the norm when there was nothing normal about it; ever. She couldn't discount it all because the light out of her time with Clyde was her children. What she accepted in how a man treated her became crystal clear and she hated that she hadn't gotten away from him sooner. She'd been on many dates with Clyde and now she knew what had been missing that she hadn't taken note of before. Every time she and Clyde went out or even were home alone and they conversed, every discussion was about him – what he was thinking, how he felt, what he was going through. If she tried to insert what was going on in her life, he would over-talk her and turn the conversation back to him. Only he had mattered, never her.

Over dinner with Perry, he was open about who he was and the events that made up his life. More importantly, he was interested in what she had to say. He didn't interrupt her and showed honest interest in her thoughts on all kinds of subjects. Though she could see women checking him out from all over the restaurant, and she couldn't blame them, he made sure she knew that he was completely focused on her and them being on a date together. She felt all warm and gooey and every time he looked at her, she felt like the most beautiful woman in the world.

With Clyde, she felt like she was always jumping through hoops to get his attention and to see that she was worthy of love. There was something wonderful in the way Perry looked at her and she loved how it made her feel.

When they got back in the car to head home, the minute he put music on, her body just started moving. She couldn't remember the last time she'd felt this good. The best idea anyone has ever had was when Perry asked her out to dinner.

When one of her favorite songs came on, she couldn't stifle the hum that escaped her lips. She mouthed the lyrics and it wasn't until she heard Perry snicker that she realized she was actually humming as loud as the song was playing.

Whitney Houston was still her favorite singer of all time and hearing her sing made her think of the love Whitney had once shared with Bobby Brown – a love not many understood, but she knew was undoubtedly there.

"You're laughing at me?" she asked, smiling.

"Never, sweetheart; never. I'm enjoying seeing you smiling and dancing around in your seat."

"I love to sing and dance, but not sure I'm great at either one."

"When we danced at the restaurant, I enjoyed every second of it. You were a perfect dance partner. I look forward to doing it again and soon."

Hearing the low tone of his voice, it resonated through her body, causing it to tingle. That deep, intoxicating tone covered her body so completely that she was glad she was already moving around in her seat. Perry would never know her embarrassment of how the erotic tone of his words stirred a sexiness in her that she forgot existed.

"I enjoyed it very much too. This was a refreshing night out, one that was definitely needed."

"We have something in common?" he asked.

Gizelle was puzzled.

"What?" she asked, turning her body more toward him.

"You're humming. That's the name of the song."

"Oh, yes. I love this song. Those were some of her happiest days. You could see it in her eyes and this song with Bobby Brown has always been one of my favorites. I was sad to see their relationship end."

"So was I, but you know, I'm not sure they were ever healthy enough together as a couple to make it last forever, though I had high hopes because they appeared to really be in love. I just believe they were fighting an uphill battle. I grew up loving their music and I followed their love story through the many songs and movies made about them. I saw it as a true love story that just didn't have a happy ending as a love story is expected to have. They had a rough time of it."

"Many relationships are, but I know they don't have to be. I've learned a lot from my relationship and marriage to Clyde."

"And that was?"

"Are you sure you're okay talking about this? I don't want to bother you with my old relationship problems. I hear women shouldn't talk about an older relationship with a new man who shows interest in her. I've made some stupid mistakes in judgement and I let it continue when I knew better."

"No topics is off limits. I believe for two people to build something, if that's what we could possibly have together, the only way to get there is with open and honest trust and communication."

This kind of open conversation with a man was new to her. She'd been stifled for so long that she felt simple as a grown woman trying to figure out how to communicate her thoughts and feeling.

"I thought I had a lot in common with Clyde when in fact, there were no commonalities. He's older and I thought that he could rescue me from my doldrum life when he swept me off of my feet. Back then, he had a little money, a house, a nice car and a pretty good job. He was the picture of what a good provider would be, though I had no real exposure to that since my own father was never around as a provider. What I failed to take note of was the fact that I didn't love him. I wasn't in love with him even when we got married. He was an escape from a father who never really wanted me and a mother who died never really knowing how to show me love. I was a burden to her because she longed for my father and to her, I could be that link to him coming back to her; he never did."

"How old were you when your mother died?"

"Nineteen. I got a job and tried to take care of myself. In fact, I had several jobs and two roommates. Those were lean, hard times. One day, when I was working at this diner, I met Clyde. He flashed a smile and money and I thought I'd hit the jackpot when he convinced me that he could take me away from a life I hated and give me anything I wanted. He bought me things and took me places that I'd never been before. He asked me to marry him, or rather told me we were getting married and I thought I was ready. We got married three weeks after we met. I moved in with him and two days later, he didn't come home and when I questioned him, he told me that as long as he was providing for me, he could do whatever he wanted. When I say we had nothing in common, I wasn't kidding. We didn't like the same food, movies, music and his friends were all sleezy. He didn't even care that they came on to me all the time. His response was that his friends knew he had a hot wife and he felt good knowing his friends wanted what he had."

"This guy," Perry said, but didn't continue his thought.

"He was horrible to me and yet again and again, I gave into him and tried to make the marriage work. He cheated on me with women I knew and he kept tabs on me even if I wanted to step out to go to the supermarket. When I became pregnant with Carrie, he got angry and said he didn't want any children and thought I had taken care to make sure I didn't have any. After I got pregnant with Brody, he wanted me to get rid of him. When I refused, he barely spoke to me during that pregnancy. He never showed me much love and barely showed any to the kids. I got this job at a law firm as a receptionist and that became my saving grace. I didn't have to be at home all the time to deal with his wrath. The kids were in a good daycare and when Brody was about six months old, I knew I was going to leave, but I was afraid to. I didn't have much. I would put money away, since before I had Carrie and he never knew that I did. I knew that one day I would need to be able to take care of myself and my children and I would have to do it without Clyde's help. He never wanted them anyway. I didn't want them to grow up and see how he treated me and think that what they saw is how a relationship should be. I'm embarrassed by how I allowed myself to be treated, just for survival. I know that relationships are more than that and should be more than that."

Gizelle stopped talking when she saw the solemn look on Perry's face. She thought that perhaps, she'd said too much.

"Did I overshare?"

"I'm sorry that your experience with love and marriage was not a good one. It should have been. You are an amazing woman and you deserve much better than what you had. You have nothing to be embarrassed about. We all make mistakes in life and in love and thankfully, you lived through your nightmare and now have a chance to find love again."

"Am I wrong to feel connected to you? I have since the moment we first met."

Gizelle could feel her heart beating a million miles a minute. She'd never been forward with a man enough to give the impression that she was more than casually interested. She didn't want to lose the vibe that had been going on between them.

"No, not at all. I agree with you there. The fact that we have so much in common is almost scary. I've never connected so well with a woman after one conversation."

"I felt the same way. I was out with Heather that night and when we left, I couldn't stop talking about you."

"So, you like me!" Perry exclaimed.

She laughed with him and even playfully punched in him lightly on the arm.

"That's all you heard?"

"That's all I needed to hear. I can admit that your beauty drew me in immediately and I knew you could feel my eyes on you all night until I approached you."

"Heather noticed it first. She kept telling me that you were watching me and I was afraid to look your way. I didn't know if it was from being scared after dealing with Clyde or the fact that I hadn't dated anyone since my split with Clyde and I wasn't sure if I was ready for any man to have an interest in me or for me to be interested in him. Once you came over and said hello and then asked me to dance, something happened. I was nervous when you took my hand to walk to the dance floor. Then you took me in your arms and the nervousness went away. Slow dancing, I could hear your heart beat and you hummed lightly in my ear. Your arms around me felt good and strong, the way a woman wants to feel when she's being held. I felt it that day. Tonight, I felt it ten-fold. It's not just that you help me and my kids out, but I know you genuinely care about us; that matters."

"Showing someone you care is what matters and treating a woman as if she is the most precious thing on earth is important when you find one who makes your world go 'round. She shouldn't just hear a man talk a good game; she should see and feel it."

"Have you ever been in love?"

"I have; once. That relationship didn't work out because she hated the ranch and ranch life. She was more interested in big city living. I respected that. It wasn't just the city life, but it was the glitz and glamour of Hollywood that attracted her. My family, especially my brothers and I, have friends who are in the entertainment industry and we are often invited to some very high-profile events. She became obsessed with the lifestyle she saw. My family has money, but we're not flashy with it. We work to build wealth, not to flash it around as if we're surprised we're wealthy unexpectedly. She wanted to be in the center of the celebrity lifestyle and that just isn't me. I like my quiet life here in Bozeman."

"What? How could *anyone* not like the ranch? I've been there a few weeks and I already dread the day the kids and I will have to leave and get back to our life. I love animals; always have. I've gotten to know Parker and she lets me bring the kids around the animals. I think Brody wants to be a cowboy. He woke up this morning in a tizzy when he couldn't find that stuffed horse Parker gave him the other day. I mean, he was so upset that I raced around like a madwoman trying to find it. It had fallen between the bed and the wall. He takes that horse everywhere and he gets so excited when he gets to go to the stables to see the horses. I've always loved animals and I want my kids to love and respect them. The ranch is amazing, especially the visitor side. Brielle told me about all the events and the ideas for expansion and it's exciting. The ranch is a magical place; a happy place. I can't imagine anyone not finding it a wonderful place to be and to experience having your love – why would anyone deny themselves all that you are? I was born and raised in the city, but in my heart, I'm all country and animals and so are my kids."

"That's good to know considering how much I like you and yes, I see the love your kids have for the ranch. They remind me of my brothers and sister when we were little. We were mesmerized with our life on the ranch."

"It's definitely a wonderful place. I see why the kids call it magical."

"Why haven't you dated since Clyde? Is it out of fear of the unknown of another relationship?"

"That's exactly why and to also protect the kids. At first, I didn't know what Clyde would do when he found out I took the kids out of state. He didn't show up for the final court date when the judge was awarding custody, so she gave me full custody. I was on edge for a while and then when I heard nothing from him, I began to relax, but not to the point that I was ready to date. I promised myself that I would take my time and make sure the relationship was right and healthy for me and for them."

As they reached the entrance to the ranch, Perry turned just as they drove down the long road to get to the gate.

"I like you."

Gizelle heard the words and if he was going to say more, she didn't need to hear it to know he meant it. When his free hand reached over and closed over hers, it was like she was experiencing a brand-new day.

"I like you, too."

"No rush on anything. As I said, I would enjoy more dates with you like tonight."

"I'm glad you asked."

"I'll be asking again real soon."

Gizelle wanted to say more, but wanted to also live in the moment. In silence, she waved to the guard, as Perry did, as they entered through the large wrought iron gate to the ranch.

"How much security do you usually have at the entrance? I know there is more since I arrived, but what's the normal number?

"We usually have two guys on this gate around the clock. There are also guys whose only job is to drive around the ranch their entire shift. There are hundreds and hundreds of acres and any breach in the fences around the property are checked every day. Some of the other gates may have three or four, but this one has two checkpoints. The other is coming up in a few seconds. I know you haven't encountered them much since you haven't been off the ranch that much since you arrived. They are more visible as night falls. Someone coming on the ranch has to pass through both entrances. I tightened security to make sure you and the kids were protected. I don't know this Clyde person, but I don't want him getting access to you. I'm hoping he's gone on about his business and not looking back, but we never know. I think he's gone back to Chicago. There is too much of a risk for him to hang around here. People know outsiders when they see them."

"Do you think Clyde really has left Montana? I mean, it's been weeks and there has been no sign of him. I'm thinking he was so angry that day and that his plan was to scare me and when I still wouldn't go back to him, he gave up."

"Marcus tried to look into his life in Chicago and he hasn't returned their as far as family and friends are concerned, but that doesn't mean much. He knows that if the cops are looking for him even in Chicago, that his place and that of any family or friends would be the first place they would look. No one has seen him and it appears the last person to see or hear from him was you at your house here. I'm sure he's in hiding, but I don't know where that place could be. Do I think you're safe to go back to your life? I can't say that I believe he's actually walked away, but yeah, things have been quiet and by now, if he has been checking, he knows you're no longer living at your house and possibly assumes you've left Bozeman."

"That would be good. Maybe he'll just go away for good since he doesn't know where we are. I'm feeling better about things every day and I haven't been this happy in a long time."

"I hope I'm a part of your happiness."

"You're a big part of my happiness."

They both looked toward the main house as they drove by, heading toward her house."

"How long are you going to continue staying with your parents? I feel bad that the kids and I have put you out of your house. I know you love it and I'm sure you miss it."

"I'm going to move into one of the cabins on the ranch, the one just down the road from you. You can see it from the side windows. We're about to pass it in a few seconds. There is no rush to move you out and move me back in. You feel safe and so do the kids. I feel better having you in it anyway."

As Perry pulled his car down the long path to his house, they rode in silence until he pulled up to the circular car path in front of the three wooden steps that led to the wraparound deck and the doubled door entrance.

"I should have asked if you wanted to stop at the main house to check on the kids or to pick them up. I know they're supposed to spend the night with my parents, but I know how you like to have them close."

Gizelle laughed.

"I bet if I went to try and get them to come home with me, they wouldn't want to go. Your mom and dad have surpassed me as their favorite person. I was in a late meeting at the school earlier this week and your dad came by to get them from aftercare. Brody was jumping up and down when he saw your father as if he'd just seen Santa Claus. My kids love your parents and when they heard they could stay the night, I didn't have to ask them to go pick out pajamas. They ran to their rooms and grabbed almost a full drawer full of clothes and ran to the door ready to go even before it was time for them to leave."

"I'm telling you, it's the cookies!" Perry joked.

"I wouldn't dare pull them away. I haven't seen my kids laugh, smile and play like this in a very long time."

"Just checking. I can go back up the road because though you are sexy as hell in those heels, they would kill your feet to walk back to the house from here if you wanted to check on them."

"Yeah, these shoes were not made for too much walking. They were made to be cute in."

"Well, you achieved your goal because you are stunning in them."

"Thank you. I'll call your mom when I get in to see if they behaved and I'm sure the answer will be yes. It's past their bedtime anyway. I'll take advantage of this quiet night and probably watch some television or do some reading. What are you going to do tonight after I go inside?" she asked.

"I may check with the staff to see how things have been around the ranch this evening and I may check on the new horses and foals we purchased that arrived today. Let's get you inside because it's getting late and colder out here. I want to be sure you're inside with the door locked and the security alarm on before I leave."

Gizelle nodded and watched as he got out of the car.

"Feels like more snow is on the way. It's really cold out tonight," she said the moment he helped her out of the car and closed the door behind them.

When they reached the door, Perry turned to her. They stood face to face in the cold and yet, she was feeling warm all over. The words, longing and desire came to mind as she found herself getting happily lost in his gaze.

"Are you okay?" he asked, pulling her close to him; she happily moved into his embrace.

She didn't know what to say because she wasn't okay. She was far from okay and unlike the recent event that occurred in her life that contributed to her not being okay, this time, the feeling was welcomed.

"I don't know. I'm not sure of the etiquette at the end of a date when I'm not ready for the date to end yet. I'm not usually forward and I'm not even sure if women should be forward. All I know is that I don't want to go inside by myself."

"Are you afraid? I was planning to go inside and look around before I left so that you would know that no one was inside. I'm trying to work on being protected myself when it comes to you," he said.

"I don't understand. You need protecting from me?"

"My heart does. I really like you, Gizelle and I'm not going to be shy about that."

"I don't want you to be. I thought that maybe I could make us something hot to drink and we could watch a movie, pop some popcorn?"

"Sounds perfect."

Gizelle moved quickly to unlock the door so that he wouldn't have time to change his mind. As he walked around checking the house out, she walked over to light the fireplace, something she did every time she came home. The fire always gave her a since of calm and peace.

After he exited the kitchen and made his way upstairs, she walked into the kitchen and pulled out everything she needed to make hot chocolate and a big bowl of popcorn. Hanging her coat over the back of the chair, she moved quickly and was practically humming again as she did so. That's how Perry found her when he entered the kitchen and she turned to see him leaning against one end of the counter black and white marble kitchen counter.

"Are you going to stare at me or help by pulling out the popcorn machine? I take it you love fresh popped popcorn. The machine has been used a lot!"

"I do and I'm glad you're finding it useful as well."

She started to speak, but her tongue lost its way the minute he took his coat off and she was reminded of just how good looking he was. His all black attire added to the mystique that spoke of how debonair he was.

"Now, who's staring?"

Gizelle fake coughed through her embarrassment of ogling him.

"Was I?" she smirked and moved about aimlessly, finding herself off-kilter. Her mind raced to what her reaction was seeing him fully dressed to what it would be to see him stark naked. She already knew the view would be magnificent.

"Come here, Gizelle," Perry whispered.

Like a moth to a flame, she moved into his outstretched arms and leaned her head on his chest. She loved being this close to him. So far, she only got the opportunity when they were dancing. He felt and smelled good; he smelled all-man, a woodsy, musk scent.

Her entire body quivered when he raised his hand and caressed her neck lightly with one finger before using the back of his hand to caress her cheek. She'd never felt so uninhibited in her life. Her desirous mind had him picking her up and making love to her right on the kitchen counter. She shook her head, not knowing where that thought came from. It had to be from those sexy romance novels she loved reading and her desire to be loved and not taken. There was a difference, but the latter is all she knew when it came to sex. Her body never sizzled like it was doing now. She was more than ready to go with whatever was next.

"Whew, it sure got warm pretty quick," she said softly. She had to clear her throat to try and erase the nervousness.

"Did it, really? I hadn't noticed since whenever I'm around you, there is warmth like right now. Do I scare you?" he asked softly.

"No."

"Are you sure?"

"I'm positive. I've never met a man like you before. I can tell from your actions and your words that you want to make sure I'm not nervous or scared or worried and I'm none of those when I'm with you."

"That's good to know because the way I make you feel is important to me."

When Perry's eyes dropped to her lips, her pulse quickened and her heart raced out of control. Was he going to kiss her again? Her mind willed for him to do so. The kiss at the restaurant wasn't enough. Without thinking, she licked her lips to moisten them just in case a kiss was coming. Watching him watch her tongue was one of the most erotic moments of her life.

"Damn," Perry said.

Gizelle could see his pulse quickened in the way his neck throbbed. She was so turned on, she was ready to jump into his arms.

When his head dipped down close to hers, she prepared herself for whatever the feel of his lips on hers would bring. It had to be good, even better than the first time. She had no doubt that everything with Perry Sullivan was good – great even.

In the next moment, she felt him. She felt his arms tighten around her waist and as he held her close, she felt him and the feeling of his hard and thick erection against her didn't frighten her. And then it happened. His lips closed around hers. He kissed her so soft and so determined that she closed her eyes so that all she could do was feel. The kiss was ripe with desire. It was filled with passion and the promise that anything that followed would be just as sweet. Just as she placed her hands on his chest to grab a hold of his shirt to hold him in place and to keep from melting to the floor in a heap of desired flesh, she felt Perry pull back and she quickly stopped moving and opened her eyes.

"Did I do something wrong?" she asked. She had to question his sudden movement to stop the kiss just as it was getting really good.

"No, not at all. I want you to look at me. Don't close your eyes. Keep them locked on mine. Now that I have you in my arms, I want nothing more than to kiss you with everything I have in me, but I want to be sure that you not only feel my kiss, but you see me when I'm kissing you. See me, feel me. I can't apologize for how you've been handled in the past, but I can guarantee you that when you look into my eyes, look into my face and feel my arms around you, every bit of me desires and wants you. My desire isn't harsh or abrasive nor is it demanding, unless there comes a time between us when you will have your way with me and in that case, I say go for what you want. Knowing you trust me, even with a kiss, matters to me. Look at me, baby," Perry whispered against her lips.

Gizelle melted in his arms. As their eyes stayed connected, he kissed her deeper this time and she enjoyed every touch and feel of him. He caressed her lips with his, moving from one end of her mouth to the other and her legs shook. He cupped her cheeks and kissed her passionately, caressing her lips until she opened for him and that was the moment she knew for sure that she was in love.

As he made love to her mouth, she melted in his embrace, allowing the kiss to temporarily ease her thirst for him. She wanted more and knew the kiss held the promise of more. Not wanting to only received, she kissed him back just as passionately. She reached her arms up and placed her hands on his shoulders and lifted up, even in her heels and gave as good as she was getting. As much as she knew he wanted her, she needed to make sure that her kiss left no doubt that she wanted him just as much.

When they broke apart slowly, to her chagrin, she leaned into his chest again and listened to the rapid sound of his heart beating, knowing hers was doing the same. The kiss was powerful and magnetic and was exactly what she needed. She needed to feel this desired by a man and not just any man; she knew it had to be Perry.

"Um, if not being able to breathe and happy about it was a picture, it would be me," she smiled and looked up at him. Before he could speak, she reached up to wipe the silky sheen from his lips from the gloss that had once been on her lips.

"Don't wipe it away. I need to keep the essence of you right there for the rest of the night. I was planning on sharing it right back with you sometime after you and I make this popcorn and find a good movie."

"You get the bowl and I'll start the Keurig to make some hot chocolate. Any particular movie you want to watch? You have a lot of them in your library or we can find something on cable."

Gizelle moved way and worked hard to gather herself. She was actually glad that Perry had ended the kiss. She wasn't sure what would have come next. The hope of it was sustaining her sanity.

She watched Perry move around her as they fell

into what seemed like a normal routine of spending the evening together. This was their first time doing so without the kids with them.

"I recommend watching something that I could keep up with even if my eyes aren't constantly on the screen. I need to be able to keep up even if the desire to kiss you comes over me again."

She turned in his direction.

"I'm all for that."

And she was. She was all for Perry. Being with him was helping her forget that her life outside the ranch was still crazy, but for now, he gave her the peace she wanted and needed and she couldn't ask for more than that. With her life going so good right now, nothing could disturb her happiness.

13

Heather walked into the small house she'd been renting for the past couple of years and noticed that the blinds were closed tight.

"Hurry up and shut and lock the door! No one followed you, right?"

Without hesitating, she did what she was told and turned around letting her eyes land on Clyde lounging on her sofa with his feet up on her cocktail table in his thick mountain boots which she could see were covered in dirt. Clumps of matted dirt now covered one side of her table. She sighed out her anger and rolled her eyes at him.

"Why would anyone follow me? No one knows you're here besides me."

Clyde stood from the small sofa where he'd been sleeping and walked over to her. She prepared herself to be on the defense, since most of their time spent together, that's the stance she found herself in.

"You know what I want to hear and it's not your

smart mouth. What happened with Gizelle?"

"I called her like you asked. I don't get to see her since she's not working at the law firm with me anymore. I told her I missed her and asked how she was doing. I tried to get information on where she's been. She told me what happened with you at the house and how she was hoping that you were gone back to Chicago. You really hit her?"

"Don't worry about what I did or didn't do. Did you convince her to come over here to visit you?"

Heather stepped back when Clyde grimaced at her as if he was about to pounce out of anger and impatience with her.

"I tried to. I asked her if she wanted to come over here and I'd make us lunch this weekend. She said she couldn't because she was having lunch with Brielle. Her family owns the ranch where Gizelle and the kids have been staying. I did get that much out of her. She said she was afraid to go back to the house because she didn't know if you were still hanging around. You terrified her. What did you do to her?"

Though she knew Clyde wanted to avoid the subject, she needed to hear him say it. In her brief conversation with Gizelle, she left their chat feeling disgusted that the man who had harmed her was the same man that she herself was in love with.

"I thought you said she told you," he snarled and she moved around him toward the sofa, out of the line of danger. He was known for striking out without warning.

"She only said you came looking for her and the kids and that you frightened them and messed up her house or something. She said you hit her and I asked her how bad, but she didn't answer me. That was it. What did you do?"

"Where did she say she was going with this woman for lunch? Are they leaving that ranch? I tried to find a way on that ranch after you told me about that family and that place is locked up tighter than a prison. I tried to find a way in without being seen for hours and I found nothing. I can't get to her on the ranch. She has to come off of it. Where is she working? She's not doing that anymore?"

"She's working on the ranch. I don't know what she's doing specifically. She said something about working at a school or center or something. That place has a lot of buildings and businesses on it, so she could be working at any of the places on the ranch. She just said that the owner found a job for her and she was glad because that meant until she was ready, she didn't have to leave the ranch."

"What about this guy? You said there was a guy who liked her and who she may be staying with on the ranch? Is she having sex with him? Who is he?" Clyde shouted at her, causing her to flinch and the piercing nature of his words.

"He's Perry Sullivan and he's not someone you want to mess with. He wields a lot of power in

Bozeman and I don't think they're having sex, but I wouldn't know. She hasn't said anything like that. We don't talk about our sex lives, hers with anyone else or mine with you. I know that he really likes her and she likes him too. That's all I know. They may be involved in some kind of way, but to what extent, I don't know."

When Clyde's head snapped around toward her in fierce anger, she tried to look away. His anger could be lethal and she didn't want to be on the other end of it tonight.

"Involved with? You think she's actually seeing this guy or is he just helping her out?"

"I don't know. All she said was that he came by the house when he hadn't heard from her and he saw what you did and got them out of their quick."

"That whore!" Clyde yelled.

"Quiet before someone hears you."

"You haven't told me *anything!* For all I know, she could be sleeping in his bed every night. I don't care who this guy is. He better not be sleeping with my wife or she'll have hell to pay when I get my hands on her. That's for sure."

Heather crossed her arms over her chest as she fumed over the way Clyde was still obsessing over his ex-wife. She wished he would put this kind of energy into her.

"Why are you worried about that? I thought you were over her. Are you trying to get her back? I thought you wanted me. You told me you wanted to be with me and not her. Every guy in this damn town looks at her like she's a beauty queen and I'm some kind of troll and I'm sick of it. I may not have her body or beauty, but I'm not some ugly duckling either. You said it was me that you wanted and yet you're talking about being upset over another man having her! What if she is sleeping with him? Come to think of it, I think I remember her telling me that the sex with him was the best she ever had!" Heather yelled and then reeled back when Clyde angrily reached for her. She tried to get far away from his grasp, but before she could get out another word, he grabbed her by the throat and pushed her down on the sofa. She took in as much air as she could as she struggled to catch her breath.

"You better be lying. I don't want to hear anything about another man touching her. Nothing!" he growled in her face. She tried to turn her head away from his hot, nasty, beer and cheese smelling breath.

The way he growled his words had her terrified. She'd never seen him like this. She fought against his grip and when he let go, she took in large gulps of air and coughed when she found it hard to breathe.

"What did you do that for?" she stuttered out through breaths as she tried to calm her breathing.

"I'm sorry. Thinking of her with another man made me mad."

"I thought you only wanted to get your kids back. You lied to me?"

"No, no, I didn't lie. That's the plan and you and me and them kids can be a family. I'm just mad that I can't see my children. I do plan to make her pay. She will wish she'd never met me and had those little runts. Because of her, I can't go back home and there is a warrant out for my arrest here in Montana and in Chicago. The police have contacted my family and when I called my mother, she told me to never contact her again because I was too much trouble. Gizelle has taken everything away from me and I want it all back. I'd like to get my hands around her neck and choke the life out of her. She's more trouble than she's worth. I should have taken my kids when I had the chance a few weeks ago. I won't miss the chance again. I don't know how to get to her. If I am caught, I'll go to jail for sure," he said.

Heather watched Clyde pace back and forth, gnawing on his fingernails. He was definitely wired up and she hated that it was all because of Gizelle.

She and Gizelle had been friends back in Chicago and she still couldn't believe how stupid she was on those nights when Clyde should have been at home with her, but instead he would find his way to her apartment and have the kind of wild sex he said Gizelle never gave him. He once told her that Gizelle was colder in bed than a block of ice. Little did she know that her own friend was the one that Clyde was having an affair with. There were times when she would be in Gizelle and Clyde's house and when

Gizelle would go and tend to Carrie as a baby, she and Clyde would slip off to another room and have sex right under her nose. She hated Gizelle and even more than that, she hated that Clyde still held a torch for her. There wasn't a man around who didn't desire Gizelle and she often felt like no matter how tight her own clothes were or how much cleavage she showed, no man looked at her if she was with Gizelle.

She had to bite her tongue when one day, Gizelle had called her from Chicago. She, herself had moved to Bozeman after she'd lost her job in Chicago and didn't have a place to stay. She headed to Bozeman to follow a man she thought wanted her, but he only wanted the ideal of how freaky she was in bed. He commented on how he enjoyed that with her, any goes. That relationship didn't last long and when he broke up with her, she was able to afford a small place by herself, something she would never be able to afford in Chicago, so she stayed. When Gizelle needed to leave Chicago, she offered her and her kids a place to stay in Bozeman until she'd moved into the house where Clyde found her; a house that, when Clyde called her to ask about Gizelle, she gave him the address of where she lived.

When Gizelle told her about the finality of her divorce, she acted surprised at hearing the news, but Clyde had already told her about it during one of their weekend romps when she flew to Chicago to meet up with him. He wasn't the best catch when it came to men, but she was able to steal him away from Gizelle and that made her feel good. It was her revenge for every man that she liked who then turned out to have eyes for Gizelle once they saw her. Some might call that jealousy but she didn't care.

"You won't go to jail. We're going to get your kids and make a life someplace else far from here," she said.

"Whatever! I need a beer so I can think. Go get me one!"

Jumping at his command, she rushed to the kitchen as she heard his loud boots on the wood floors following behind her.

"What are you going to do?" she asked.

"I have to find a way to get to her, but I can't be seen."

"As long as you stay in here, no one is going to find you."

"Right because no one, especially Gizelle would think that one of her friends would be bedding her ex-husband and helping him hide from the law."

Heather ignored him since being facetious was a rule of thumb for him and when he was this angry, there was no way to reason with him.

"What are you going to do to her?"

"I just want to reason with her to let me see my children."

"Oh, okay. It's just that you told me you were over her and everything and that you wanted me, but you sound different right now," she said.

"I do want you," Clyde said.

Walking back to the living room, Heather plopped back down on her sofa, caressing her neck where his hands were and shifting in her seat as he came and stood above her. When he leaned his body down to cover hers and forced his mouth on hers hard and demanding, she felt reassured that he was all about her. As quickly as the kiss started, it ended, leaving her wanting. His kisses never satisfied her and she knew it was because he took and never gave.

"That's better, but a little rough," she said, rubbing her lips where his lips had just been, not because she was savoring the kiss, but because she wanted to soothe the immediate soreness she felt from the coarse kiss.

"You like it rough or have you been faking?"

"No, I do."

"Stop complaining then and get back to telling me what else was said between you and Gizelle."

"She said that she was happy and she and Perry were getting close. When I asked how close, she gave me a look and when I told her I know what she meant, she shook her head to confirm it."

"Wait – you *saw* her? I thought you only talked to her?"

"We were video chatting. I didn't actually see her in person. She did say she wasn't concerned about you anymore. I think she feels that she's safe."

"Does she ever leave the ranch without him or anyone else with her? I need her to be off the ranch alone."

"I didn't ask."

"You need to get her off the ranch."

"How?"

"You said you like to hang out sometimes. Maybe ask her to hang out or something. Try anything to get her to leave the ranch."

"I don't think that will work. It will have to be something where she would leave the ranch for a quick run and go right back."

"Think of something."

"I will. I shouldn't be helping you with this. I could get into trouble, too."

At first, she was upset of what Gizelle said Clyde had done to her. She wouldn't dare tell him all that she knew. She felt sick to her stomach that she was helping him, but then she found herself jealous of Gizelle at the same time because she drew the eye of Perry Sullivan.

There was a time when she had hoped Perry or one of the other Sullivan brothers would be interested in her, but so far, no such luck and then Gizelle comes along and snags him right away. She didn't deserve Perry, one of the most eligible bachelors in Bozeman. Why should she have a man as fine and rich as Perry while she has her pick of the lowest, dirtiest, creepiest men around town? Whatever Clyde does to her, she deserves.

"She's trying to ruin my life and all I want is my kids. You can understand that, right? I mean, I just want to be able to see my kids and she took them from me and ran off to this place as if I don't matter. Fathers matter, right baby?" Clyde said, reaching for her, playing on her sympathy and lust for him. She knew it and fell for it anyway by turning and sliding onto his lap now that he was sitting next to her.

"You're right. No woman should keep a man from his children. I like your kids and they like me."

"Well, when I get them, we'll get to spend time with them together. Wouldn't you like that?"

"I would."

"Good. We'll put our heads together and think of some way to get her off the ranch alone. For now, I've been waiting here all lonely while you were gone and I think you should make it up to me."

"Okay, do you want me to cook something?"

"No. I want you in the bedroom and undressed in less than a minute."

Heather kissed him passionately and though she was putting her all into it, she could see that he was preoccupied, no doubt with thoughts of Gizelle. She wanted her out of their lives and if helping Clyde was going to be the way to see to that, she would help him.

With the kiss not working, she jumped up and walked toward the bedroom. When he stood and walked by her, she knew what they were about to experience wouldn't be filled with words of love and devotion, but in her mind, that's what she'd make herself hear as she closed her eyes and faked yet another round of unsatisfying sex for her.

**

Gizelle entered the house expecting to hear Carrie and Brody running about or playing loudly, but the scene before her was the complete opposite and to her surprise, warmed her heart. Closing the door behind her to keep out the brisk winter cold, she removed her coat, scarf and gloves and moved about quietly until she walked up to the kids who were sound asleep. What surprised her the most was how they were snuggled up on either side of Perry who was also sound asleep. The television, on the Disney channel, was watching them.

After last week's date night with Perry, she had run into Brielle that next day who told her that she'd seen Perry's truck parked outside the house and asked if they were getting close. She'd had few girlfriends growing up and that was by choice. She and her mother moved around so much that she never had a chance to really connect with anyone until meeting Heather in high school.

Since being on the ranch, she'd been spending time with Brielle and Parker and they began feeling like sisters. When Brielle asked her to dinner for some real girl talk, she leaped at the chance. Marta had offered to pick the kids up from aftercare, but when

Perry overheard that she was going out, he offered to look after the kids until she got home. She had no idea she'd arrive home and find the perfect vision – the three of them snuggled up and from the sounds of it, they were snoring, a beautiful sound to her ears.

She stood for a few moments and took in the view. This is something every mother would love to see, kids who felt comfortable and cared for. They've never had that before from anyone else other than her.

Clyde never liked for Carrie to even ask him for a hug or to pick her up. He would tell her that her mother gave better hugs than him, an excuse to keep from having any kind of a connection with her. He had been that way as a husband as well. Other than the closeness needed for her wifely duties, as he called their sex life, he was never affectionate to her or to the kids.

Looking around the room, there were toys everywhere and a half-eaten bowl of fruit and cups of water were on a side table. The kids weren't in pajamas yet, something she would remedy shortly after cleaning up the room. She didn't want to wake them, but the moment she reached for the remote and turned the television off, Perry snapped right up, fully awake and looking around for who was intruding. It didn't escape her that when he did, his immediate reaction was to pull the kids closer to him. Oh, what a man, she thought to herself.

"Hey," she said quietly in order to not wake the

kids.

"Hi there. You're back. How did your girl's dinner go?"

"It was perfect and I see you were zonked out and it's not even eight o'clock yet. Tired? Did they wear you out?"

"Not at all. My work day started at four this morning and for the first time in a long time, I asked to not be disturbed by anything work related. I forgot how to relax and not think about work. The kids and I had a ball. Sarah made us some chicken nuggets and fries and then we had fruit and have watched *Peppa Pig* a million times. When they fell asleep, I realized I couldn't keep my eyes open another second."

"Thank you for looking after them."

"Thanks for letting me or I never would have gotten this downtime in the middle of the week. You had fun?"

Perry stood and walked right over to her. She exhaled when his hand cradled her chin and without any words, he leaned down and kissed her fervently. The kiss was so purposeful and full of images of what else they could have together that she dropped her purse to the floor and wrapped her arms around his waist and held on while the kiss swept her off her feet and to a place where only they were. Not just a safe place, but a place filled with love.

When they leaned apart, she wondered how many more of his kisses like this would she be able to handle before she stripped and led the way to the bedroom.

"Um, you asked me a question, I think," she said and laughed when Perry laughed.

"I got you like that?" he joked.

"Yeah, you do," she blurted out without thinking of the meaning.

Perry leaned close to her lips as if to kiss her again, but this time, he spoke right against them.

"You're not alone and when the time is right for us, I promise that I will quench every thirst and stroke every desire you have. Just be ready for me, baby. I'm going to go so that you can get those two in bed. Do you need my help getting them up to bed?"

"No, I'm going to let them sleep right there for now while I clean up."

"I can help with that."

"No, you had better go or I'm going to shout to the roof just how ready I am for you right now."

Perry kissed her sweetly on the lips, grabbed his coat and winked as he opened the door.

"Lock up and I'll call you when I'm settled. I need to hear your voice when I'm falling asleep."

She walked to the door, right up to him.

"There were times when I would lay awake at night and dream about a man who was kind, gentle, caring and loving – all the things I was missing. I saw a movie once and I heard that all I had to do was dream. My dream was delayed, but thanks to you, it wasn't out of my reach forever. You've shown me that men like that exist. Thank you."

"Only the beginning."

When he turned and left, she knew he meant those few words and she was not bothered by starting over with a man like him. He is worth the dream and the wait.

"What a man!" she said. "I'm ready."

14

Perry came down the back stairs of the house that led directly into the kitchen and smiled the moment he saw Sarah, up early and already preparing breakfast for the day. From the looks of the kitchen counter where she was kneading dough and somehow also cutting potatoes and then moving to lay bacon on a metal pan for oven baking, he knew she was in her element. At six in the morning, his father would usually be up by now, and figured with an empty house other than his parents, Sarah no longer got up with the birds at this hour, yet here she was. Though he'd moved into his own cabin a week ago, he'd been up late at the house going over business plans with his father until the wee hours of the morning and he was too tired to go to his own place. Instead, he went upstairs and slept in his old bedroom.

"You should still be asleep," he said, dropping his overnight bag at the foot of the steps and resting his cowboy hat on top of it before taking a seat at the high oak kitchen set which sat ten.

"I knew you would be up and heading to the airport and I wanted to make sure you got breakfast before you left. Your mother figured you would be up late going over details for the meeting you were traveling to New York for today. You know I can't stand the idea of you grabbing fast-food on the run when you travel. Nothing beats a home-cooked meal and this morning, I'm making your favorite, oven-fried bacon, grilled ham, fresh biscuits, home-fried potatoes with onions and eggs over-easy. It's all done except the eggs which I'm going to make right now."

"You don't have to cook for me."

"You kids still don't get it. The best part of my day is seeing each one of you and then after that, feeding you. I've always done it and as long as I'm breathing I always will."

"You have been busy. I was planning to make some coffee and get to the airport early."

"Nonsense and you have plenty of time to eat a hearty breakfast, so sit still and just eat. How are things going with Gizelle and her kids?"

Perry kept his eyes on her as she rushed about placing food on several plates in front of him and just when he was about to stand to get coffee, she pushed a freshly brewed, steamy cup in front of him.

"You think of everything."

"I've been with you kids since you were running around here in diapers. I know all of your habits, what you like to eat and especially the fact that you like nice hot coffee on a cold winter morning. Gizelle?" Sarah asked again.

"They're doing good. She had a good time when she went out with Brielle last week and she loves the job. She's happy."

"Is that crazy ex-husband of hers still out there somewhere?"

Perry's smile quickly turned to a frown at the thought. He wanted Marcus and his team to catch Clyde, but so far, the man had been elusive.

"He is out there somewhere. If he tries anything, I'll be ready for him," he boasted.

"Don't go getting yourself into any trouble. There is security on the ranch for a reason and they are the best. So, you and Gizelle? What's going on there?"

Perry chuckled as he ate. Sarah wasn't going to let him get away with not giving her details on a more personal level.

"When there is more to tell besides she's safe and I think she's wonderful, I'll let you know. I still love to tell you everything, but there's nothing to tell; not yet."

"I'll take not yet, for now. Just make sure you don't go getting in any trouble that could impact there being more to tell. That crazy man isn't worth it and Gizelle is worth everything. You don't think I see, but I see. Still, I'll wait until you're ready to share. Let the law do their job and you stay out of it."

"You sound like Pop and the only thing I can promise is that as long as Marcus or someone else gets to him first, he'll survive to see another day and his day in court. I can't make that promise if I get my hands on him first. That's all I'm saying."

"He's someone who needs to be taken down a peg or two."

"Leave a few jabs for me!" Brielle yelled, coming up behind him before heading to the sink to wash her hands, no doubt, coming by early for breakfast.

"How did you know there would be food? I swear, you show up at the most opportunists of moments!" he joked.

"Well, we all grew up with Sarah. Anytime anyone is at this house and is up early to take care of business, she would be in the kitchen making enough food to feed an army. I knew you had a flight this morning and I didn't have to think twice about whether she would force you to sit down and eat before you left and I wanted to see you off."

"Brielle, you come here just about every morning for breakfast, so don't even try that with me. You have your own house with a fully stocked kitchen and you still don't cook? Why did you move out when I know you still spend all of your time here?" he asked.

"I love my house, but I love this house; it's home. Besides, I can cook, but why should I when there is always good food here? Been doing anymore babysitting lately?" she jokingly asked.

"Very funny."

"Seriously. Now that I know you've got skills with kids, Gizelle and I can hang out more often."

"She needed me and I was happy to help and besides, they're great kids."

"Sounds like you enjoyed it. I never thought I'd see the day when you would be babysitting. You hated keeping an eye on me when you were forced to do so."

Perry looked at her and stuck his tongue out at her like he did when they were kids.

"Yeah, that's because you were hard-headed and spoiled rotten, thanks to Mom, Pop and Sarah!" he replied.

"You're all spoiled, not just Brielle, but you're the good kind of spoiled, not the bratty kind, thank goodness," Sarah chimed in.

"Oh, please – Brielle is a brat and you know it. By the time she came along, they were too exhausted to be as hard on her as they were on us boys."

"All of you spoiled Brielle because she was the only girl and you still do; each of you still give her whatever she wants even though she's a grown woman. I can't wait to see the day when she gets really serious about a man and he tries to fit in. He'll never have a chance," Sarah said.

Perry laughed out loud when Brielle faked choking on the water she was drinking.

"Brielle has brought plenty of dudes around here that she thought she was going to date and none of them were good enough for her. Any guy would be risking his life coming around here talking about he's all in love with my baby sister. She would be better off staying single and waiting until she's in her fifties to start dating!"

"You're crazy and I date plenty. You just don't see because like Sarah said, no guy will ever be good enough, that is, until he is. You'll see when that perfect guy comes along – you'll be happy for me. I only hope that you and Nick don't run him off from the start and instead will give him a chance. Dayton and Shelton, I trust, but you and Nick are another story. You've always been the problem, yet I can't have a vote when all of you meet women and bring them here to the ranch. I didn't get a say about Gizelle, though I think she's the best woman you have ever been involved with."

"I'm not involved with her. I mean, I'm not sure if I am or not. We've shared some moments."

"Oh, is that what they're calling it these days?" Brielle joked.

"Don't go there with me. Gizelle and I are building something, not running a marathon."

"I'm just saying, she's ready for a man like you to love her and care for her. She senses that being with you is not like being with that demon she was married to. She's been through a lot, but you're ready for more and I believe she is too. I see it every time you talk about her or are around her and you actually babysat her kids! That's huge! I have never, ever seen you sit with anyone's kids for any reason."

"Has she said something to you?"

"I wouldn't tell you if she did or didn't because that's girl talk and you're not privy to that. I will say that even though I know she's been through a lot, you make her happy, you make her smile and that's not divulging anything. Anyone who is around the two of you together for more than a few seconds can see and feel that. The way you look at her, I've never seen before, not even when you dated Veronica. You have a different kind of look when it comes to Gizelle. There's something serious there. What are you waiting for?"

"I'm feeling pretty serious about her."

"I have always been closer to you than Nick, Shelton or Dayton and it's probably because you are the oldest and I'm the youngest and with the age difference, you've always been more like another parent than just a brother. I know you've always looked out for me and had my back any and every time I needed it. I've been lucky to have you as a brother; to have you all as my brothers, but especially you. I want so much for you. I never liked Veronica. She was never the woman for you, but Gizelle is different. She is amazing and she'd be grateful to have a good man like you."

"You never told me you didn't like Veronica until after we broke up."

"That's because I love you and I want whatever

makes you happy and at that time, you were happy. I felt like she was hiding something and she made your relationship with her about her and only her all the time. That's not a real relationship. I'm glad you finally broke up with her and moved on, though you didn't move on to any one woman in particular. The number of women in and out of your house was crazy for a while. I was actually worried!"

"No need to worry. We were scratching each other's itches and I never introduced any of them to the family, so you knew there wasn't much there."

"And Gizelle?" she asked.

"She's my dream girl; period.

"See? That's what I'm talking about. Every woman wants a man who says that about her, not just to her face, but in her absence like you just did."

"I want to be everything she never had and that's not because I feel sorry for her, but because she's an amazing woman and I want her to be mine."

"Perry, you wear your heart on your sleeve and you always have. The moment you brought her and the kids here after finding them that day, I think we all knew that she was special and since she's been here, you've bent over backwards to make her life easier. There isn't a woman in the world who wouldn't want to be sought out and loved by you and you do love her don't you? I mean, I'm not trying to be too far up in your business, but I can't seem to help myself. I've been doing it since I was a kid and I'm not about to stop now. One day, my perfect man will care about me and look at me the way you do with Gizelle."

Perry looked at Sarah and was glad she was focused as he leaned in close to Brielle's ear.

"I am in love with her. I've never told her that. I came close last night when we talked until the middle of the night, but I held it back. I can't understand how her ex-husband could treat them the way he did."

"No one knows why someone would treat his wife and kids that way or why a woman would stay with a man who treated her the way Clyde did Gizelle. Remember what mom would tell us about her aunt Jean? Her sister didn't think she was worthy of a man better than uncle Terrence who ended up killing her. Even after they split and she tried dating, she didn't think there was a man who could truly love her unconditionally. Mom said that she had a messed up view of what love was supposed to be and the problem was she never had a man who came along and showed her, proved to her that real love actually existed. Because of that, she kept going back to uncle Terrence because he was familiar territory. I don't think Gizelle would do that, but you love her and you would never hurt her. If you know Gizelle is who you want, why would you wait to show her what real love looks and feels like? What if she is ready for you now? What if she is ready for a real man in her life? You will never know if you don't tell her that your help isn't because she is a damsel in distress, but because you genuinely care about her. You love her and that's all that matters, especially now. If she isn't ready, she'll tell you, but at least she knows that there are good men out there and she's entitled to have one despite what her life has been like. Anyway, I'm going to wrap some of this food up to go. I'm heading over to check on the setup for tomorrow night. There is still a lot that needs to be done for tomorrow's Valentine's Day dance. Have a safe flight and holler when you get back. I'll see you tomorrow night in whatever fly outfit you'll have on, complete with your staple cowboy hat and a very beautiful Gizelle on your arm, I hope. You're crazy if you don't ask her to go as your date and yeah, I said it!"

When Brielle reached over to hug him, Perry embraced her and thought about the advice from his baby sister who was definitely wiser than her age.

"I'll get some foil for your plate and Perry, you better get going if you're going to make your flight," Sarah said.

He had been so engrossed in his conversation with Brielle that he forgot Sarah was in the kitchen with them. Before he could respond, they were joined by his mother.

"Morning, mom," he said along with Brielle who kissed her on the cheek and rushed to the door.

"I'll come by later, mom!" Brielle yelled as she closed the door behind her.

"Perry, you're still here?" Marta asked. "Good

morning, Sarah."

"I'm just about to leave. I couldn't pass up this feast Sarah prepared. I've got some time."

"Is Buck dropping you off?"

"No, I'm driving myself. I'll leave my car at the airport. My truck is behind the house. You and Pop going to the big party for Valentine's Day tomorrow?"

"Depends."

"Depends? On what? You have other plans or something?"

"It depends on whether I need to watch Carrie and Brody for Gizelle. Do you know if she's going to the dance? She hasn't said anything, but I think it would be nice for her to go and have some fun."

"I was actually going to ask you about daycare for kids of the parents going to the party tomorrow night. Last year, the center was open for drop-ins until midnight so that parents who couldn't get baby sitters could come out and have a nice evening of dinner and dancing. I should have asked Brielle before she left and I forgot."

"Yes, we're offering that again this year. You're not usually in the loop with that because you don't have any children. Yes, that's being provided again this year and there are a lot of activities planned for the kids. Security will be tighter and we've hired extra staff from one of the daycare centers in town. It was easy to get the extra help when they realized they could make a week of their salary in one night."

"Yeah, that's a great incentive."

"And Sarah is baking her famous cookies for them to enjoy. The chef is making hot dogs, nuggets, fries and other treats. There are games and arts and crafts. So far, we have over fifty kids registered. I didn't see Gizelle's name on the list of parents who signed up. I told your father I was planning on helping with the kids unless he was dying to go to the event and he said he was planning on taking me away for a special Valentine's treat in a few days and so going to the dance wasn't a big priority if I wanted to be on hand for the kids. You know how I feel about those children."

"I'll call Gizelle later when I think she's up. She may not realize we have that available. I'm going to ask her to be my date for the dance."

Perry waited for any shrieks or screams of joy from his mother, but he was disappointed when she composed herself. He started to repeat himself in case she didn't hear him, but then he got his answer.

"Music to my ears and I won't say a whole lot more about that right now. Let me know if you need me. If for any reason she's not comfortable, I can keep the kids here and Sarah and I can have some fun activities with them. I do hope she'll register the kids. It's the same staff she's used to working with every day at the school."

"I'll let her know that."

When Marta started clapping, Perry laughed out

loud. That's the sound he'd been waiting on from her.

"You go ahead and get going. Have a safe flight and call when you land."

"Make sure Buck keeps an extra eye out. If Gizelle needs to leave the ranch for any reason, make sure someone accompanies her."

He didn't like having to be away and have his eyes on the ranch, but he still had ranch business to take care of and this time, that business was taking him out of town.

"Don't worry. I don't want that on your mind when you'll be states away. Your father and I will make sure the necessary precautions are in place. Love you, son."

"Love you too and love you too, Sarah," Perry added.

"Fly safe," Sarah said.

Perry stood, grabbed his hat and bag and headed to his car parked out front. As he stepped out into the cold, brisk morning air, he thought about going by the house to check on Gizelle and the kids before he left, but the hour was still pretty early. He wanted to ask her to the dance knowing he should have already done that. They've been spending lots of time together, hugging, kissing and enjoying each other and he hadn't even brought up the dance with her. He shouldn't have missed that Valentine's Day was coming up and that there was a dance. It's a time made for those in love, which he was and the first thing on his agenda should have been to ask Gizelle to be his date and really put his cards on the table for the next step in their budding relationship.

Heading off the ranch to the airport, the first thing he would do when the hour of the day was better, will be a call to Gizelle with a plea to be his date and an apology for not asking her earlier. He was looking forward to having her in his arms as they danced the night away.

**

Gizelle smiled when her phone vibrated and Perry's number appeared on the screen. She knew he'd flown out of Bozeman earlier for a meeting and though she hadn't said so out loud, she missed him already and couldn't wait for him to get back.

"Hey you!" she said, stepping away from her desk at work and crossed the hall to the teacher's lounge.

"Hi, beautiful. How is your day going?" Perry asked and her day was made brighter just hearing his voice.

"It's going great. I can't believe how fast the days go by while working here. That never happened when I worked at the law firm. Time seemed to stand still there."

"You've been couped up behind a desk all morning and you love it? I'm an outdoors kind of guy."

"You're a cowboy, Perry, and cowboys love being outdoors. Is your business trip going well?"

"It is. My flight just landed and I was thinking about you and thought I would check to see how things were going."

"I'm glad you did. I was thinking about you and wondering if you had landed safely. I guess I won't be seeing you around the ranch today. You didn't mention when you're returning."

"I'll be back tomorrow just in time for the dance tomorrow night."

Gizelle felt nervousness in her body at the thought of the dance the ranch was hosting for Valentine's Day. She had been wondering if Perry was going and if she would be out of place if she asked him to go with her. She had hoped and thought that he would have asked her, but so far, he hadn't said anything about it. She had given up hope that he wanted to go with her.

"I was helping Brielle out an hour earlier with some of the decorating. The party looks like it's going to be nice. She mentioned there is a live band and a popular R&B artist coming to perform. I was looking at the menu and my stomach started growling at all of the delicious treats I saw being delivered, especially the strawberry cheesecake, my favorite dessert."

"So, you were planning on going?"

Gizelle bit her bottom lip. She wanted to go, but didn't want to go with anyone other than him. She didn't know how to make that obvious.

"I want to go. Your mother was here today and she mentioned that there would be child care for the children of any parents who wanted to attend. I told her I would think about it."

"Would you like to be my date for the dance? I'm sorry it's last minute. I wanted to ask you a few days ago and got distracted and then this morning, I was going to call you, but it was so early when I got up. I would really love to have you on my arm as my date if you're open to that or we can do something else. I don't care what we do as long as we do something together."

"Are you serious? I would love to go and be your date. I was hoping you would ask."

"Then it's a date. I'll be back tomorrow morning. I'm so use to seeing you and the kids every day and I already miss you."

"You could have done that. You can call me any time of the day or night. I would have liked that."

"Well, now that I know that, I will make a point of doing that. Hearing your voice right now makes my day. I can get through my meetings with an extra pep in my step after talking to you. I'll let you get back to work. I wanted to say hi and to ask you to be my date for tomorrow. I'm running to a meeting and I'll get in pretty late. Can I call you later tonight after you're in for the night?"

Gizelle was so excited and inside, she was feeling like a blushing school girl waiting for the most popular guy at school to call her.

"I'm going to wait up for your call."

"I can't wait to see you for the dance tomorrow night. I know you'll be in something cute and sexy. The image of you in that red dress that night we went on our first date is etched in my brain."

Gizelle thought about that and wasn't sure she had the perfect outfit for a Valentine's Day date with Perry, but she played it off.

"We're going to be the *hottest* couple there!"

"All because you'll be beautiful and no one will be able to take their eyes off of you the way I never can when I'm around you. I miss you," Perry said.

Gizelle swooned at hearing the words. She felt new to dating because Perry said all of the sweet things women love to hear.

"I miss you, too. I can't wait for you to come back tomorrow."

"I'll call you later, sweetheart. Until then, I'll think about your smile and that'll carry me over until I get back."

"You make me feel so special, Perry."

"You are special and you deserve it. Until tonight."

"Until tonight," she replied.

The moment the call was over, she danced around the room, smiling and giggling and then remembered she could be seen and she stopped. Just as she was about to return to her desk, she thought about the dance the next night and her smiled turned to a frown when she realized she didn't think she had the perfect dress for the party. She had that pretty red dress, but

Perry had already seen her in that. She had some other nice things, but nothing she'd want to wear to a dance for an event on Valentine's Day. She had to call Brielle. She would know what to do.

"Hey Gizelle."

She sighed with relief that Brielle wasn't too busy to answer her call.

"I hope I didn't catch you at a bad time."

"Never. What's up?"

"Perry asked me to be his date for the party tomorrow night," she said eagerly.

"Yeah!"

"Right, but there is one thing – I don't have the perfect dress."

"Girl, any dress you put on will be a perfect dress. Have you seen how beautiful you are? I'm jealous!" Brielle shouted.

"Do you have time to go shopping with me after work? Maybe we can grab a bite to eat after?"

"Of course. I love any excuse to shop."

"Great. The kids and I will be ready when you're finish for the day."

"Do you want to see if my mom will keep an eye on them? They'll probably be tired after a full day of school."

"Do you think she'll mind? She helps out with them so much and I don't want to take advantage of her kindness?"

"What? Please! She would have them every day if

she thought she didn't have to return them to you. I can't tell you how much my mother wants grandchildren and she's getting good practice with your kids. I'm sure she'll love to. I'll give her a call and I should be able to meet you right when you're getting off. I'm excited! I finally have another sister to shop with. You and Parker are the sisters I never had. At first there were none and now I have two! I'm going to call and see if she wants to go. There is a boutique in the city that's owned by a friend of mine and they will have everything from a dress to accessories. Is that okay with you?"

"Of course. In fact, I'll stop over and ask her in a few minutes. She's here at the school for a meeting. I'll see you later and thanks for helping me out. Your brother is special to me and I want the perfect dress."

"Perry will love you in anything. I'll see you shortly."

This time, Gizelle looked around and not seeing anyone, she danced around and pumped her fist in the air. She was going on a date on Valentine's Day. Clyde never gave her as much as a flower on that day, let alone took her anywhere to dance. Her life was finally turning around and she was running with the feelings she has for Perry. She thought about how it felt to be kissed by him and hoped more of that was on the table for them. Maybe even a little more. Who was she kidding, she wanted a lot more. Was she ready? Before she could second guess herself, she already knew the answer. She was ready for everything with Perry. He was the perfect man and if not her, then it would be someone else. He was more than she ever thought or expected and she wanted to be that for him. She hoped he was ready for her because she was going to be ready for him.

15

Parking his car in front of the police station, Perry rushed inside with a purpose-filled stride, especially after seeing Nick's truck already parked a few spaces from where he'd parked. He checked his phone to see if he'd missed a text or phone call regarding any sightings of Clyde. He'd checked in with his family several times while he was out of town on business and nothing had changed. Still, he knew that didn't mean Clyde was gone. The couple of times he'd called Gizelle, he kept their conversation light and didn't bring up anything about her plight with Clyde. He wanted their chats to be about them and how much he was looking forward to dancing and holding her in his arms at the dance. He was anxious to get to the ranch, but he wanted to check in with Marcus first. When he drove to the station and saw the Sheriff's car, which only Marcus drove, he decided now was a good time to get an update.

THE WAY YOU LOVE ME: The Sullivans of Montana

Putting his phone away, he turned to Nick, who was standing at the front desk beaming the minute they saw each other.

"Bro! You're back!" Nick exclaimed as they fist bumped before hugging.

"Yeah, I just landed and I see we've had some snow overnight."

"Yeah, and a fire. I stopped by to give Marcus an update on it."

"I still can't believe my brother is a fire chief! Still loving being back here in Bozeman?"

"More than you know. I can't believe I stayed away so long, but never again and besides, my life with Parker is every man's dream; she's every man's dream woman!"

"Man, what did you do with my brother? You must be some kind of alien out here shouting in public all loud about a woman."

"Yeah, whatever. I'm not the only one all wrapped up in a woman, though you're still trying to play it cool. Did you go by the ranch to check on Gizelle and the kids before coming by here?"

"No, not yet. I came straight from the airport. I want to find out if there is any update on finding Clyde either here or back in Chicago."

"Cool. I saw Gizelle this morning talking with Brielle while they were doing some last-minute setup for the party tonight. I also hear you're going."

"I am and I'm looking forward to it. This has been

some year already and I'm ready for some uninterrupted fun with a beautiful woman in my arms, just as you are."

"You got that right! The women have had their heads together since yesterday about tonight. They went out shopping and from what I know about Parker, get ready for some of the sexiest women this side of Montana. I tried to get a look at her dress and she practically tackled me to the floor when I tried to look in the bag. Brielle took them out and the word I heard was they're going to knock our socks off with what they're wearing. I know I'm ready! You?"

"More than you know."

"You and Gizelle getting close, huh?"

"We are and where I have been going at a snail's pace with her, she's surprising me with impatience that I'm going too slow for her," he laughed. "Can you believe that? I am not known for going too slow when it comes to women, so that's a first."

"That's because you're in love and being with a woman hits different when it's about love and not just lust, though I know both play a role in what you're feeling for her. I don't blame you. I didn't think I'd fall in love with Parker as fast as I did, but when it hit me that she was everything I could want in a woman, I didn't let anything get in the way of making her my woman and in a few months, she'll be Parker Sullivan and hopefully shortly after that, they'll be some little Sullivans running around the ranch."

"Bro, I've never seen you like this, not even with..."

"Perry stopped short of saying the name of Nick's first love, Sienna McCorn, who was the center of his world back when he was a teenager until the day she died in Nick's arms after a horse-riding accident that he blamed himself for. He didn't want to visit past hurts when Nick was so happy now, living back in Bozeman after years of being away and living in New York out of the self-imposed guilt he'd laid on himself.

"It's okay to say Sienna's name and I'll always love her. I didn't think I'd find that kind of love again. Parker entered my life at the perfect time, when I didn't have a choice but to be still and reflect on my life after the fire accident in New York."

"Well, I'm glad you're back and Bozeman is lucky to have you as fire chief. What about this fire you mentioned?"

Before Nick could respond, Marcus walked up to them.

"Hey, you're back! I was wondering if you would stop by here today. Before you ask, there have been no sightings of Clyde anywhere. I'll also get an alert if he shows up in Chicago and is spotted or picked up for any reason. Why don't you both come into my office where we can talk privately.

When Marcus turned and walked away, Perry fell in step behind him, followed closely by Nick. As they entered the office, he took one brown leather office chair in front of the desk as Nick sat in the other.

"No news is good news," Perry spoke first.

"True and I hope it stays that way. I hope that whatever his plan was, he's moved on after being unable to find Gizelle and the kids. I sent some guys out to check around the Baxter property and they noticed some tire treads in the snow that appear to match the same ones we saw the day we got Gizelle and the kids out of there. I have no doubt that Clyde came back, but I'm not sure if he's still around or not. Only time will tell, but we're ready for him," Marcus said.

"Yeah, well, so am I. I'm not going to tell Gizelle about the tire tracks at the house. She's been doing good and not worrying as much and I don't want to upset her with the possibility of him being here. He will regret the day he tries to hurt her again. I'm serious when I say you better get to him first because if I do, I won't hold back on showing him what happens when a man hits a woman. He's used to overpowering women, but I don't think he's ever come up against a man with a plan to teach him a lesson," Perry exclaimed.

"Perry, do not get into anything with this guy. I'm not saying that for your sake, I'm saying it for his because I know what you'll do. Nick, remember that guy, Jonah, who at nineteen pushed Brielle off the bleachers at one of the high school football games where she was a cheerleader? She was like sixteen or

THE WAY YOU LOVE ME: The Sullivans of Montana

something like that. He had asked her out a few weeks before that and she declined, only for him to see her out on a date the night before with the star football player.

Nobody saw Perry coming when all of a sudden, that guy was lifted high in the air, off of his feet and found himself face to face with you and then that turned into fist to face. If it hadn't been for your brothers who pulled you off of him, he would have ended up with more than a broken nose. I mean you gave him a whooping that day that none of us will ever forget."

Perry huffed at the remembrance of his antics back then. He had a hot temper then, especially when it came to Brielle getter older and guys started sniffing around her.

"Yeah, he deserved that. No man should ever harm a woman, especially my sister. It's a good thing my brothers were there because I didn't even see his face. All I saw was someone who hurt Brielle and needed the breath knocked out of him. It sucks that your father, who was the sheriff back then, had to lock me up."

He thought about how Marcus' father, as sheriff, was not to be played with. It was no surprise that when he retired, Marcus, who grew up to be his deputy, had taken over as sheriff.

"I know. I remember that day and he hated doing it too, but you needed to calm down. You were only in

217

a cell for like an hour and no charges were filed after Jonah's father let him know that he deserved what he got. I hear his father gave him worse when he got home," Marcus said.

"That day was crazy and none of us could calm Perry down. It took my father coming to get him released that he finally calmed down. You have always been that protector of all of us, especially Brielle and that guy probably still has no idea what we saved him from when we finally got you off of him. We don't want to see you in any trouble with this Clyde guy. Though I always have bail money on hand, I don't want to have to use it. Let Marcus and his team do their job if Clyde shows up and you encounter him."

"No promises about not hurting him, but I will promise to contact Marcus immediately."

"Nick, I already know that's all we're going to get. Wait, I just remembered something else about that football game and the incident. What was the guy's name, the football player that Brielle dated? I can't think of it," Marcus asked.

"Cordell. Cordell Marshall," Nick shouted.

"Yeah, that's him. Did you guys know that after Perry beat him down, a few days later, Cordell went after Jonah at the diner and re-broke his nose after it had been reset after Perry broke it? I had to put him in a cell that night, but let him out after a few hours. Man, his father said that for days, Cordell fumed in anger that Jonah had hurt Brielle and even though he was warned to not retaliate, he put all that on the table along with his football scholarship and went after him with a severity that I've only seen with the Sullivan bunch."

"Yeah, I heard something about that," Nick said. "Brielle came running into my room and begged me to have my dad go talk to your father about letting Cordell go. By the time my father got to the station, Cordell's dad was there and your father was already in the middle of letting Cordell out. Whatever happened to Jonah?"

"Died in jail in New Jersey. I remember hearing the story about a hometown guy who, along with some other guys, tried to rob a bank in Manhattan and a teller ended up dying. That teller was the younger sister of some badass guy in New Jersey and he made sure Jonah and the other two guys responsible never saw the light of day again," Marcus explained.

"Wow, street justice," Perry said. "I didn't know about Cordell going after him like I did. No one told me about that. I always liked that kid."

"Yeah, and when Nick remembered his name, it sounded familiar and now I know why. He's doing great things. He could be one of the top draft professional football picks this year. The town is planning some big celebration. I knew the name, but didn't make the connection to Brielle until just now. I only know about it because we have to be notified of all large public events that may need security,"

Marcus said.

"Yeah? That's cool. He sure was in love with Brielle back then, but my parents wanted her to focus on school and after graduation, he went away to college to play ball and I don't think he came home often. Never saw him again," Nick said. "His family is still here?"

"They're in Livingston now, but still consider Bozeman home. I'm sure you'll hear more about the event with the draft coming up in a few months," Marcus said.

"Cool. I have to jet soon, so let me bring you up to speed on the fire. The investigator met me this morning at the place of last night's fire and what he initially thought was a deliberately set fire, was actually an accident. Old man Jenkins was drinking again and was pouring out liquor as he was walking out of the house, while also smoking. He stumbled at the doorway, dropped the cigarette and forgot about it. He got in his car, drove away and ended up in a ditch. One of your sheriff's deputies found him a few hours ago, still asleep in his car. He'd run out of gas and if he had not been found, he would have frozen to death."

"Yeah, Peters alerted me to that right before I came out to see the two of you. I'm expecting a briefing shortly," Marcus said.

"Luckily, most of the damage was from water, though the fire damage was still pretty significant. I'll leave a copy of my report out front on my way out," Nick said standing. "Perry, I'll see you on the ranch later. I need to get back to the firehouse."

"I'll see you at the dance," Perry said as Nick walked out.

"Dance? You're going? I was sure you'd be at the Farmer's Association meeting here in town tonight," Marcus said.

"Yeah, at any other time, I would have been, but that was before Gizelle. I am not missing a chance to spend an evening removing any bad memories with good ones. She needs a night like Valentine's Day so that she can see and feel what it's like to be cherished. I'm going all out!" Perry said.

"Really? Well, do tell, my friend."

"I have flowers that are being delivered to her today, which should be happening about right now," Perry said checking his watch.

"Okay, I see you."

"I have some delicious Godiva chocolates coming in about an hour after that. I checked with Brielle, who wouldn't tell me anything about what Gizelle was wearing other than the color and how the neckline was made. I ordered a beautiful platinum and diamond necklace and bracelet for her to wear tonight and every hour on the hour from noon until six this evening, there will be a different card given to her where I wrote my own messages inside to her, letting her know that she's an amazing woman who deserves an amazing life. I also have some other gifts that she's been getting throughout the day that I hope she loves. I just wanted her to know that I was thinking about her and that I want today to be special. I want her to know that a man is supposed to love on her, not hurt her. He is supposed to care for her, not take her for granted. He is supposed to shower her with love and never harm her. I want this day to be special for her. I also sent gifts and candy to the kids."

"Oh, you really did it up nice! I'm glad my lady doesn't know about all of that. I see I'll have to step up my game," Marcus joked. "I've known you to always do special things for women, but never on this level," he added.

"I never have before, but when I think of Gizelle, I think of happiness and love and I wanted to relay that, especially today. Her life hasn't been the best before now, but that's all changing for her and Carrie and Brody. I better get out of here too. Sounds like there isn't much to really talk about when it comes to Clyde, but you know how to reach me if you hear anything," Perry said and stood.

He turned toward the door and then looked back when he heard Marcus moving around as he stood as well.

"Perry, let me repeat again - don't do anything crazy if you run into Clyde before I can get to him if he is still in Bozeman. If he's here, he's hiding pretty good or he has someone who is hiding him. If he's

THE WAY YOU LOVE ME: The Sullivans of Montana

gone, good riddance, but that doesn't mean he won't appear. Call me. Don't hesitate and don't take matters into your own hands. Let me do my job of keeping you out of jail. Unlike my father, who was Sheriff before me, I won't be able to handle putting my best friend in a jail cell and definitely not for murder. I know the rage you're carrying, but remember that Gizelle and her kids need you. You are no good to them if you're in jail. Protect them, but let me handle Clyde."

"I hear you. Are you and Donna coming to the dance tonight?"

"I may for a bit just to check things out. Donna is in Canada visiting her parents. Her father is ill and she wanted to get back here today, but I told her to take the time she needs. We'll have Valentine's Day whenever she returns. That'll give me a chance to get on your level of gift giving before she gets back," he joked.

Perry left Marcus' office and headed straight for his car. After getting in, he smiled as he dialed Gizelle's cell after seeing several texts from her of her delight of the flowers she'd received. She thought he was still in the air on his flight and pressed him to call her as soon as he got her message.

Smiling as he pulled off, he didn't see the blue truck that pulled out of a spot a few spaces down from his and followed him as he headed for the ranch.

16

"Ugh! So frustrating!" Gizelle yelled into the floor-to-ceiling mirror in the master bedroom. She was worried that what she was seeing in the mirror would not appeal to Perry the way she wanted to appeal to him.

Turning around and around and looking at herself from head to toe, she was either disappointed at what she saw or just nervous. Either way, her frustration with herself was growing by the minute. She didn't know if she had what it took to really get and keep the eye of a man like Perry, oh but she wanted to. It wasn't just the ideal that he had come to her rescue when she needed someone in her corner, but even before that, going back to the day they first met, she remembered the butterflies in her stomach when her eyes locked with his. His heated gaze, the sexy way he sat in the chair and then the way his body moved and swayed when she saw him out on the dance floor. She wanted him then as much as she wants him now.

Fast forward, to today, a day that she feels is critical to what happens next for them. What she didn't want was for him to lose interest in her when she was in love with him. This love felt different than what she thought love was. If she were being truthful with herself, she knew her heart was falling for Perry that first day they met, specifically, it was one small action that only resonated with her when he wanted to make sure she and Heather got home after they danced all night. Since she had driven them, Perry had followed her to Heather's place and then fell in line behind her as she drove to her own home. If it had been anyone else other than Perry, she may not have been open to the idea, but they were well known and no one ever had a bad word to say about any of them, especially Perry. Once she was home, he waited until she was inside before he pulled off. She stood in the doorway as he turned to leave.

As he drove off, he had tipped his cowboy hat to her and smiled so bright that her heart melted. For the next month, they'd spoken several times and when she would be out, he would make sure she and Heather got home safely. It had become a staple for him and she loved every minute of it. Then, Clyde had shown up and all hell broke loose, just when she thought she and Perry may be on to something. Life dished her a big bag of lemons; or so she thought.

Tonight, she was looking forward to making

lemonade. She thought about all the sexually satisfied women in the world and looked forward to the day that she could add her name to that list.

Her own intimate life had been very unsatisfying. Clyde had been her first and only and she was ashamed to say to anyone that even until today, she had never experienced an orgasm that she hadn't given herself. Clyde was self-serving when it came to sex and she had faked her way through to the end. She had wanted children and never would she regret having either one of them. She still longed for that feeling of true intimacy with a man who knew how to please a woman or was open to hearing from a woman what she had to share about what pleased her. She had wanted to do that, but learned early in her rushed marriage to Clyde that what she thought, wanted or needed was of no concern of his. She endured as long as she could and once she had children, her focus shifted from Clyde's needs to those of her children.

She knew from the start that Perry was different. Even as friends, he'd shown her more caring and support than any person in her life. They had shared a kiss here and there and even now, thinking about how sensual his kisses were, she reached to her lips as if she could still feel his lips on hers. When her eyes closed as she stood still thinking about him, she longed for so much more. She thought she wouldn't be ready, but then after the first kissed they shared, she had to ask herself what she had been waiting on. She had inwardly prayed for a good man and now that she had one who clearly cared about her and wanted her, she didn't want to wait. She was more than ready for more, much, much more.

As she looked to the bed, she smiled as she glanced at the candy, cards and other gifts that had arrived throughout the day from Perry. The first had been the flowers, two dozen roses, one dozen in red and the other in orange that had arrived around noon. Even Carrie and Brody were excited when Buck brought the two huge arrangements by the house. Perry had mentioned that any deliveries would be brought by Buck or one of the other bunkhouse boys.

After the flowers had been the chocolates and then cards, every hour on the hour, each more beautiful than the last. Gifts had consisted of jewelry which was exquisite and would go perfect with the black, form-fitting dress she'd brought to wear for the dance. When she tried the necklace on, it had fit perfectly along the neckline of the dress. She spotted it on the bed and smiled.

Other gifts were a beautiful thick, winter coat in pink and white, her favorite colors, a pair of black and white flannel pajamas that matched the sets he'd also given to Carrie and Brody as gifts. There was a pair of beautiful butterfly earrings in red with small diamonds around the wings and several DVD movies that she mentioned she'd never seen. In the note that accompanied the movies, he mentioned that he couldn't wait to sit in front of the fireplace and enjoy them with her. She couldn't wait either.

Hearing a knock at the front door and knowing the kids were taking a nap, she rushed to answer it and found Brielle standing there.

"Hey!" Brielle said greeting her with a hug. "I see you have the dress on! You look amazing."

"Ugh, I don't think I like it as much as I did in the store. I don't know if Perry will like it."

"Girl, stop it. Perry would like you if you showed up in a cloth sack. You are beautiful and it has nothing to do with the dress. I think I have a solution for what I think is your problem. Come on," Brielle said, taking her by the arm and walking up the stairs to the bedroom.

"What am I missing?" Gizelle asked impatiently.

"It's the bra. I say that because you and I have large breasts and with this type of dress, the bra is the key. Because of how the dress fits like a second skin, the straps of your bra are digging into your shoulder because of the weight and it causes a sort of dip on the shoulders where the straps are and it's noticeable under the dress."

Gizelle turned toward the mirror and realized that's what she was hating. She could see the seams of the straps on her shoulders.

"Wow, yeah, I missed that."

"Tell me you have a strapless bra in black or I can run out to the store and pick you up one."

"No, I don't want you running out to do that. You should be home getting dressed for the dance. Perry and your mom had the rest of my things picked up from the house and I have several strapless bras in the bags I haven't gone through yet. Let me check. While I'm doing that, are you bringing a date to the dance?" Gizelle asked, smiling when she came across the bags in the bottom of the closet and poured the contents out on the bed.

"I almost forgot to give you this," Brielle said.

When Gizelle turned around, Brielle was holding out a card to her.

"From Perry? He has you delivering cards too?" she asked, tearing at it with an eagerness to get to the message inside. The cards had made her day perfect and she loved looking around the bedroom at how she'd placed them all around the room.

"Just this last one. He wanted to be sure you got it before he picked you up and you've got like two hours left."

"I know. He called to say he was back and would be tied up with work until he picked me up for the dance. I'm so excited and nervous."

Opening the card with nervous fingers that shook uncontrollably, she was surprised and ecstatic to see five words that brought her love for Perry to the surface. The words read, "*Will You Be My Valentine?*"

"Yes, yes!" she screamed.

"Yes, what?" Brielle asked.

"Your brother officially asked me to be his Valentine. Whew, how I love that man!"

Before she could take the words back, Gizelle looked over at Brielle who was now grinning from ear to ear.

"Don't be shocked that you said it out loud. I already knew. You and my brother can barely keep your eyes off of each other. Perry is a great man to be in love with and I'm not just saying that because he's my brother."

"I know and yes he is. He is everything any woman could ask for."

"Wait – have you and my brother been doing 'the dirty'?" Brielle asked and fell on the bed laughing.

Gizelle almost choked when she understood what 'the dirty' meant.

"Oh, my goodness. No, we haven't done that yet and I swear I'm about to explode every time I'm around him. I keep wondering when it will happen and just when I think it will, it doesn't. He's being a gentleman and I think he's waiting for a sign that I'm ready for that next step with him."

"You ready?"

"I've been ready. All the dreams I have about your brother at night lets me know that I'm beyond ready."

"I can't think of a more perfect night than tonight. My mom will have Carrie and Brody and I'm sure she won't mind if they stay the night. If not, they can stay with me tonight."

"You didn't answer my question about a date for tonight. You're going alone?"

"I am. Can I tell you a secret? I haven't even told any of my friends or Parker and you know how close I've gotten to her. The two of you are the sisters I would long for growing up."

Gizelle wanted to cry and tried to hold back the tears that threatened to fall. The Sullivans had made her feel like family from the moment she'd met them and she loved connecting with Brielle and Parker as the sisters she herself had never had.

"You and Parker have been the best little sisters."

"Well, as your little sister, I'm going to share a secret and you can't tell anyone," Brielle said.

"Sisters honor."

Gizelle laughed as she kissed her two fingers and placed them over her heart to signify their bond as sisters and her oath to keep her secret.

"I've been seeing someone. He's a guy from my past, but my family doesn't know. I dated him back in high school, but then he went away to college, to the delight of my family who thought he and I were getting too serious too fast. I was sixteen and he was eighteen and a senior, but I was in love and nobody could tell me different. We lost touch for a long time and a few months ago, he sought me out on Instagram. When he can find the time to come to town, I've been sneaking off to see him. He's not in town right now due to a commitment around his career, so yes, I'm going alone tonight, but I'll be so busy, it won't matter."

"Why the secrecy? Your family doesn't like him?"

"They did back then. I don't know how they feel about him now. He has a son who is three years old and there is some drama with his son's mother. She knows he's seeing someone and has made all kinds of threats and demands and that could bring drama. My family won't like that and would want me to stay away from him and what they'll call baby mama drama. There's more to it, but I won't go into that right now. The time will come when I'll tell my family, that time is not today, especially since he won't be here anyway. Now, back to you and my brother."

"Here is one! I found one of my sexiest strapless bras."

Gizelle held it up and beamed.

"That'll work. It will make a huge difference. Us busty women have to make sure our 'girls' are set up right in the perfect dress like the one you have for tonight. Now, sexy underwear, sexy dress, beautiful jewelry, Parker did an amazing job with your hair and I can help with your make-up. I would say you are on your way to the perfect night of seduction."

"Seduction? I wouldn't even know where to start. I've never been that forward and I've only been with one man in my life."

"Then, you, my sister, have been missing out. There is nothing wrong with initiating what you want.

You just have to be prepared. Condoms? Do you have any? I know my brother keeps boxes of them. I know you know he's no angel, but do you have any? Are there any here at the house?"

"I don't know and I don't have any," Gizelle said nervously. The idea of initiating sex with a man scared her.

"No worries. I have some. I'll bring them over before Perry gets here to pick you up. I'm no expert on men since I don't have as much experience as I would like to have, but Cordell and I get it in when he's in town. He was my first back when I was in high school and he has learned a lot since then."

"I'm so nervous."

Gizelle watched as Brielle stood and walked over to her, taking her by the hands.

"Don't be nervous. Go with the flow of the night. It's Valentine's Day, a day meant for lovers and you and Perry are meant to be together. I would say forever, but I don't want to scare you even more."

"Until I met your brother, I never thought on terms of forever because of what I'd been through, but Perry is an incredible man and I'm a lucky woman that he's patiently waiting on me. I don't want to make him wait any longer. Thanks for the condoms. I've never even bought any before. I wouldn't know the size to get or anything. I will say that from what I hear..."

Gizelle didn't get the rest of her words out before

Brielle put a hand in front of her face to stop her.

"Okay, you're about to share more than I need to know about my brother. Don't forget, I live in this town and I've heard the stories about my brothers and I know what they say about Perry. I'll bring plenty of the gold packs for you because you'll need them. I keep plenty on hand for Cordell. Now, let's get you ready for your night."

"I'm glad we got those pedicures, manicures and most of all, the waxing of important womanly areas. I'm going to switch bras and I'll be right back," Gizelle said, running off.

In the bathroom, she turned and looked in the mirror, this time seeing herself differently. The bra would fix the look, but to her, she saw a confidence in herself that she'd never really had before. She was ready to put the past behind her and walk into her future; one she hoped included Perry.

17

From the ride from the house all the way to the event hall, Perry had yet to say another word other than what he'd said to Gizelle the moment she opened the door and he found her beauty standing on the other side. If he thought she was stunning before, she outdid herself. When his eyes landed on her, he could feel his mouth gaping open as he took in all of her, from her head to her feet. He knew she would be a knockout, but she took her vivaciousness to a whole other level, one that hit him like a ton of bricks. He felt like a high school kid foaming at the mouth at the most beautiful girl in the school who agreed to be his date.

As he handed the valet the keys to move his car to a reserved spot, he helped Gizelle out of the car and after placing her hand in his, they walked to the door. He smiled looking down and seeing the red and white corsage he'd given her prominently displayed on her wrist. The necklace and bracelet he'd sent her gleaned in the beautiful, starry night and under her coat, he knew what he would find when he helped her take it off. His first sight of her dressed to the nines nearly had him forgetting about the dance and all he could think of was making love to her until she writhed under him like a wild woman, finally freeing herself of any reserve.

Once inside, they went to the coat check area where he took his time helping Gizelle remove her coat slowly down her arms so that he could get an extra look at her and his eyes did not deceive him. He'd lost all form of speech. His tongue would not work beyond telling her how beautiful she was. For the first time in his life, he was tongue-tied. When Gizelle turned to him and he smiled at her without words, he saw a look of worry on her face.

"Is something wrong?" she asked him.

"Wrong? Why would anything be wrong?" he asked as he took her hand and began walking toward the registration table. Even though everyone knew him, he still required family and staff to follow every instruction Brielle had in place including making sure they stopped at the registration table.

"You didn't say anything on the ride here. Did I do or say anything wrong? Are you upset with me? You don't like the dress? It's too much right?" she asked.

Perry felt her nervousness where their hands were clasped together. He could feel her shaking. He didn't want her doubting anything about herself, him or about them together. Before going inside of the large ballroom, he pulled her to the side and walked down one of the hallways where they would have some privacy. He needed to set the record straight and let her know that his behavior was all him and his desire to focus on anything other than how sexy she looked so that he didn't embarrass himself with his body's reaction to seeing her. The hardening of that certain part of him would be evident to anyone who looked his way. He'd never been in a constant state of arousal like he seemed to always be in when she was around. Tonight, he was hard as a rock and he needed the time in the truck to focus on something to alleviate his reaction to her so that they could enjoy the night without him having to sit cross-legged all night long.

When he looked around and didn't see another person in sight, he moved to the side wall next to some long, gold curtains so that they would not be seen. He leaned back against the wall and pulled her flush up against his body.

"Baby, let me make something very clear – you have done nothing wrong and I don't think you ever could in my eyes. I apologize for my quietness, but you were so beautiful when you opened the door and I was trying to figure out how I got to be this lucky that you said yes to being my Valentine. Nothing is wrong – everything is absolutely perfect. You are absolutely perfect. Your dress is perfect, your hair is perfect and I love it in the pinned-up style. I know you like to wear it down around your shoulders. Without being too forward where I usually am forward, your body in this dress is about to give me a heart attack. You are perfect and I guess I didn't want to say the wrong thing. What I really want to do is this."

With no other words needed, Perry lifted her chin up even higher and just as she was about to smile brightly after hearing his compliments, he leaned down and kissed her deeply. Now, was not the time for soft and slow. If he was ever going to relay to her just how much he desired her and get it out of the way before their evening moved ahead, he needed to go all in now.

His heart raced when without seeking approval to deepen the kiss even more, Gizelle opened for him and accepted the kiss with the same vigor in which he was giving the kiss. He felt her rising up on her heels as she reached up and circled her arms around his neck as far as she could reach and when she pulled him closer to her, he reached down and practically lifted her off of her feet so that he could get even more of her than he was already getting with the illicit, seductive kiss, one he knew was so intoxicating that it had to be against the law. As his mouth melded with hers, Perry felt lightheaded as if he'd been struck by lightning, but he refused to release her mouth. He savored her sweetness and when she moaned into his mouth, he returned his own low growl as they feasted on each other.

Finally remembering where they were, he slowly pulled back, though deep down, he didn't want to. Placing Gizelle back down on the floor, on her feet, he took in deep breaths of air as he tried to get his breathing to return to normal. Looking at Gizelle, she was struggling with the same reluctancy that he was to be apart.

"Okay, so, damn! What was that? I mean, we have kissed before, but that was something out of this world. If we were anyplace other than here at the dance, that kind of kiss would still be going on and a lot more after that. Whew, you consistently take my breath away, sweetness," Perry admitted.

"So, that did just happen. I didn't dream that powerful kiss? I think we need to find chairs because my legs are weak after that. You, uh, you mentioned more would have taken place. Is that more off of the table since we stopped kissing?" Gizelle asked.

Perry knew what he wanted to say, but he had to make an appearance at the dance when what he wanted to do was get back in his car and take her straight to his house and strip her of every stitch of clothing that has shielded his eyes from her natural beauty.

Reaching for her, Perry pulled her back against his body and this time, he held her close enough for her to feel how much he wanted her. When he heard a hitch in her breath as she was about to speak, he knew that she'd felt him.

"Question answered?" he asked.

"Clear as day."

Looking into her eyes and locking on, he made sure she didn't look away.

"I would love nothing more than to finish the 'more' now, but we just arrived and I want you to have a nice time at the dance, but leaving no confusion about you and me, I want you and I have since the moment I met you."

When Gizelle looked at him sheepishly, he knew she was falling back on her shyness and he was okay with that. Not all women knew how to go for what they wanted or needed and he was as patient as she needed him to be.

"But you never made that kind of move. The few times I thought you would, you backed away. I thought you didn't want me in that way," she said.

When she looked down, Perry drew her attention back to him by lifting her eyes back up to his with a raise of her chin.

"Baby, don't you ever think that I don't want you. I thought that you weren't ready after all that you had been through. I don't want to be a man coming after you to satisfy my own desire for you. I want you badly and it's not about the sex. If we become intimate, I want you to be sure about it. I mean, I need you to be absolutely sure that I am who you want because being with you isn't like any other casual, friends-with-benefits type of thing. I have a very healthy sexual appetite and I can admit that I haven't been active since I met you because I want you and only you. I want there to be an us. I really like you and trust me, I am not like the man you have been involved with in the past. Our involvement is just as much for you as it is for me and you, my sweet, would be my priority. I want to not only make love to you, but I want to love and care for you. I want to show you the way a woman should be loved because the way I will do that, you will never have to wonder if it's real or not. Are you ready for that? Are you ready for that with me?" he asked.

Perry hadn't planned on laying his heart on the line like this at this moment, but he had a feeling this was the perfect time to have this conversation. When she didn't look away again, he waited for her answer while still holding her in his arms.

"I've been ready for that. I've been ready for you – for us. I've been waiting. I have some condoms."

Perry smiled the minute she said the words and covered her mouth, looking down as if she were ashamed. He cleared his throat and moved his head around until he captured her eyes and kept his eyes focused on hers.

"Do you? Well, that says a lot. I guess you are serious about being ready. I'll tell you what – I have them too, so no worries. I think we've both been holding out waiting for the other while both of us have been ready to move to the next level. What do you say we enjoy ourselves for a few hours and then head out for some alone time? My mother is planning to take Carrie and Brody home with her from the party the kids are having at the school. I'm going to call her to see if she can keep them overnight and you and I are going to have a beautiful night. How does that sound?"

"How long are we staying?"

"Baby, I'm ready to leave this joint now, but let's make an appearance, dance a few dances, eat a little food and then make our exit."

"Are we going back to the house?" she asked.

"I don't think so, unless you want to. I have other plans in mind that I'm going to make as soon as you find your way to the ladies room to fix your lipstick which I have completely messed up. That way, I'll have time to let my body calm down, and I do mean every part of me and I'm going to make a call. My family owns a building of condominiums in the city where we put up guests who prefer hotels over the ranch life. Shelton and I have condos in the building. I'm going to call my service and have them send someone over to set up my place for a night of romance. How does that sound?"

"It sounds like something I've never experienced before; something put together for a queen."

"You are my queen. I never want you to doubt that. You are my queen, baby, today and for the unforeseeable future. It's me and you."

"I'm not dreaming?"

"After tonight, you won't be able to ask that ever again. Nothing will feel more real than the night we're going to share. I'll take care of everything. Go ahead and fix your lipstick before everyone gets a look at you and wonder just what I've been doing to you."

"Oh, right. The kissing did a number on my lipstick I'm sure. I'll go do that while you make your call. Will I have time to go back to the house and pack an overnight bag? Do you want me to call your mother and ask her about the kids while you make your call?"

"I don't want you worrying about anything other than enjoying a wonderful night and I'll take care of everything else. Just enjoy – that's the name of the game for you tonight."

When she was out of sight, Perry first called his mother who told him that she was already planning on the Carrie and Brody spending the night after the three of them left the party for the kids. He asked if she needed pajamas and other stuff from the house and she told him that she already kept extra night clothes, regular clothes and toiletries for them at her house. After telling him to enjoy his night and to give Gizelle a hug, she hung up and told him not to come get the kids before twelve noon the next day and that she would be fine if he decided to stay away for an extra day or two. His mind went to what he and Gizelle could do with several days alone and he just may do that.

He then called the concierge for the condo building and gave instructions for everything he wanted set up at his place including clean linen, candles, flowers, fresh fruit, wine and most of all, he wanted red rose petals on the floor in every room and for them to leave enough that he could place some in the tub. He was going all out and as he gave his last instruction and had them read back to him over the phone, he walked back toward the entrance and went in search of his lady.

**

"Why aren't you dressed yet? I need you to tell me what's happening at that dance. You said Gizelle was going with that guy from the ranch. I followed him for a while until I got the feeling that he knew I was behind him or that someone was behind him. He started making weird turns earlier today and finally I gave up just in case he spotted me. Since I can't go anywhere near that place, you said you would scope things out for me."

Heather rushed around trying to finish getting dressed while listening as Clyde berated her yet again.

"I told you I was sorry that I had to work late. That was unavoidable and the dance is going on for a few more hours. It started at seven I think and it's only eight-thirty. I'll get there in plenty of time."

"She knows you're coming right?" Clyde asked, pacing back and forth across her brown carpeted bedroom, leaving heavy footprints as he moved about.

"Can you take your boots off? You're wearing a tread in my carpet," she said.

"Shut up about your damn carpet. Who cares about your carpet? If you were gone, we wouldn't even be having this conversation. Hurry up!" he yelled over her shoulder as she almost tripped trying to put on her shoes while standing.

"Okay, I'm going. Where are you going to be?"

"I'm going to be here. I can't trust being out. I'm sure the cops will be out in full force tonight because of it being Valentine's Day. I'll be fine here. You go and get information of what's happening between Gizelle and this guy Perry you showed me. I can't believe she's already sleeping with some other guy. He will regret the day he touched my wife. He'll regret that!"

"Ex-wife. I keep having to tell you that. You are obsessed with her. Why are you messing with me? How do you think it makes me feel to hear how you only talk about her? All day and night I have to hear Gizelle this and Gizelle that. You're with me now," Heather said and turned to see Clyde's fiery red eyes staring back at her. She could see his fist balling up as if he was preparing to hit her. She knew what that felt like and she didn't need any bruises going to the party.

"Shut up and leave. You better not be too late. Find out if she's having sex with him and how close they are. You need to also tell me if my kids are on that ranch and where they are. I want my kids from that witch!" he yelled and then pounded his fists on the top of her redwood dresser.

"Don't break anything. I'll see what I can find out. You're getting crazy about this."

"Shut up! Just shut up and go."

When Clyde stormed off into the bathroom and slammed the door shut, he heard Heather grab her keys and head for the door. He was glad she was gone. Next, he was sure she was going to bring up the fact that it was Valentine's Day and he hadn't given her anything or made any plans other than for her to go and spy on Gizelle for him. That would have caused a brand new argument and he needed her. He can't get to Gizelle without her and once he did, if Heather continued to run her mouth, he'd get rid of her the way that he was planning to get rid of Gizelle. There were many places to hide and he would have to after what he has planned for her.

Clyde smiled to himself in the bathroom mirror.

"Your time is almost up, Gizelle."

18

If this was how women are treated by men who care about them, Gizelle never wanted to forget what was in front of her. She had entered the condo and stopped in her tracks before Perry had a chance to close the door behind them. What she saw took her breath away. When he said he was preparing a special night for them and she wouldn't have to worry about anything other than enjoying being catered to, she didn't know what that would look like; now she knew and it was more than she could have ever imagined.

"You did this? You made a phone call and did all of this without even leaving the ranch?"

Before her was a room filled with flowers and not just a few here and there. There were vases full of roses in white, red, pink and orange and they filled every table and ledge that she could see. There had to be dozens and dozens of them. She saw balloons floating up to the ceiling and some fluttered around on the floor. To make sure she wasn't dreaming, she kicked a few and laughed when they flew about.

When she turned around and faced Perry, he had a smile that said he was proud of what he was able to accomplish with little notice.

"I did and it was my pleasure. I told you that tonight was all about you."

"I know, but it's Valentine's Day and it's supposed to be about you too. I have a gift for you. It's not a bunch of things like you got for me, but I hope you like it," she said handing him the bag she'd grabbed when they stopped first at his parents' house so that she could say goodnight to Carrie and Brody and then by her house where she packed a bag for their night together. She even added a few extras after he told her that he was thinking of staying away for a few days, not just one night. Excitement streaked through her at what that could mean and she couldn't wait.

After leaving the ranch, they headed straight for the condo and now here she was standing and looking around at how the place was sweetly done in decorations for lovers.

As Perry closed and locked the door along with activating the alarm system, he touched a switch on the wall and the two fireplaces that she could see came to life adding another level of coziness to the room. Going further into the wide-open space, she saw wine on ice, platters of fresh fruit, cheese and crackers and in the next instance, sounds of jazz music poured from speakers throughout the condo. The room was decorated in shades of blue throughout,

Perry's favorite color. She knew that was his favorite color since the house she was currently living in that was his also had hues of blue throughout. There was navy blue leather furniture in a large family room with a television that covered the entire wall. It had to be at least a one-hundred-inch screen.

"Go ahead and take a look around. I'm going to check out the other arrangements to be sure everything was done per my specific instructions. Get comfortable and remove as much or as little as you like, but at least get out of that coat. Here, let me help you."

Gizelle felt Perry's arms come around her from behind and she shivered the minute she felt his lips on the back of her neck. She was glad she decided to wear her hair up. She'll have to thank Parker again. Leaning back into him, she allowed her eyes to close for a moment and focus only on the feel of his strong arms holding her close.

"This place is amazing," she said when he finally removed her coat and hung it up in a hall closet.

"Check the rest of it out and I'll take your bag to the bedroom."

"Open your gift first. I hope you like it."

When Perry reached into the gift bag, Gizelle held her breath, praying that he liked what she'd bought for him.

"Gucci Guilty cologne for me. It's my favorite and I'm just about out of mine. How did you know? I love it, baby, thank you."

"I inhale every time I'm close to you and when I was out shopping, I could smell it in the store and asked the sales clerk what I was smelling. I had to get it for you. I didn't know what else to get and then you started sending me so many gifts that I wasn't sure I had done enough."

"You are enough of a gift for me every day. I love my gifts, the cologne and you."

When Perry kissed her, she got all the thanks she needed.

"Whew, yes! Now I can go check out the rest of this place."

"So that you don't get lost, there are three bedrooms, this large room here is the master suite with its own bathroom. The other two rooms have their own and there is another full bathroom in the hall off the media room. The kitchen and dining area are to your left and if you want to look out over the city and mountains, there is a switch on the wall that will open the curtains and raise the blinds on all three walls. We're on the top floor so there is a lot of privacy. On a warmer day, we can check out the balcony. There is a hot tub out there, but it's too cold and besides, I have other ways I plan to keep us warm."

She nodded without words. The image of him keeping her warm is all she wanted to think of.

When Perry walked out of sight, she did walk

around and loved everything about the place. Each bedroom was decorated in a different color, one in red and black and the other in shades of brown and beige. In the room decorated in red and black, there were pictures of Brielle with a lot of her friends and now that she focused better, she assumed this was where she stayed when she was in the city. The room was all girl.

Going back out into the main area, she headed toward the master bedroom in search of Perry. Just as she reached the room, he was coming out of it and moved to the side to give her a peek inside.

"Wow! You did all this? Flowers everywhere, rose petals throughout and even more wine chilling in here. Is there anything you didn't think of that would impress a woman? I mean, is there anything else? You thought of everything," she said.

"Well, I do have dinner in warmers in the kitchen if we get hungry and the makings for omelets in the morning which I can make, competing with any chef. I told you I was going to make Valentine's Day special."

Gizelle smiled. He had gone far beyond just special.

"I love it, Perry. Thank you. I can't thank you enough for how incredible this day has been and it continues."

"It does and it will, not just today, but beyond today."

When he walked up to her and pulled her close,

she went willingly into his arms and allowed her gaze to sweep over him.

"I want that too."

"I want to be clear with you about something. I know I said this already, but now that we're here in this space and it's just me and you with this night turning out however we both want it to, no pressure, you need to know that once we cross a threshold tonight, there is no going back. For me, there is no one nor do I want there to be anyone but you. I'm not a saint or an angel when it comes to women but know that what I feel for you isn't temporary or casual. I'm looking for more and I want more with you. If we spend this night together, then I will know that we're on the same page and you want more with me too."

Gizelle's heart was beating so fast and had swelled so big with love for him. Nothing had ever felt righter than every moment she's spent with him.

"I'm all in and no more talk of not having this night together. We both have a past and that's just what it is; the past. I'm with you for the long haul."

"Baby, as long as we are together, I will go anywhere with you. Now, how about a glass of wine."

"I'd love that. First, I want to freshen up and change into more comfortable clothing. I love this dress and heels, but I'm already over it."

"Go right on into the bedroom while I get some wine and then we can eat when you come back out. How's that?"

"Perfect."

Leaning up and kissing Perry on the lips, she walked around him and into the bedroom where her packed bag was waiting for her.

Unzipping the black and red overnight bag, she began taking out several different options to change into. There were two pair of black leggings, which she loved to lounge around when at home. She had also packed a few t-shirts. Setting them to the side, she thought about what else she had in the bag and wondered if she would be too forward with what she wanted to change into. Perry was preparing them for dinner, but she wanted to eat later and get to the later part of their evening, right now. She was always led, never the leader; she was never the aggressor. She never felt comfortable sharing her wants and desires, but with Perry, she felt like a new woman. She felt like she could be the sexy, vibrant, desirous woman Perry saw with his eyes and the way she wanted to be seen. She knew that he'd gone through a lot to make this night special for her, but she wanted to make it just as special for him.

Changing her mind, she pulled out the black seductive lace gown with a deep plunging neckline and a scalloped trim that would cup and brace her large breasts with a look that she knew would be an open invitation for him to get a closer look and feel. The bodice of the gown was floor length and made her legs look long and sexy. What she loved about the gown was the way her back would be left bare and the matching thong panties covered her womanhood with more lace with ties made of a thin, satin material that tied at her hips. In her bag, she also included a new pair of high-heeled, seductive slip-on shoes in black, something she'd never owned before. Clearly, she'd already had plans for a night like this with Perry when she'd gone out shopping with Brielle when she picked up several sexy numbers like this one. She'd never owned lingerie this sexy before, but just looking into Perry's eyes and the way he looked at her had her thinking of all kinds of sexy things she could get that would entice him.

Looking around the bedroom, she saw flameless candles all over the room, soft music was playing and there were roses and rose petals everywhere. Perry had done his part and now, she wanted to do hers by showing him that she wanted him and only him. She felt connected to him in a way she'd never felt with a man before. She felt empowered to have the kind of life and love that she'd often dreamed about but never had before now. She was in love and ready to show Perry every ounce of love she had for him.

Grabbing a few toiletries and the nightie and panties, she threw the bag on the floor near the door and headed into the bathroom. Excitement ran through her as she quickly changed and looked at herself in the mirror. She didn't even recognize herself. Every part of her body was exposed and she loved all of it. All she needed to do was add a little more light lip gloss to her lips and she was set. Her hair was still perfect and her makeup was light and soft like she wanted it to be. She looked down her body and smiled at how she was able to see that she was more than she had ever been told she was.

Feeling bold and ready, she left the bathroom and headed toward her destiny. She was ready to take control of getting the love she deserved.

**

"What do you mean she wasn't there? I thought you said she told you she was going and with that Perry guy! You are useless. That means tonight was a waste."

"I tried Clyde. I went, looked for her and even texted her. She wasn't there. I know she was going because she went shopping for a dress for the party in order to get something extra special for him. I guess they decided to make other plans on their own."

"I'm going to kill her! I swear, if I get my hands on her, I'm going to get rid of her for good and I don't have to worry about who she's with anymore. Then I can get my kids and make a life in Mexico or someplace like that."

"You're taking me with you, right?" Heather asked.

Clyde looked her way and didn't think the time was right to tell her that once he got rid of Gizelle for her blatant disrespect, he had no plans of dealing with her anymore either. He would deal with Gizelle and then hightail it out of town because his plan for her would send the cops from all over looking for him. He was going to be out of Bozeman and in Mexico before anyone got wind of him ever being in town. He only needed a few more days and Heather was going to help him.

"Of course, I am. First, you need to get her off the ranch. Tell her you have an emergency and you need her and convince her that she needs to meet you and that it's private so she has to come alone. Tell her it's life or death. Tell her something, but get her off that ranch and you have a week to do it. One week, Heather, or I'm leaving Bozeman and heading to Mexico without you."

"I'll do it. I'll come up with something to tell her. I'll do it before the week is out, I promise."

"Good, now get in the bedroom because I need to be taken care of. It's Valentine's Day and I want to know how much you appreciate me and the life I'm going to make for us in Mexico. Anything for me, right?" he asked.

Clyde watched as she moved from the couch and walked ahead of him into the bedroom. He may not be able to have Gizelle like he wanted her, but once he was in the bedroom with Heather in the dark, he was going to be picturing Gizelle. Every woman will always be Gizelle.

19

On wobbly legs, Gizelle walked out of the bedroom, more nervous than she'd ever been in her life, but loving the newness of the moment. She walked slowly toward the kitchen area where she knew Perry was. She found him with his back to her, standing at the island scooping food out from pans onto plates for them.

"I thought I would have to eat all of this food by myself. I was concerned that you'd gotten in the bedroom, saw that inviting bed and fell asleep on me," he said, still not turning toward her.

She didn't reply. She wanted her reply to be what he saw when he turned around and looked at her. She straightened the flowing part of the gown and stood in her sexiest pose with her hands on her hips and her head held high.

"I'm far from sleepy," she said seductively.

"Well, are you thirsty?" he asked her.

"Are you?" she countered and waited.

And then it happened. Perry turned toward her with a glass of wine in each hand and then everything around them ceased moving. No sound was heard and the world consisted of only the two of them. Her pulse quickened and her heart raced, but she stood her ground and waited for what seemed an eternity for Perry to say something. What she got was him standing before her like a mannequin. His eyes bulged, his mouth hung open, yet, he still hadn't moved a muscle. He still held the glasses in his hands but remained where he was. She stood still as his eyes landed on her and he took in every voluptuous curve. He was seeing that sleep, in fact, was the furthest thing from her mind.

"Um," was the only thing he could say. His brain was fried from desire.

Perry had to have died and gone to heaven or someplace, the planets were aligning in his favor because in front of him was the most delectable sight. Gizelle was before him looking like a goddess. His mouth suddenly went dry and any moment, the air in his lungs would dry up. He wanted to reach for her but couldn't move. Dinner and the wine were the last thing on his mind.

Gizelle smiled. Everything in her told her that he loved what he was seeing. His reaction was exactly what she wanted it to be; it was priceless.

"See, not sleepy at all. Are sleepy?" she asked softly.

"Sleep? What's that?" Perry replied.

She stood still and let him get his fill.

"It's something I hope I won't being doing until much, much, much later," she replied.

Perry's eyes pierced through her as he remained stoic, still not moving. She waited patiently as his eyes went from her eyes and traveled slowly down her body. When they reached her feet and traveled back up, she moved a little, doing a little spin to give him a view of the back, knowing that her bare back and bare behind would be on display. One thing she did know was her body was on point and shaped like the original Coke bottle, but with a lot more to see on top. Her big breasts always garnered attention from me, but tonight, the only man she wanted to gaze at them now and forever was Perry.

"Damn! Is that what you were doing in there all that tine? That's what you had in mind when you said you wanted to put on something comfortable? Damn!"

Gizelle laughed out loud.

"You do realize you said damn twice, right?"

"Baby, you look incredible – amazing and right now, I think I'm thirsty, but not for any wine and most definitely not sleep."

When Perry turned and placed the glasses back on the counter and turned to her, she exhaled deeply and feeling every bit of her early nervousness dissipate. All she felt now was desired.

"You like?"

"Is like even a word? Baby, I love it."

Like slow motion, she watched him walk over to her and leaned down and captured her lips so softly and methodically slow that she quickly felt lightheaded. She had to reach up to hold on to his shoulders to keep from falling in the floor. He was making love to her mouth in a way that had her body quivering and longing for more. She felt his hands on her hips as he pulled her closer and deepened the kiss. She tried her best to get more, to get closer and moaned out her want for more of him. As if he could read her mind, she felt herself being lifted into his strong arms. They continued to kiss as he walked with her in his arms into the bedroom.

She'd wanted to be with Perry like this for a long time and now that nothing was holding her back, she was leading into a life and love with him that would erase any idea that she wasn't worthy of this kind of love. Perry was showing her that she was worthy, plus some.

She felt herself being lowered to the soft bed and could feel the soft red rose petals against her back and the powerfulness of his body as he lightly covered her body with his. She wiggled around in a heightened state of arousal at the feel of that strong length between his legs that grazed against her body letting her get a feel of what was in store for her.

"Thank you for tonight and every night before and after this one," she whispered against his lips.

"We're just beginning, baby – just beginning."

Gizelle welcomed the words and the attention Perry lavished on her.

"You don't mind us eating later on?" she asked breathlessly as she felt his lips kiss their way down her neck and around to the center of her chest where he stopped, leaned back and removed his shirt and she smiled when she saw his muscled, sculpted chest – the sign of a man who stayed in perfect shape. She ran her hands over his chest and traced each muscle within her reach with the palm of her hands.

"That food will be there, but right now, I have other plans for us. How could I not when I set my eyes on you standing there like the perfect gift, not just for Valentine's Day, but for every day."

"You feel incredible. So strong and powerful and the way you look at me like you did when you saw me standing there makes me feel empowered and secure. I don't know that I've ever really felt that way," she admitted.

"You will from this day forward. You are everything a man could ask for and if you have ever gotten a different vibe from anyone, then they are the problem, not you. I look at you and my heart practically stops because of the gut punch to my very being knowing that I'm a lucky guy."

"I'm lucky too," she said.

When she thought more words were coming, none did as Perry, keeping his eyes on hers, leaned down and kissed the area between her breasts. The minute she felt his lips on her again, she closed her eyes and focused on feeling. She let her hands run up and down his strong arms and around to his back. She practically leaped off the bed when she felt his lips kiss her nipples through the thin layer of the gown. When he used the pad of his tongue to add pressure, a loud moan escaped her lips and she reached to cover her mouth.

"Don't do that. However you feel and any sound you want to make, you do that. No suppressing anything around me," Perry said and to prove his point, he repeated the action and when she felt the desire to emit a cry of pleasure, she did so and let it out. The feeling was exhilarating.

She delighted in the feel of him sliding the sleaves of the gown down her arms and the minute her full breasts were exposed, she watched Perry's perusal and his pleasure. She loved that he wasted no time in feasting on them, first one and then the other – going between them as if he couldn't decide which side he loved more.

As he slid further down her body, he pulled the gown down with him. When he slid it from her body, leaving her only in the panties and shoes, she spread her arms open wide and gripped the bed cover. She didn't know what was coming next, but she wanted it as much as she wanted her next breath.

Perry slid the shoes from her feet and used his

teeth to untie the strings of the thong at her hips. When the panel fell away, he removed it from her body and then stood and looked at her. She started to feel exposed, but then relaxed when he smiled.

"My goodness, you are so beautiful. I had no idea you were hiding all this under those leggings, jeans and t-shirts you like to wear."

"I know. I always felt comfortable that way and self-conscious about my breasts because of their size."

"Never again because I feel incredibly lucky to get a look at you and your beautiful breasts. You are perfect, baby," he said.

Gizelle didn't know how to reply. She kept her eyes on Perry as he removed the remainder of his clothes and stood before her completely naked. His manhood pointed straight at her. To her delight, it was long, thick and powerful. His size alone had her squirming around. Her womanhood jumped and ached in a nice way. As he reached for a condom, she kept her eyes on that part of him that she hoped would fit comfortably. She didn't know men were actually that large.

"That is really something," she said and then wished she hadn't said it out loud when Perry followed her line of sight where it landed on his penis.

"I promise you it will fit and I won't let you out of this bed until you are exhausted from enjoying it."

She smiled and put all reservations aside. She was already feeling a need so strong and one unlike anything before and that feeling coated her insides. When Perry's eyes landed on her womanhood, she felt brazen and opened her legs wider for him to get an even closer look knowing that sexy strip of hair she wanted left after her trip to the salon would dazzle him; and it did.

"You're already glistening for me. Is there anything about intimacy that you don't like?" he asked, rejoining her on the bed.

Gizelle had to think about it and didn't know how to respond. She'd never been asked before.

"I...I...I don't think so," she stuttered out.

"What do you like?" he asked

She was now embarrassed and looked away.

"I'm so stupid, acting like a silly girl," she said.

"Talk to me. We can do this anytime, but I need to know that I am pleasing you the way you like. Trust me, I know about pleasuring a woman and I'm not concerned that I don't know what to do. I love knowing what turns a woman on the most. What makes you orgasm the hardest?"

Now she was dumfounded. Should she really tell him the truth?

"Talk to me, Gizelle. You have a perplexed look on our face. What's wrong?"

"I've only ever orgasmed by touching myself with my own fingers or my B.O.B."

"You've never climaxed with a man? Only with touching yourself and with a battery-operated boyfriend? Yes, I know the term," he said.

When he smiled, Gizelle did too. He was keeping the conversation light and comfortable.

"Yes. I know I'm not as experienced as other women you've been with. Mutual satisfaction has never been my experience, but I want to."

"And you will, trust that. Always tell me what you like and don't like. Making love is not a one-way experience just for me. I already know I'll get my pleasure because that's how much I want you. We won't visit where you've been. I'm only concerned about where you're going with me and you will never, ever leave a bed with me and be unsatisfied. What you want and need matters."

Gizelle shook her head, afraid to speak because if she did, she may cry. She didn't know men could be this caring and concerned about her pleasure; she's never had that before. She watched him open the condom wrapper and slide the contents of the gold packet over himself.

When he turned to her, covering her body with his she wanted to cry at the intense look of desire she saw in his eyes. How could she have survived never seeing that look before? How could she have not known that a man looking at a woman like that existed?

"Perry?"

"Yes, baby."

She hoped her words didn't come out and caused the night to be ruined.

"I love you," she said and waited. Would he be happy? Would he get up and say he didn't feel the same way?

"You do? That's wonderful because I love you too. I've wanted to tell you. I told Brielle and she told me I was crazy for not telling you, but I thought you weren't ready for love."

"I didn't know I was until I met you."

"I'm yours and you're mine."

"You're mine?" she asked.

"Oh, yeah, I am," Perry said and before she could get any more words out, he kissed her. He loved her mouth and she returned the fervor by giving as good as he was laying on her and it was good; it was amazing; it was intoxicating and she loved it.

"I want you; I want everything; I love you so much," she whispered against his lips. She knew she was repeating herself, but she needed him to know. She wanted and needed to be open and ready to live in their love.

"It's me and you from this day forward. Let's love," he said.

This time, as his kisses traveled down her body, she closed her eyes as her body moved of its own volition. His lips touched her skin and she felt like she could burst into flames any moment. She felt him all over, though his lips traveled across her neck from one side to the other. She lifted her head to give him better access. He wanted to be everywhere and that's where she wanted him. When his lips rolled across her breast, she thought she would die from the pleasure. His hand caressed one while his lips bathed the other passionately.

As his lips traveled further down her body, she moaned and lived in the feelings his touches brought out of her. The air sizzled and her body was inflamed with need. All she could think was that she wanted more and more and without her saying so, that's exactly what Perry gave her. She needed to see him. She needed to see the man who expressed his love for her. She wanted to see him as they made love.

Opening her eyes, she caught sight of Perry just as he disappeared between her now wide-open legs. She caught a glimpse of his smile as his head dipped toward her womanhood. A feeling so intense, unlike anything she'd ever felt before came over her as she felt his mouth close over her. There was nothing she could do to hold back the scream of pleasure that escaped her lips while her hips shot up from the bed. She wanted the feeling to last forever.

She watched his eyes as they locked on hers. She focused on his tongue when he lifted his head long enough for her to see it just before he went back to pleasuring her with his mouth. She felt a pressure building up that felt new and invigorating and in the next second, the world around her head exploded and she saw white sparkling lights everywhere. She screamed not caring that anyone else could hear her.

She couldn't hold her response to his love back. She let go and fell into the soft clouds of love that surrounded them. Her body thrashed about, seeking more, wanting more and getting more.

Gizelle felt movement as her body still rocked from the pleasure bestowed upon her. She hated that her eyes had closed, knowing she wanted to see as well as experience everything. When she opened them, Perry was back near her face, lowering his head to kiss her and she grabbed and held onto him, never wanting him to be more than a few inches away from her ever again. They kissed, their mouths loved while at the same time, she felt Perry spread her legs open and fit himself between them. When she felt him entering her body, she held her breath, feeling full and one with him. He moaned into her mouth and she accepted it and him. She said she wanted all of him and she was getting that.

"Baby," he whispered.

"You feel so good," she uttered.

"Are you okay?" he asked.

Gizelle knew he was speaking of the restraint he was using in entering her body, knowing that she felt tight and he was engorged beyond anything she'd ever felt.

"Yes."

"More?" he asked.

"Yes!"

That time she screamed her response and didn't

care how desperate she may have sounded. She'd never felt anything so wonderful in her life.

As Perry moved his hips slowly back and forth, she felt him go as far as he could and then he increased the pace. His head dropped down to the space between her head and her shoulder and the sound of their rapid breaths was a turn-on. The sound vibrated throughout the room as the bed moved around them, adding to the moment.

Her body was going through an unfamiliar feeling when it came to intimacy with a man. Her only orgasms had only been self-produced and not only did Perry love her to her first one, she was on her way to a second explosion. Her womanhood tingled and the sound of them loving each other drove her to a height she had never been to before. She could feel her body climbing higher and higher and then it happened again. She let go as her hips moved wildly with his. Her release touched every part of her body. Her toes tingled and curled up, her legs shook uncontrollably and her arms held Perry tighter.

Against her neck she heard Perry's moans of pleasure as he increased the pace of their lovemaking. When he groaned out his pleasure, she reached up and lifted his head, locking their eyes and like he once said to her, she wanted him to see her at this most pivotal moment for them. Love surged through her as he surged lovingly into her body and together, they rode the wave of pleasure that sealed their love like

Perry said, forever.

As their bodies calmed and their lovemaking movements slowed, Gizelle held tightly to Perry, caressing his back as he breathed through the work he'd just put in to bring them pleasure like none she'd ever felt. This is what she'd been missing. The connection during lovemaking with a man who stoked her embers not just intimately through connecting their bodies, but also by melding their hearts together. If this is what being as one meant, yeah, she's been missing out for a very long time.

Perry leaned up and looked down at her and she leaned up and kissed him. This man above her was hers and she felt a sudden need to claim a kiss between them.

"Are you okay?" he asked.

"Mmm, I am more than okay."

"Feeling good?" he added.

"I'm feeling great; I'm feeling wonderful; I'm feeling amazing!" she shouted.

She and Perry laughed together. When he tried to move away, she held him close with her arms and locked her legs around his waist.

"Okay, you're holding me hostage now?" he joked.

"You feel so good right where you are that I don't want to lose the feeling."

"Baby, you're not losing anything and we have all night to revisit this feeling again and again."

When Perry rolled to the side, she turned and

faced him as he pulled her closer into his embrace.

"All night?" she asked.

"All damn night, sweetheart. You every wish is my command and I take instruction very well especially when it comes to making my lady feel the way she feels right now. As long as I can look into your eyes and see satisfaction like now, I do mean all night. We still need to eat, but I don't think I can move."

"Food! I completely forgot that there was food. I don't think I have the energy to move either."

"Are you happy?" he asked.

"I am. I can't remember a time that I was this happy. I will say that I'm happy to be on this end of what I've heard about you. You know women talk, right?" she quipped.

"Oh, I know, but from this moment on, you'll be the only person who will be able to talk."

"Yeah, well, I'm not giving any woman insight into what we share. You're all mind. You said that and you can't take it back."

Perry kissed her sweetly on the lips and she sighed deeply with a happiness that every woman should have.

"I never plan to. What I do plan to do is feed us and then we'll get back to this bed where we'll feed each other in another way, but first, more kissing and cuddling until my legs decide they want to work again."

"You know, you've unleashed a now sex-crazed

woman and I don't know if I'll be able to settle for all night only."

"Well, my mom has the kids for a couple of days if we want to stay locked in this bed together for more than just a night."

"Don't you have business to tend to?" she asked.

"Baby, all the business I need to tend to is right here with me in this bed. We eat tonight, make love some more and then in the morning, I'll cook for us and we'll love some more. I say we love all over this place and take advantage of this time alone. You up for that?"

Gizelle looked down at the area between them and noticed something that was pretty much sealing the deal for her.

"Looks like you're up for it and I love it."

When Perry rolled over on top of her, looks like their dinner was about to be put on hold for a little longer.

20

Perry slipped out of bed as quiet as he could in hopes that he wouldn't wake Gizelle. They'd been up late making love well after putting Carrie and Brody to bed. For the past two weeks, he'd spent several nights with them and always woke before the kids did. Though they weren't shielding them from the relationship, he still wanted to protect their innocent eyes from seeing him in bed with Gizelle in the morning. It was still dark outside, hours before she would have to get up and get the kids ready for school and get to work herself. The morning must be cold because there was a chill in the bedroom. Slipping out of his flannel pajama bottoms and into his jeans, he headed downstairs to turn up the heat. Coming back upstairs, he checked in on the kids and made sure they were covered up. Thankfully, their rooms were warm and toasty. He went back to finish getting dressed and was surprised to find Gizelle wide awake, in bed looking over at him.

"Good morning," he said.

"Yes, it is. After a night like last night, I was bound to have a good morning. You're leaving? It's barely five in the morning. You can't possibly have a meeting this early," she said.

"I don't," he replied, buttoning up the shirt he'd worn the night before. "I've been leaving before the kids get up and I was hoping to not wake you. I am meeting Nick and Shelton around six-thirty before a meeting Shelton and I have with a banking association later this morning."

"Busy day ahead of you?"

Perry paused her with his hand when he saw her making a move to get out of bed.

"Don't you dare get up. When I leave, you need to catch as much shut eye as you can before you have to get ready for work."

"I don't like that we have to sneak around," she said.

"Baby, we are not sneaking around. There isn't anyone on this ranch who doesn't know that we're in a relationship. It's been two weeks since we sealed our relationship on Valentine's night and I have never been happier in my life."

"I can't believe we stayed in your condo for the rest of that weekend."

"Yeah, you mean the weekend when you turned into a she-devil and gave me the workout of my life?"

"It's all your fault. You released something in me that I didn't know had been asleep for my entire adult life. If I didn't miss the kids so much, we would have stayed longer – oh, and of course there was that work thing that we both had to get back to, especially since your dad decided to whisk your mom away for a few days to an undisclosed place. I used to think that couples married as long as your parents didn't still take the time to keep the fire rekindled like those two do. Did you see your dad when he grabbed her behind before they got into the limo that picked them up at the house? And that hot kiss?"

"Ugh, stop it. I struggle with getting that image out of my head. I don't want to think of my parents that way."

"What way? In the way that they still get busy after all these years and after five children? Where do you think you get it from!"

Perry rushed around to the other side of the bed and reached for her just as she moved out of his reach, giggling like a school girl.

"You like it," he exclaimed.

"Oh, no, lover – I love it! I want to love you openly like that."

Perry heard a sullen tone to her words.

"Remember, we talked about treading light around the kids when it comes to me being in bed with you. We need to sit down and talk to them. Though they won't understand most of what we are saying, let's talk to them about how they may see me in bed with you when they wake up in the morning just so that they are not shocked. They are used to seeing you in bed by yourself or even with them, but not with me. There will come a time when we'll be a family and it will be the norm," he said.

"We will?"

"Baby, I love you and there is no one else for me, but you. We're in a good place and on a great path. Do you agree? Do you feel that way?"

"I love you, too and yes, I'm in this with you until the wheels fall off. Isn't that a saying that stands for forever?"

Perry, unable to resist the beautiful woman with the morning glow who looked like his angel in waiting, leaned down on the bed and covered her body with his, taking in her scent to carry it with him throughout the day.

"Forever is what I'm going for. Right now, I'm thinking about getting undressed and rejoining you in this bed. If I remember correctly, you only have on my pajama top and absolutely nothing else."

When she lifted the cover to show him exactly what was waiting for him, he was ready to strip his clothes away and join her nakedness. They were so hot and spicy together that he never seemed to be able to get enough of loving her completely.

"I wish you would. I was hoping for a little something, something to get me through the day."

"Baby, you have done things to me that no woman ever has. I swear I remember you telling me that you didn't think you could satisfy me because of your lack of experience, but I beg to differ. For now, what we had last night and throughout the night will have to last. Get some sleep and I'll call you later. I thought you and the kids and I could get off of this ranch for dinner. I'm thinking nice steak dinners for us and burgers and fries with ice cream sundaes for them. What do you say to that?"

"You spoil us. You have time after work today? You won't be too tired? I know you said you have meetings all day, with two of them being in town. I don't have a very busy day at work and plan to get off on-time."

"I don't care how tired I may be, I want time with the three of you and then we can come back here and watch movies in front of the fireplace. Besides, I want to talk to you tonight about what our forever will look like. Up for that?"

"I'm more than up for that. The kids and I will be ready when you are and if you're late, it'll be fine. I need to call Heather when I get off. I try not to call her during the day because when we get on the phone, an hour later, I find that I've lost track of time. I can call her while we're waiting on you. She'll help me pass the time."

"How has she been? I know the two of you haven't had a chance to really hang out much. You have been one busy woman."

"She's fine and I love, love, love my job and I get to look in on the kids throughout the day. I love it here. I love this ranch," she said.

"I hope we can make a life here or someplace close by."

"My life and the life of the kids will be wherever you are. On this ranch, off the ranch, doesn't matter to me. I want to be close by because I love your family. I've never had a family like yours and it feels good having them. Were you thinking of off-ranch?"

"No. We'll talk in detail about it tonight, but I'm thinking about adding on to this house so that Carrie and Brody can have bigger rooms and a play room. Once we're married one day and decide to have more kids, if you want that, we'll need more space."

"You're serious?"

"Baby, I am dead serious. I'm not looking to find anyone else. You are it for me. What would we need to wait for? I've waited a lifetime for someone like you. I know this isn't any kind of proposal, which I will do the right way. I want to plan our life out together with us on the same page."

"Perry, we are on the same page. Don't think you have to question that. I love you so much and I want to be with you in our forever space. We'll talk about it later and yes, since you brought it up."

"Yes, what?"

"Yes, I want more babies. I won't say how many

more because I don't want to scare you, but I want more. We will have a lot to talk about tonight. I'm excited."

"Sounds like a plan. Tell your friend hello."

"I'm thinking of inviting her to the ranch to have lunch or I may go with her to one of our favorite spots to eat. I think she's feeling like I don't want to be bothered with her since I've been living and working here on the ranch."

"Enjoy time with your friend. If you go off the ranch, let Buck know and he'll send someone with you. He's at the other end of the ranch overseeing some digging, but he can get on the radio and have someone accompany you."

"You think there is still an issue? It's been weeks, well over a month or so and there has been no sign of him. By now, he probably is back to living his life someplace else not caring about me anymore. I don't want to take anyone away from their work here on the ranch."

"Gizelle, just do it for me, okay. Maybe over the weekend, I can take you to meet her someplace and I'll stay out of sight and ready to bring you back when you're ready. You said she's a long-time friend, right? Someone from back in Chicago?"

"Yeah, she has been through a lot of bad times with me. She's been that shoulder and good friend that I need. She's been calling all week and I've been so busy that I haven't gotten back to her. I'll call her later and plan something for the weekend. Don't worry about it. Go have your breakfast with your brothers and get your meetings done. The faster you do all that, the faster you'll get back to me. I love you."

"I can't wait to have a life with you – an extension of what we've already been living."

"I do want to talk to the kids. I know they are three and four, but I want them to know how much I love you and you already know how they feel about you."

"I want us to be a family. I enjoy the mornings when I get to wake up with you in my arms. I feel complete when I'm here with the three of you."

"Then do that every night, if you want to. You're here all the time anyway and this is your house. I don't like the idea of you being in that cottage alone at night and you could be here with us. What do you say?"

"I say that I think it's a great idea. I see we have even more to talk about tonight and we can't get to that if I don't get out of here to start my day. Get a little more sleep and call me later."

He watched Gizelle get up and walk toward the bedroom door.

"Get in that bed, woman. I can see myself out and lock up behind myself. I love you."

"I love you more," she said.

After one final, luscious kiss on the lips, Perry rushed out of the house, looking forward to getting through the day in order to get back to her waiting arms.

**

Gizelle made her last call for the day to order the remaining school supplies and books needed for the rest of the school year. She'd offered her resignation after the incident with Clyde because she was afraid to go back to places where she may encounter him again. Being on the ranch gave her a sense of security. Not only did she love her job, but she loved the ranch. Where she thought she would only be living on the ranch temporarily, it had been almost two months since she'd arrived and now that she and Perry were in a relationship and in love, she was happy enough to never want to leave and live anyplace that did not include him.

For the past week or so, she'd been venturing off the ranch more and more, but still not alone. She and Perry went out often and most times with the kids with them. They went the movies, dinner and even took the kids bowling, something they'd never done, but loved. She didn't even know that bowling alleys had balls small enough for children Carrie and Brody's age. They would venture off for pizza and visits to bookstores. Thankfully, there had been no signs or discussions about Clyde. She had come to believe that he was gone from Bozeman for good after all this time had gone by. There was no way he'd still be around. What would he do to make money and

CHERYL BARTON

survive? Where would he be living that someone wouldn't spot him and turn him in. She was still cautious and kept an eye on her surroundings. Tonight, she was going to plan a night out with Perry and the kids and focus on that.

She loved warm cozy nights by the fireplace with Perry and the kids and then hot steamy nights with Perry after the kids were asleep.

Needing to make copies of some documents on her desk, she stood just as her cell phone rang. She saw Heather's name and took the call. They hadn't spoken a lot lately and she rarely saw her, though Perry suggested she invite her to the ranch for a visit sometime. Gizelle was mad at herself that she never did so. Heather had been there when she had no one else in Bozeman to call a friend.

"Heather! It's so good to hear from you."

"Girl, where you been? It's been ages since we've seen each other. I miss my friend."

"I miss you too and we will again, real soon. How are you?"

"I'm in a bind and I need your help. I'm less than a mile from the ranch where you're living and my car broke down. I was actually coming to the ranch to see if they would ask you if I could visit and the car stopped working just short of the entrance. Can you come out and give me a ride? I mean, even if coming on the ranch isn't a good time, maybe you can give me a lift back to the office. It won't take long at all. Please help me. It's freezing out here. The snow on the ground from the last storm is keeping it freezing cold out here."

Gizelle thought about what to do. She never really left the ranch much alone, though she had gone out a time a two and came right back. Heather did say she was right by the ranch and it was cold out. She was right that it would only take a few minutes. She contemplated and decided.

"Sure. You can come here on the ranch and hang for a while."

"Oh, that would be great. I can call a tow truck and when it comes, I can ride back with it to a garage. I can't wait to see you. It's been so long and I know you have a lot to tell me about Perry since you're having sex with him and everything now."

Gizelle looked around shyly as if someone else in the office could hear Heather's end of the conversation.

"I told you that in confidence," she whispered.

"No one's listening. It's just me and you and I promise not to tell anyone. Are you coming now? I'm really getting cold. I don't think I wore the right kind of coat for this weather."

"Yes. We have to make it quick. I really shouldn't leave the ranch and the kids will be out of school soon."

"No worries. You know by now that Clyde is long gone. You have nothing to worry about. I bet he's already moved on to terrorizing another woman he claims to love. I'll be on the side of the road. Come before some crazy person tries to kidnap me. You know how hot, sexy and tempting I am. Maybe you can introduce me to one of the other Sullivan brothers who is single. I hear Dayton will be in town soon. I may be too old for him, but that Shelton is a sexy beast. Is he on the ranch? Can I meet him?"

"How about we get you here safe and warm and we can talk about all that later. I'm on my way."

Gizelle hung up and grabbed her purse and told the others in the office that she was stepping out for a few minutes to help a friend whose car had broken down right outside of the ranch. She promised them she would be right back. As she rushed out, she grabbed her phone and looked for the cord since she didn't have much power left on it. Realizing she may have left it at the house when she left for work, she shook it off knowing that she'd be right back.

Rushing out of the door, she pulled her black, faux fur trimmed coat around her and jumped in her car, immediately turning on the heat. She drove off not waiting for the car to warm up. By the time she picked up Heather and drove back, the car would probably still be cold.

**

Clyde dialed Heather's cell phone again. From his vantage point behind a group of thick trees where he was hidden, he could see her standing in the cold shivering and he wondered what was taking Gizelle so long. Maybe Heather wasn't as convincing as she said she could be. This time he watched her answer.

"Do not ignore my call. Where is she?" he shouted.

"She's on her way, so stop calling me every two seconds. She said she's coming and I believe her. She wouldn't leave me standing here in the cold. Don't forget, she thinks I'm her friend."

"You are her friend, just not a very good one. You've been sleeping with her husband and that doesn't make for a good friend," he said.

"Well, you weren't a good husband cheating on her the way you did and don't forget, you're not married to her anymore. You keep speaking of her as if you're still married to her."

"Well, she better hurry up and get here. I'm going to change the plan up a little bit," he said.

"Change it to what? You said you wanted to talk to her to convince her to let you see your children. What are you talking about now?"

Heather was nervous. She knew how devious Clyde could be and hearing that he was changing the plan from just talking to Gizelle didn't sit right with her. She didn't want to be involved with anything that could hurt Gizelle.

"She'll never let me see them, so I'm going to remove her as a road block and then I'll take my children off that ranch and leave."

"Wait – what? You never said that. You said you wanted to talk to her. What are you going to do to her? She's coming. I see her car. What are you planning to do Clyde? Don't you dare hurt her. You promised you wouldn't hurt her again."

"Hurt? I'm going to make sure she never sees my kids again and I didn't promise anything. Get off the phone and I'll take over when she drives up. Don't you dare get in that car. Do you hear me? Do what we planned!" Clyde screamed loudly.

"I'm not doing this. I change my mind."

"I will kill you if you mess this up and you know I mean it. Stand right where you are and don't move."

Without giving her a chance to say anything else, he disconnected the call and waited.

Clyde's body itched with excitement. He would teach Gizelle a lesson about crossing him and getting him in more trouble. If he was going to be in trouble, he may as well make it worth his while and really teach her a lesson that she won't need to forget because she won't live long enough to remember it.

He watched from behind the tree as Gizelle pulled up in her car. He didn't see anyone with her and smiled. She would be his. His face would be the last one she'll ever see.

The minute her car stopped and Heather walked slowly toward the passenger door, he snuck around to the back of the car and waited for Gizelle to unlock the door to let Heather in. As soon as he heard the click, he raced to the driver's side door and snatched it open, surprising Gizelle. The look of shock on her face will be one he will never forget; he saw terror.

"I'm sorry Gizelle. He made me," Heather cried out in fear.

"Shut up!" Clyde yelled. "Why don't you tell her that you've been screwing me since before Brody was born and that you've been hiding me in your apartment since I got to town. No? Well, shut up then and get in your car."

When Gizelle tried to scream as he dragged her out of the car, Clyde pulled her kicking and tossing around behind the closest tree. He could hear Heather crying and asking him to stop, but he ignored her. He no longer cared about her. He only wanted Gizelle. He wanted her to feel his pain. When her arms began to flail as she tried to grab a hold of him, he leaned back and with a force that contained every ounce of hatred and love he had for her, he balled up his fist and hit her so hard that she fell back against the tree and collapsed to the grown in a heap. He hoped he hadn't killed her with that punch because he was hoping to complete that act with her looking in his eyes as he choked the life out of her. He needed to get off the road.

"Clyde! Stop it!" Heather cried louder.

"I told you to shut up. Get in your car and get out of here."

"You can't hurt her. She's the mother of your

children. Let her go!"

"Oh, now you want to be her friend? I'm leaving here with her whether you like it or not and whether you get in your car or not. Go away, Heather. I never want to see you again. We're over!"

Without saying anything else, Clyde looked left and right and saw no other cars on the road. He ran to Gizelle's car and popped the trunk. Checking again, he still saw no one. He picked up Gizelle's limp body and without a second thought, he threw her in the trunk of her own car.

"Clyde, please don't do this. We can run away and forget about this. I can give you children. Please don't do this!" Heather screamed.

"You're stupid enough to think this is about the kids?" he laughed.

At this point, he didn't care what Heather thought or said. He got into the driver's seat and sped off in the opposite direction of the ranch. He got what he came for; he got Gizelle back and it was time to make her pay.

21

"Marta, there's a call for you from Ms. Maria on the house phone from the daycare center. It's something about Gizelle's children not being picked up. Were you supposed to pick them up for Gizelle today?" Sarah asked.

"No, not today. I would have remembered that. I've never missed getting them when Gizelle needs me."

Feeling some kind of way about there being a mix up, she reached for the phone and paused. A bad feeling washed over her just as it did the day she got the call about her sister Jean. She had been expecting Jean on the ranch the morning that she went missing and when she didn't show up or call and the phone rang, before she picked it up, she had a feeling in her spine that something was wrong. She was having that feeling again, right now.

Her hands shook as she picked up the phone and hit the button for the house line, already lit up on her phone.

"Oh," was all she heard Sarah say.

"Maria, is there a problem?" she stuttered out before Maria had a chance to say anything.

"Hi, Mrs. Sullivan. It's five in the evening and Miss Gizelle hasn't picked up Brody and Carrie. She usually picks them up by four-thirty and she's never been late. She would tell me if you, Mr. David or Mr. Perry were coming to get them. Since she works here, I checked with the office and they said she may have lost track of time after she left around three. She left saying she was meeting a friend who called her with some kind of emergency. She told the office staff that she'd be back in about an hour and she never returned. I was told something about a woman named Heather, I think, who called and Ms. Gizelle went running out. What should I do?"

Marta stood up so suddenly that the office chair behind her turned over and clashed to the floor. When Sarah moved to set it back up, she stopped her. The chair was the least of her concerns.

"She left the ranch?" Marta asked.

"I believe so, but I'm not sure. Do you want me to pass you to Ms. Gathers? She's still here."

Yolanda Gathers was the director of the daycare center and may have more information than what Maria was giving her.

"Yes, get her on the line."

"What's wrong?" Sarah asked her.

"Get Buck on the line immediately. I need to know if he's with Gizelle off the ranch or if he sent someone off the ranch with her."

"Mrs. Sullivan?"

Marta exhaled hearing Yolanda's voice.

"Yes, Yolanda, sorry to bother you. I understand Gizelle left and didn't pick the kids up at her usual time."

"That's true."

"Is there a reason I'm just getting this call? She's an hour late picking up her children and you know that never happens!" Marta shouted as images of her own sister's broken and battered body came to mind. She shook off the thought in order to focus.

"I'm sorry. I wasn't aware she hadn't returned until just now when Maria told me. I was in a meeting and hadn't realized she wasn't at her desk. I told Maria to get you on the line right away to see if someone else was scheduled to get them. I'm sorry. Do you think something is wrong?"

"I do. There is no other reason of why she would not pick them up. I'm going to reach out to Perry to see if he knows anything about where she went. He's off the ranch at meetings today. Maria mentioned someone named Heather?"

"Oh, yes. She was talking to her and said she had an emergency and it would be really quick, so she would be right back. That's all I know. I didn't speak with her. Audra gave me the message and that was right before three earlier today. I'm so sorry I didn't have someone reach out sooner."

"Don't worry about it. I'll take it from here. Please stay with the children until I get there. I'm on my way. Do not let the kids out of your sight. Lock the doors and I'm going to have Buck send some guys over there for extra security. I don't think anyone could get on the ranch, but I'm not taking any chances either. Only me, Mr. David, Perry or one of Buck's guys that you know are allowed anywhere near the school. If you see anyone else, you know what to do. We ask questions later, right?" she asked.

"Absolutely. I'm taking the necessary precautions right now. We're on lockdown and I'm armed."

"See you in a few," Marta said and hung up just as Sarah told her that Buck was on the line. She switched lines immediately. "Get my cell and call Perry," she addressed Sarah.

"Ms. Marta? Everything alright?" Buck asked.

"Are you with Gizelle? I think she left the ranch."

"No, but I'm headed your way to get to the entrance. I just spoke with Kibby, who is on duty at the gate, about an issue and he, on the side, asked if he should have gone with Gizelle when she left a while ago because he didn't see her come back. He said he saw her talking to a woman outside the ranch and then a delivery truck showed up and he didn't think about it. I'm speeding that way right now. She told him she was going right outside the gate and would only be a few seconds, yet he failed to call me or check when an hour later, she hasn't returned. She said something about a friend in need who was on foot with a broke down car and Gizelle went to pick her up and since it was so close, she didn't think anything of it being unsafe."

"Was Kibby alone at the gate?"

"No, Nelson is on duty at the main gate also. Mike and Sean are on duty at the first gate and I called them and they told me they thought she was going to have Kibby or Nelson go with her. It's messy, I know and I'm sorry. I'm on it. She's still not back?"

Marta could hear the hurriedness in his voice.

"No, and she didn't pick up the kids from school. Something is wrong. Go find her, now! Also, check with your men at every entrance, including the other side of the ranch. Priority number one is to find her."

Marta hung up the phone and was about to ask Sarah if she was able to raise Perry on the phone when the front door slammed open and in walked her husband followed by Perry and Shelton.

"Ma? What is it? What's wrong? Sarah called all frantic saying something about Gizelle? We were already here on the ranch coming back from a meeting."

When she couldn't get any words out, David stepped up.

"Honey, what's wrong? What happened?"

Moving beyond the lump in her throat that

something may have happened to Gizelle, she turned to Perry first.

"Gizelle isn't with you?" she asked cautiously.

"No, I tried calling her about an hour ago and I'm waiting for her to call me back. I assumed she was busy at work or with the kids. I actually came here thinking she may be here with you."

She shivered and her hands shook as David took them in his and looked down where their hands met. He could feel the terror without looking in her face. Her hands were noticeably shaking uncontrollably.

"I'm worried," she slurred out when the lump she thought had cleared her throat returned.

"Is there a reason you're worried?" David asked.

"Perry, the Maria called. Gizelle left the ranch and didn't come back to pick up the kids. They are still there and she's nowhere to be found."

"Wait – what? What do you mean she left the ranch? Alone? Where's Buck? She didn't pick up Carrie and Brody?" Perry shouted and Marta felt his fear.

"She didn't. Kibby let her leave thinking she was picking up a friend walking on the road by the ranch. He saw her stop and even saw a woman walk toward the car and then he looked away when he got sidetracked by a delivery. He didn't think to check on her and just went on with his work forgetting she didn't return and he no longer saw her car. We now know that she never returned."

She watched Perry pull out his phone and frantically dial Gizelle's number.

"She shouldn't have left the ranch without an escort. I know it's been a while, but we have still been on guard. Why did she leave? Who did she meet?" he asked.

"Heather. That friend of hers that she used to work with."

"Where's Buck?"

"Out looking for her."

Everyone paused as Perry put the phone to his ear and waited. He then dialed again and then again.

"I keep getting her voicemail. It's no longer ringing anymore."

They all turned in the direction of the door as Brielle walked in chipper and humming a song.

"Whoa, hey everybody! What's going on? Why does everyone look so serious?"

"Have you seen or talked to Gizelle?" Perry asked.

"Yeah, about three or so. That friend of hers, Heather had her car break down right outside of the ranch gate and Gizelle was going to go and escort her onto the ranch and help her get some help for her car. She's not back yet?" Brielle asked. "She said Heather called her frantic about her car out of gas or flat tire or something and she was right outside the ranch gate, walking distance. I assumed she would take someone with her. I told her to call me when she got back. I was in a meeting about an upcoming event. I thought maybe she forgot to call me and that I would find her here. I was going to take the kids to the barn for an hour or so."

"She didn't take one of the guys with her. Kibby let her leave without checking with any of us. Make sure he's fired immediately," Perry said to Marta.

All she did was nod her head, knowing Perry was right. There could be no gap in the chain when it came to security.

"I told her to take someone with her and when she didn't respond, I assumed she would do that. Why would she leave by herself? Oh my god, where is she?" Brielle asked.

"She's had a new level of comfort lately and things have been going so well. I still wanted her to be careful, but she kept telling me that she has to get back to a normal life sooner or later. I didn't want to push, but I was still telling her to be careful. She's not in prison on the ranch. I just wanted her to be careful," Perry explained.

"Does anyone have a number for Heather?" Marta asked.

"I'm going to call the law firm where she works and demand they give me Heather's number!" Perry shouted. "The kids? Where are they?"

"Yolanda has them at the school and she's armed. I'm heading over to get them now," Marta replied.

"Good. I want them here with you."

"I'm sure she's fine," David chimed in.

"We don't know that, Pop," Perry said.

"She wouldn't forget the kids," Marta added.

"Your mother will get a number for this friend and maybe we'll find that they are together and perhaps Gizelle's phone has died. Let's all stay positive," David said.

"Pop, she would never be late picking up the kids and if so, she would have called one of us considering how late she now is. She must not be able to call back. Something is wrong," Perry said as he dialed Gizelle's cell again hoping that she would pick up.

"Here is the number to where Gizelle was working before. I have it from when I requested information on her employment record," Marta said handing the number to Perry.

She waited and quickly wrote down another number he rambled off after speaking to someone.

"That's Heather's cell phone according to Jim Robeson, her boss."

"Good," Marta said as Perry disconnected that call and dialed Heather's number.

"Uh, heather. It's Perry Sullivan. Is Gizelle still with you? She's not? Didn't you call her? What's going on, Heather?"

"Perry what's wrong?" Marta asked.

"She's stuttering over her words and she sounds strange. Like she's been crying."

Marta took the phone from him.

"Heather? It's Perry's mother, Marta. Tell me

what's going on right now or I'll have the sheriff on his way to you. Where is Gizelle. The school said you called with an emergency and she went to meet you and she has yet to return. Where is she?" Marta demanded.

"Ma?" Perry asked with worry.

Marta listened to Heather and from what Heather was telling her, things were worse than she thought; than any of them could imagine.

"You did what? Why would you do that? Do you have any idea how dangerous Clyde is?"

"Mom?" Perry pleaded.

"You've done enough and you better pray nothing has happened to her."

Marta hung up and turned to Perry.

"Clyde has her. From what I could gather, Heather tricked Gizelle into leaving the ranch alone saying she was right outside the gate and needed her help when in fact, Heather is the one who has been hiding and helping Clyde all along. She told her she was cold and scared and could barely feel her toes because she was close enough to the ranch and started walking toward it and Gizelle went running since she was right outside the gate. Heather said she didn't know what Clyde had planned. He told her he only wanted to talk to Gizelle about seeing the kids and then at the last minute, he told her he was going to hurt Gizelle. He pulled her out of the car when she stopped to let Heather in and hit her. She saw Gizelle hit her head on a tree and then she wasn't moving. Clyde put Gizelle in the trunk of her car and took off in the opposite direction. Heather got back in her car and has been driving around not knowing what to do."

"What!" Perry yelled.

Before anyone could stop him, Perry rushed for the door and was in his truck and gone before anyone could catch up to him.

"Perry!" Marta screamed, knowing that there was no hope for Clyde if Perry got his hands on him.

"Ma, get the kids," Shelton yelled as he started to run after Perry with no hope of catching him. Perry had taken off at a high rate of speed.

Feeling someone place a coat around her arms, she didn't realize she was outside. The cold of the winter did not penetrate her skin.

"David, go after him. Shelton, go get him. Don't let him kill that man. I know he wants Gizelle back, but if he gets his hands on Clyde, we all know it's over," Marta screamed.

As David pulled her into his arms, she cried softly and then looked up as Nick came barreling toward the house in his own truck. He'd been off for the day and last she heard, he was at the veterinary office helping Parker out for the day.

"I called him," Brielle said when everyone looked at Nick as he leaped out of his truck not bothering to turn it off.

"I'm going to get more guys on the road to keep

up with Perry. We'll find her," David said.

"I'm going too. If Perry calls, keep us posted," Shelton shouted as she ran down the front steps and hopped into one of the ranch trucks parked on the side of the house.

Marta heard David and Shelton talking as they walked toward their trucks.

"Call in the guys who are off for the day. I need as many guys as possible out looking for Gizelle and at this point, Perry too. Get extra men on the gate and get Kibby off the ranch right now! He's fired," David shouted.

Marta knew they didn't usually have security issues, but they liked guys who were always alert and aware and Kibby proved that wasn't him.

"He's not crazy enough to come here, Pop," Shelton said.

"True, but we don't know if he's working alone or not and right now, the ranch is on red alert. No one on for any reason on either side."

"Pop! What's the latest?" Nick asked approaching them. "Brielle called me," he added.

"Your mother will update you. Shelton and I have our marching orders. I need you to focus on Perry. Find him and get him to tell you where he is and where he's going. He listens to you over all of us and you're the only person who can talk him down from the ledge. He's like a wild man right now and he knows that Clyde has Gizelle. He'll kill him if he reaches him. Find him, Nick," David ordered.

"Nick, I'm going over to the school to get the kids. Clyde has Gizelle in the trunk of a car and he's driven off someplace with her. Where, we don't know. Perry left here on a mission to find them and you know how he feels about her. He will go through hell to get her back."

Nick shook his head and raced off toward his father before he pulled off in another of the ranch's trucks.

"Pop, I just got the word that Gizelle's house, where she used to live, was set on fire about an hour ago. I have crews over there and there is a lot of damage to the kitchen where it looks like some kind of bottle with flammable liquid was thrown through the back window. That room is toast; it's completely burned out. There was no body found inside, but I suspect Clyde may have set that fire. Gizelle's car was seen leaving the scene by a neighbor who recognized her car and then he saw the fire and called emergency.

"What the hell is going on?" Marta shouted.

"My god. This man is insane. We have to find Gizelle. We have to," David yelled and drove off.

Nick's head turned her way in shock. He'd never heard his mother curse before.

"I have that under control. I need to see what Perry needs right now," he responded.

"I know. It's just so much is happening at the moment and it's hard to take it all in and process it logically. It's that crazy husband of hers doing all of this. Your men have the fire in their hands and so you get to Perry and see what he needs," she suggested.

"I'm on it."

**

Clyde drove around aimlessly not sure what he wanted to do. He had a plan or at least, thought he had a plan, but he didn't stick to it. His first mistake was riding with Heather to get Gizelle when he should have taken his truck because now that he was driving off-road, Gizelle's car wasn't handling the trek well from icy roads to muddy unpaved roads.

Once Gizelle woke up in the trunk, he had to get her out before she kicked it open and fell or jumped out and then someone might see them. He had to find a place to get her to a place where he could tie her up and cover her mouth and he could only think of one place; her old house. No one would suspect he'd go there since it had been months since anyone had last seen him thanks to Heather who was as stupid as a bag of rocks. She actually thought he wanted a future with her.

When he got to the house, he pulled around to the back, the only part of the house that was hidden from the road. He had hoped there would be some kind of rope or something else he could use to tie Gizelle up until he figured out what he was going to do with her. He didn't know Bozeman enough to know where the good spots were to hide a body. With her kicking and screaming in the back, he had to silence her temporarily until he could do so permanently with her looking him in the face as he snuffed out her miserable life. He had to get off of the main highway because by now, every cop and hick from that ranch was probably out looking for him. Seeing what looked like a road that led far back behind trees, possibly leading into the mountains, he took that and hoped that in a couple of hours, he could be on his way out of town and onto a new life with his past taken care of.

Bouncing along, he rolled down the window when the windshield wipers stopped working as ice and snow from the road covered the front windshield. Inhaling, he could smell smoke in the air, no doubt from the house fire he'd set after searching Gizelle's house and finding just enough rope to tie her up with.

When he had opened the trunk, he knew she would try to flee, but he grabbed her before she could get away and using the rope he'd found after breaking into the house, he tied her hands even as she begged and pleaded for him to let her go. Tired of hearing her talking, he stuffed some rags in her mouth that he'd found in the kitchen. Haphazardly, he had an idea to set the house on fire because he hated the place she moved to trying to get away from him. Finding oil in the kitchen cabinet, he wasn't sure it would work, but it did and as he drove away after putting Gizelle back in the trunk, this time tied up and muzzled, he smiled at the flames he saw in the rearview mirror. Thinking back, it was a mistake. That fire would bring more than just the police. By now, even the fire department was probably told to be on the lookout for him. He saw a man eyeing him as he drove by and since he appeared to be a neighbor, he as sure the man recognized Gizelle's car and saw the fire and would make the call. There goes his idea of getting rid of Gizelle and getting out of town unseen.

Not sure of where he was going, he knew he had to get rid of Gizelle quick and then drive back to his truck which he'd hidden behind some trees not far from the city line. His reason for being in Bozeman and his patience was about to pay off. Dancing in his seat, Clyde thought of how good revenge felt; in fact, it felt damn good!

Seeing another road, he turned and ended up back on the main highway where ahead on the left, he saw a better path that had been cleared of snow and would be easier to get down. Turning onto it, he was halfway in when the front of the car started smoking and he could see flames under the hood. Stopping, he jumped out, knowing the car was toast and he ran to grab Gizelle out of the back. He could leave her inside and be done with her and let the fire consume her body, but he had to get the revenge he sought. He had to be looking her in the eyes as her life ended. Opening the trunk, he snatched her out, untied her legs so that she could walk and drug her across the ground. By the time anyone discovered where they were, she would be dead and he would have no regrets; one.

**

Nick dialed Perry's number as he walked back toward his truck. His mother and sister were still close by as he talked to Perry who finally answered.

"Perry, where are you, brother. Where are you? I'm coming with you," Nick said.

"He has her, Nick. I let my guard down and he has her."

Nick heard Perry's fear more than he heard the anger.

"This is not your fault."

"It was my job to protect her and the kids and I failed her."

"Perry, she left the ranch and you couldn't have known she would do that. Where are you? I'm heading off the ranch. Are you armed?" Nick asked.

Crazy question, Nick thought. None of them left the ranch without some sort of weapon, even Brielle, who had been taught to shoot at a young age. The purpose wasn't as much against people as it was against wild animals that were sometimes seen around Bozeman considering all the mountainous ranges. There was no doubt Perry had his rifle, which he never drove his truck without and he probably had a Glock in a lockbox under the driver's seat of his truck. He feared the path his brother was going down.

"I am and I'm going to use it if I find him!"

"Perry, no. Let me call Marcus. Let him handle this. Nothing will be gained by killing Clyde. Listen, nothing you can do about this, but he may have set Gizelle's house on fire about an hour ago. Not the one here on the ranch, the old Baxter house she had been renting. I got the call and put two of my trucks on it. The entire of rear of the house, the kitchen, family room and mudroom, including the back bedroom upstairs had severe damage from the fire and water damage everywhere else. Before you ask, no one was found inside, but we suspect it was Clyde. Gizelle's car was seen leaving that direction by a neighbor who said a man was driving her car. When I heard about Gizelle, I put it together that it was him," he explained.

"This bastard is crazy! I'm going to kill him!" Perry shouted.

"No, you are not. He's dangerous, bro."

"So am I. There is no telling what he's doing to her. That Heather girl said he hit her and knocked her out and threw her in the trunk of her car. He's driving her car! I'll find her and he's dead, Nick. He took my woman and that means all bets are off. He had a chance to get away with his life and now, that's no longer an option. If I go to jail, I know that she and the kids will forever have a home with you all on the ranch. I'm out."

"Perry!" Nick yelled as the line disconnected.

"What happened, Nick?" Brielle asked.

"Ugh, he hung up on me. Somebody call Marcus. He was at the sight of the fire, but he now needs to know that Perry is on the hunt and Clyde has Gizelle. Maybe he and his men can find him before Perry does. I'm going to try calling him back."

He was about to dial Perry's number and his phone rang. Thinking it was Perry calling back, he answered immediately without looking at who was calling.

"Perry?"

"No, it's Marcus. Where's Perry?"

"There's an issue. We can't find Gizelle. It seems her crazy ex-husband showed up and some woman convinced Gizelle to come off the ranch and Clyde was waiting. He kidnapped her and Perry is already on the prowl with the temper of a mad-man. You have to help us look for her!" he shouted.

Just then the radio in his truck signaled an emergency. The radio was linked to the fire station.

"I've got some news, Nick."

"Wait, I'm getting a message from the firehouse."

"I know you are. I know what it's about. It's why I'm calling. There is a fire down off of Brush Lane, that new road that leads to the lake. It's not even paved yet. It's a car fire and I just got word that the car is Gizelle's. I didn't know she was missing. Where is Perry? I'm heading to Brush Lane."

"What! I don't know where he is. We were talking and he hung up on me. He's out looking for Gizelle,"

Nick hollered, scaring everyone around him.

His mother had never seen him react like that to anything. She and Brielle rushed over to his truck."

"Nick? What's wrong? Is that Perry? Did he find her?" Marta asked.

"Mom, I have to go. They found Gizelle's car on fire about five miles from here. I have to get there. Go get the kids and I'll call you," Nick said and sped off.

"Marcus, I'm on my way. I'll call Perry. Let's pray she's not in the car. Trucks are on the way."

Nick put his truck in drive and pushed the gas pedal to the floor and rushed off the ranch and dialed Perry who didn't answer. He left a voicemail.

"Perry, listen, there is a fire on Blush Lane. The fire is Gizelle's care. Marcus is on his way and I don't have any other information. I'm on my way."

He then dialed his father and Shelton and gave them the news. He turned on the siren in his truck and prayed as he drove.

22

Perry pulled up on the scene of a smoldering car, Gizelle's car. After listening to Nick's message, he realized he was less than a mile from Brush Lane and could see smoke through the trees.

Turning onto the road, he could see the car fully engulfed in flames as he leaped out and tried to get close. He heard sirens behind him, but didn't care. He had to get close enough to see if Gizelle was in the car. His heart was pounding so hard that he could hear it over the sound of the roaring flames. He swatted at the flames that threatened to consume him as he looked for a way to get close. Risking it, he leaped forward just as hands pulled him back and arms went around him. He fought against them and screamed Gizelle's name over and over.

"Perry, stop! You can't get closer. Stop fighting me!" Marcus shouted.

Perry ignored him and continued to struggle as another set of hands held him back and his fight to get to the car was made much harder. He could feel the

CHERYL BARTON

flames close to his face, but he didn't care. Gizelle could be in the car.

"Let me go, Marcus. She could be in the trunk. The fire hasn't gotten to that part of the car yet. Let me go!" Perry shouted and continued to struggle against the hands holding him.

"Trucks are here. Fire trucks are here. Let them put the fire out, Perry. You can't get any closer," Marcus said in his ear.

Perry couldn't hear – he could only see and what he saw took the life out of him. He had to know if she was in the car or not. Could Clyde have actually killed her? He didn't want to think that way.

"I have to see if she's in there Marcus. I have to see!" he shouted.

"I know and the men will check as soon as they douse more of the fire."

Perry struggled against Marcus' hold, but his friend held him tight. He then heard his brothers and his father calling for him as they each ran over to him and watched and waited. Finally free from Marcus' hold, Perry paced and waited for the chance to get closer to the car.

A few minutes later, when the firemen put their hose down, he knew now was the time and he moved closer to the car. Before he could reach it, he was grabbed by the arm by Nick. He tried with his might to push through Nick's hold.

"Perry, just wait. If she's in there, you don't want

to see that. We'll get him. You know we will get him, but let my guys do what they do. They'll open the trunk and check the inside. Give it a minute, bro. Please, give it a minute," Nick begged.

"Listen to him, Perry. Just hold up a minute," David added.

Perry knew they were right and again, he waited. He couldn't stand still, but he waited.

"I'm going to walk over, but you wait here. Just wait," Nick warned.

Perry shook his head in agreement and waited. After a few seconds and with the trunk now opened, Nick looked at him and Perry rushed toward him.

"Well?" he yelled.

"She's not in there. She's not in the car or in the trunk. There is no sign of a body," Nick assured him.

"Are you sure? Do you know for sure?"

"I'm sure. I checked myself and she's not in there and that's a good thing. We'll keep looking for her."

"I don't care if I'm out here for weeks, I'm going to find her, even if I have to drive to Chicago in case he took her there. I'm going to find her, Nick or I'll die trying."

Perry looked around frantic as he tried to clear his thoughts and figure out his next move. He knew he had to get back in his truck, but the fire trucks and police cars were all blocking his truck in.

"Just wait and let's all figure this out," Nick exclaimed.

"No! Get your trucks out of the way so that I can get my truck back on the road. Either help me or get out of my damn way! I mean it Nick! Move!" Perry shouted and rushed to his truck.

Seeing no one move out of his way, Perry put his truck in drive and knowing it could get through anything, he drove forward around the burned-out car and ignored everyone's pleas for him to wait. Once he got beyond the car, he noticed something in the mud a few yards ahead of the car. Looking ahead through the trees, he saw foot prints. One set walking up right and the other looked like those of someone being dragged. Following the prints, he drove slowly until he came to another clearing on the right where he saw the prints continuing. He knew that about a half of a mile down that path, there was a lake. Could Clyde have taken her there? The road ahead was narrow because of the number of trees that had not been cut down. He wasn't sure his truck would make it, so he hopped out of it and ran at full speed. Adrenaline could be a beast and he was running on so much of it that he could run a marathon and not get tired. He had an end game and it was to get to Gizelle.

**

"What next, Marcus?" Nick asked. "My men will stay here and follow up.

"I have a BOLO, be on the lookout" for Clyde and my men are out in full force. We'll find him and we'll keep up with where Perry is."

"Every hand from the ranch is out in the streets looking also," Shelton walked up and said.

"Hey, where is Perry? There isn't a road that leads out from the direction he went in. Once you get beyond the clearing ahead, there is nothing but trees until you get almost a mile down to an open area right at the lake. I thought Perry was going to turn around and come back out this way," David said.

"Your father is right. There is no way out back there and Perry hasn't come out. Running around the car followed by Nick and Shelton, Marcus saw what he knew Perry saw; there were foot prints in the mud and the little snow that had not melted.

"Footprints?" Nick asked.

"Footprints and I bet Perry saw them. Look, his truck is following them."

"Marcus, Nick and Shelton took off running until they came up to a bank of trees that no car or truck could get through and that's where they found Perry's truck, still running with the driver's side door open. Nick looked inside and reached under the seat and to his chagrin, his heart dropped.

"His gun box is open and the gun is missing. Look, he's on foot following the foot tracks in the mud. Nick, go tell your father. I think Perry is heading to the lake. That may be where Clyde is with Gizelle. Shelton, with me," Marcus yelled and began running even as he barked out orders over his radio to his men to get to the lake as fast as they could. Even with all of his equipment on, Marcus ran like he did back in high school where he was a track star. Shelton, he could hear was right behind him, in the freezing cold, running as if their own lives depended on it; in a way, they were.

**

Perry was running so hard that he barely felt the tree branches smacking against his face as he ran. He didn't know how long he had been running or how far. He just followed the tracks in the snow and then the path began to clear and he knew he was getting closer to the lake. He remembered hanging out there as a youngster with friends on days when they would cut school and eventually, someone from the ranch would find them after his mother got a call from the school that he'd left in the middle of the day.

He came upon some large rocks and raced around them. He could hear voices calling out to him behind him, but he ignored them and looked along the edge of the lake. Quieting for a moment and trying to breathe as shallow as he could, Perry heard something. He could hear a man talking loudly and then he heard it. He heard Gizelle scream and he took off running along the lake and through more trees and over old tree stumps and then he saw them. In the next instant, when Gizelle screamed again, he took in the sight before him. Clyde was dragging Gizelle by the hood of her coat toward the lake as if he was planning to throw her in or perhaps drown her at the edge. They were struggling as he tried to lower her head to the water. The sound of her voice and the obvious fear pushed him on and he took off, going as fast as he could.

Without thinking, he charged faster and harder and reached them just as Clyde was about to roll Gizelle into the lake. A fear like he's never felt before came over him as he locked eyes with Gizelle who was clawing at the ground trying to grab a hold of anything to keep Clyde from dragging her into the water. The moment she saw him, she screamed his name causing Clyde to turn around.

Perry was running so fast, Clyde didn't have time to react before he was on him. With a rage he'd only seen in animals, but now himself felt, he grabbed Clyde, gripping him tightly around the neck to the point where Clyde had no choice but to let go of Gizelle in order to try and get the large hands from around his neck. Perry looked him in the eye as his eyes grew to a size so large, he thought that they would pop out of Clyde's head. Nothing else existed in the world except making sure Clyde never saw the light of day again. Picking Clyde up even higher, Perry dropped him hard to the ground where Clyde writhed in pain and struggled to get away. Before he could get too far, Perry picked him up again and this time when he slammed Clyde to the ground, he held him there and pounded away at his face and then his chest and then back to his face again. He saw the will to fight back leave Clyde's body as his body flailed around on the ground like a rag doll. Still, Perry didn't stop. With the full force of his might behind each punch, he kept hitting Clyde, even when blood began spewing from his mouth and nose, Perry kept hitting and hitting with no plans of stopping until Clyde was no longer breathing. The man took his woman and tried to kill her and he couldn't let him live after that. He thought quickly about the gun on his waist, but couldn't stop long enough from letting out his rage with his fist in order to grab it.

Hearing Gizelle screaming, he turned to her.

"Run, Gizelle. Get up and run, baby and don't stop!" he shouted. "Don't stop until you see or hear anyone. Run!"

As he struggled with Clyde, he noticed Gizelle struggled with getting up as she continued to gasp for air. He knew he needed to get to her and put an end to his rage against Clyde. Knowing what he had to do and not caring about the repercussions, he reached for the gun on his side, took it out of the holster and almost as if he was moving in slow motion, he put the nozzle in Clyde's mouth. Perry knew his own eyes were bulging from the adrenaline pouring through is veins. In the next second, he could end any chance Clyde could have of ever bring pain to Gizelle's life again.

"Perry!" Shelton yelled running toward them.

Still, Perry didn't look away. He kept his eyes on

Clyde, who by this time was barely moving. His face was so bloody, that Perry could barely recognize him. Clyde was moaning, but not moving. He heard Shelton and Marcus call his name this time and heard them getting closer.

"Get Gizelle! Get her, Shelton. I don't think she can get up. Get her away from here! Help her!" Perry yelled and then turned back to Clyde who was now more aware now that he was lucid enough to see that there was a gun in his mouth. Perry saw fear like no other looking back at him because Clyde knew that any second, his life could be over and his brains would be scattered all over the ground.

"Perry, don't do this!" Marcus yelled.

"Come near me and he's dead and you know I'm serious, Marcus. Do not move, cop or not; don't you come even an inch loser," Perry slurred out through gritted teeth.

His jaw was tensed, his eyes were like fire and the hatred that ran through his body for the man who tried to kill his woman was frightening even through hm. He'd never hated anyone this much.

"Perry!" Shelton yelled.

He ignored him too as he leaned down closer to Clyde's face, almost eye to eye with him.

"You son of a bitch! You tried to kill my woman! You piece of scum! I ought to end your life right here. Are you afraid? Are you terrorized? Now, you know what you have put Gizelle through and for what?

Because she didn't want you anymore? She's my woman and I protect what's mine. You're not even worth killing, but you will remember this day and you will remember the name, Perry Sullivan and just in case you ever get out of jail and decide to come after my family again, I want to leave you with a little more of me for you to think about before you make another move against my woman.

Tossing the gun toward Marcus, Perry let go of his rage again and pummeled Clyde again and again.

Showing no mercy and with the wildness of an untamed animal, he leaned back and put all of his power behind his fist and landed one punch after another to Clyde's face. He didn't care how much damage he was doing because rage had taken over and he couldn't let up on his assault even if he tried.

He grabbed ahold of Clyde's full body and picked him up again, lifting him high over his head before slamming him back to the ground with a loud, defining thud. Reaching down, he dragged Clyde toward the water's edge pulling him by his neck. As Clyde tried to struggle against his strong hold, he let go of his neck.

"No!" Clyde yelled out as blood poured from his mouth. Perry knew Clyde could see the water right at his face.

"Come on, Clyde. Take me on. You like to beat up on women. Try that with me, you son of a bitch!" Perry yelled and hit him again and again in the chest while stomping him with his heavy work boots. Behind him, he could hear other people running up and calling his name.

"You like dragging women by their feet?" he asked angrily. "Did I see you about to try and drown my woman?"

Even more enraged as he thought back to the image he walked up on with Clyde dragging Gizelle toward the water, Perry pulled him and then spun his body around until Clyde's head was right at the edge of the lake again. He briefly looked back to be sure Shelton had Gizelle and seeing her up on her feet, he had another surge of energy and grabbed Clyde by the neck once again and this time, he held his head under the dirty, murky, freezing cold water. Knowing Clyde was no match for his strength, he ignored his attempts to claw his way out of the tight grip on his head. Perry knew he couldn't breathe under the water and he didn't care. He saw fire. He saw his woman being dragged by a raving lunatic.

"Perry! Let him go before you kill him!" Marcus shouted running toward him.

"That's my plan. Look away, Marcus!" he yelled.

"Perry! Stop! Don't do this!" Shelton screamed.

"Perry! Enough!" Marcus screamed again the moment he saw Clyde's body give up the fight unable to breathe under water.

Perry had no plans of letting go and then Nick was pulling at him.

"Let him go, bro. You're killing him and he's not worth your life being way from us. Let him go; let him up. He'll have his day. Don't do this. Don't go to jail over killing this piece of trash. You got to release your rage and now, let him go. Gizelle needs you, let him go," Nick said in a voice so calm that Perry began to come back to himself and release some of the hate that fused through him.

In seconds, Perry felt two sets of hands trying to pry Clyde from his grip.

"Perry, it's me – let him go, son," David said. "Gizelle and the kids need you with them, not in jail for killing this slime. Let him go, please," David yelled. "Perry!"

Hearing his father shout his name brought him back to reality and he let go. When he did, Clyde's body lay on the ground, not moving. Standing and moving backwards, allowing Nick and his father to pull him away, he watched as Marcus ran over and dragged Clyde's body out of the water.

"He's alive! Evan, get an ambulance here. Tell them we need two, one for Gizelle and one for this mound of dirt here who likes beating up on women," he said. "Perry, you good?" he asked.

"Yeah, I'm good."

"Your hands?" David asked.

"My hands are fine, but you need to check his face."

"Perry!"

Hearing his name come from Gizelle, Perry turned and ran and picked her up in his arms and held her close to his body.

"Baby, are you hurt? Are you okay? How bad are you hurt?" he asked with one question after the other in quick succession.

"No, I'm fine. I ache but I'm not hurt. Look at you."

Perry tried to smile now that he knew she was safe.

"I thought..." he said and that was all he could say as he got choked up at what his mind had been telling him could have happened to her.

"You're bleeding," Gizelle said.

Perry looked down at himself and noticed his hands and clothes were bloody.

"That's not my blood, it's his. My knuckles may be bruised, but I'm feeling no pain right now. I just need to know that you're okay. I need to hold you," he said and picked her up, curving her legs around his waist, walking toward the first ambulance that had shown up.

"I'm fine. Are the kids okay?" Gizelle cried.

"Yes. They're safe on the ranch."

"I was hoping my absence would be noticeable when I didn't pick them up. I figured that would send up a red flag. Heather did this. She's been seeing Clyde and I didn't know it. She got me off the ranch without having someone with me and then I knew, I just knew someone would discover something was wrong when I didn't return to get the kids."

"Yeah, the school called mom when you were late getting them since you're never late or you have Brielle or Parker get them for you. They're fine. Let's get you looked at," Perry said as the medics came running, but he walked by them and took her straight to the back of the ambulance and sat her down.

As they began looking her over and tending to her bruised face, Perry looked back toward the lake in time to see Marcus roll Clyde over and placed handcuffs on him as a second ambulance pulled up and rushed to the lake's edge.

"You should be arresting him! He almost killed me!" Clyde yelled, barely audible. His speech was severely slurred.

Perry started to say something, but didn't when he saw that Marcus had everything under control.

"Are you serious right now? Don't piss me off or I'll forget I'm wearing a badge and let him finish what he started. You're not in a place to make demands," Marcus said and read Clyde his rights before dragging his body toward the waiting ambulance.

As a medic looked at his hands and began bandaging them up, Perry nodded to Marcus who walked over to him followed by Nick, Shelton and his father.

"Are you two alright?"

"I'm good," Perry answered.

"Gizelle? How are you?" Marcus asked.

"I'm okay. I'm more worried about Perry. Look at his hands," she said.

"Baby, I'm fine. You're okay and that's all that matter," Perry said, moving to sit beside her on the metal ledge of the back of the ambulance.

"You almost killed him, Perry. I think with a few more seconds, we'd be placing Clyde in a body bag instead of the back of a police car."

"Where's my gun?" he asked.

"I have it. I'll give it to Nick to put back in your truck," Marcus said and turned and walked toward his men.

"Wouldn't matter much to me. He's terrorized Gizelle and the kids for far too long."

"I know that, bro, but that could have meant losing you, too, though a good lawyer could have proved it would have been justified," Shelton said.

Perry leaned over toward Shelton's ear.

"Give me a few more minutes and everybody turn their heads and we could test that theory," Perry said.

"Not this time. Let's keep you free while you are free. I'm going back to my truck to call the ranch. I know they're worried crazy," Shelton said. "Gizelle, you're good?" he asked before leaving.

"I'm fine and thanks for coming behind your brother. I know he was protecting me, but I wouldn't be able to live without him if he went to jail for murder. Clyde is a monster, but I love Perry and so do my kids and we can't have a life if he's not free to have one with us. Right?" she said to Perry.

Kissing her on the lips before answering, Perry smiled, finally able to let go of some of the last bit of rage he felt especially now that he had her in his arms and she was safe.

"Yes, I know you're right. I couldn't pull it back when I saw you struggling like that knowing if I hadn't found you, this could have ended badly."

Gizelle reached up and cupped his face.

"It didn't and I'm fine."

"I wouldn't survive if anything had happened to you. I wouldn't have survived. I love you. I love you so much," he declared.

"I know and that's why we're going to let the law handle this."

"How can you be so calm after what he put you through? I still want to kill him!"

"I know, but I have you and he's just no longer a factor. I trust that there is enough against him that I won't have to worry about him. I have you, you have me and we have two kids back at the ranch who need us. I'm done letting him ruin my life."

"I think you won't have to worry about Clyde anymore especially after what he just went through experiencing Perry's wrath. No one wants to be on the other end of that," Nick said.

"Where's Pop?" Perry asked looking around for him.

"He went with Shelton. He wanted to get back to the ranch to check on mom and the kids. Knowing you and Gizelle are okay was all he needed," Nick said.

Marcus walked back over to them and addressed Gizelle.

"I'm going to have an officer meet you at the hospital so that we can get a statement after you're checked out and Perry, don't even think about saying you don't need to be checked out like her. Do it anyway so that I don't have to deal with your mother when she asks me why I didn't make you go to the hospital."

"Don't worry, I'm going. I'm not letting this lady out of my sight."

"Good. My men are going to rope off this area and get some photos while I the ambulance gets Clyde to the hospital. I'm going to have several men on him until we can get him released to us and placed in a cell. I'm sure he's got a lot of things broken, but he'll live to see his day in court. Tonight, a lot of people will sleep better knowing Clyde is off the streets. Just before I got here, I got word that there is a warrant for his arrest in two other states, so even after this case is heard and tried here where I know he'll get some time, he'll get more time from those cases, probably putting him in jail for a very, very long time. Gizelle, we also have Heather in custody. I'm sorry for what she did in all of this."

"She's dead to me, too. I'm good and thanks for

letting me know. Clyde set the Baxter house on fire," she said.

"You need not ever worry about that. I will handle helping out Mr. Baxter. Sullivan Construction will rebuild it free of charge. Mr. Baxter will understand and remember, it's all over now," Perry explained.

"Yeah, don't worry about that Gizelle. We take care of our own and look out for each other in this town," Marcus added.

"Let's get you in the ambulance, baby," Perry said helping her up on the stretcher.

"Go with her, Perry. I'll have one of the men drive your truck back," Nick said.

"Thanks. I'll call them when I get to the hospital," Perry said.

"Shelton just sent me a text that mom and dad are meeting you there. Parker and Brielle have the kids. She's going to keep them busy and make sure they don't know about any of this. Mom said Sarah was making them dinner and then Parker is going to take them to her and Nick's house for the night to watch movies and eat popcorn. She figured you and Gizelle could use a quiet evening to regroup. I'm glad you're okay, Gizelle. I'm going to head back to the ranch to check on things there. If you and Perry need anything, call me and I'll be right there."

Gizelle waved as the stretcher was loaded into the ambulance while Perry climbed in after her.

As the doors shut behind them, Perry held her as

close as he could to him as the other medic sat at the end as the ambulance took off with sirens blazing.

"Are you sure you're not hurt anywhere else?" Perry asked.

"I'm sure. How did you find us?" she asked.

"Your car was on fire and Nick left me a message while I was out looking for you. When you weren't at the car, I was heading back out to look around and I saw foot tracks in the mud and snow and followed them to the lake. Heather told us what happened when we found you missing."

"Heather," Gizelle exhaled. "I thought she was my friend."

"Don't dwell on it. Clyde's treachery didn't work and you and the kids are safe now and never again will he get the chance to come after you."

"He's never encountered anyone going at him the way you did. I have no doubt, even after all the years and years of jail time I'm hoping he will get, he won't come back this way. He learned you can't mess with the Sullivans."

"You can't mess with the woman of a Sullivan either."

"I love you, Perry."

"I love you, too, baby and that's a forever love – from this moment on."

"I love the sound of that."

"Good because we have a future to plan for me, you and the kids. I know we were planning on talking about that tonight and after today, that conversation is needed more than ever. I love you, I want to marry you and live forever with you in my arms. Today, I came close to losing you and I need us to be a family. I need to know that you, Carrie and Brody are my family and I promise to forever and ever protect you from everything and everyone."

"Marry? You want to get married?"

"I would do it today, if we could, but I won't put that kind of pressure on you, but yes, I want to marry you. I want you to be my wife and I don't care how long we have to fight Clyde, I want Carrie and Brody to be Sullivans also. They need a read father who will love and care for them and I want the job if you want that too."

"Oh, yes. I want that more than anything and yes, I will marry you anytime, anywhere," Gizelle said.

Perry wanted to shout and celebrate, but now wasn't the time. To seal their love, he leaned over and kissed her.

"For now, that kiss is our promise to each other," he said as the ambulance rushed to get them to the hospital and to the beginning of their life together.

Keeping Gizelle's hand in his, Perry leaned his head back and whispered a silent thanks that though the day was rough, it was ending with him able to continue to show Gizelle just how a man should love a woman.

23

David walked into his house and immediately knew that something was wrong. The love of his life was pacing frantically, wrangling her hands looking afraid. What he couldn't handle was more antics like what happened a few days ago when Clyde made his appearance and kidnapped Gizelle. Thankfully, the kids had been safe on the ranch and a determined Perry wouldn't let up on his search for Gizelle. Walking over to Marta, he reached for her and the minute she felt his touch, she snuggled close to his neck and cried.

"Baby, now come on, tell me what's wrong. Has something else happened? After what we've just been through, I don't think I can take anything else," he asked.

"No, no, I'm just happy. I'm just happy that this is all over and I feel it in my bones that we'll never hear from this Clyde character again. From what I hear, Perry put a whooping on him that he'll never forget," she said.

"Well, that is true. I tried to keep the details from you, but it's safe to say that anyone who hears about what happened will never step to our son, ever. Marcus came by earlier today and gave Perry an update and he said that Clyde's injuries were severe, but he'll be okay to stand for the crimes he's committed and the list of them is long. Even the doctor wanted to know if he'd been hit by a two by four piece of wood or something."

"Is Perry going to have any law issues with all of this? Is he in trouble?"

"No, dear. He's not in any trouble. Everything he did was justified. Now, stop crying and worrying. Everyone is here, safe on the ranch and it's well after midnight. Why are you still up?"

"I was full of worry, I guess. I wanted to march over to Perry's house and get another hug and kiss from them. I'm just so happy that everyone is safe back on the ranch."

"Is Brielle here in the house or did she decide to stay at her own house for a change?"

"No, she's at her place. I think she had a gentleman over, but she didn't want to tell me too much. I started to call Buck to get information on him since they had to gather it before he was allowed on this side of the ranch. I tell you, all of our kids being grown and having adult lives is a lot to swallow. Nick and Parker are getting married this summer, Perry and Gizelle are in love and I'm ecstatic about that.

Shelton, oh goodness, my poor son. He won't even live on the ranch because he doesn't want me to get a birds-eye-view of the women who parade in and out of his life and his bed according to the talk in town. I hear that condo of his gets more traffic than the freeway," she said.

David laughed with her.

"Now, I've told you about being that vested in our grown children's lives."

"Oh, please. Even before they were grown, you kept me blind to our teenage sons raging hormones. And I can't even get all into Dayton's business because he hardly ever comes home and spends his time galivanting around the world with his race cars."

"Well, soon, you'll have everybody here on the ranch for Nick's wedding and you can dig into Dayton's personal life then. Why don't you and I relax and watch a movie so that you can unwind before bed."

"Okay, but first, let me go up and check on the babies."

"Babies? The kids are here? Carrie and Brody?" David asked.

"Well, of course. I told Perry and Gizelle that they needed some more alone, quiet time after all the excitement from the past few days. He hasn't been right since the hospital kept Gizelle one night for observation and he wouldn't leave her side, not even for a minute. When she came home, I told her to leave them with me so that she wouldn't have to get up to get them ready for daycare and school. They're upstairs asleep. You know, I want to put some new furniture in the rooms for them. I've seen some online that I want to order. I want them to be comfortable here with us."

"Now, Marta, let me say this and don't get mad at me. Carrie and Brody will have to go home with Gizelle because that's where they live. Yes, we can get the rooms all redecorated for them, but know that Perry and Gizelle may decide to move off of the ranch and we'll see them during the day mostly."

When Marta moved out of his arms, David tried his best to hold back his smile. He loved that she loved them like her own grandkids, but she needed a reality check. Grandkids are those kids who visit and go home with their parents eventually.

"Who said they were moving off of the ranch? Perry loves being on the ranch and so does Gizelle. There is plenty of room for them all in Perry's house and he can even expand if they need more space. They need to be close so that we can help them with the kids. There is so much craziness in the world."

"Honey, Clyde is not coming back to hurt them. I know you're worried and that's why you want them to stay on the ranch, but they will be safe wherever they are as long as Perry is around."

"Am I being silly?"

"No, you're being a grandmother and I love it. You

know, with two of our kids getting married, not sure when for Perry and Gizelle, but they plan on it, I'm sure Carrie and Brody won't be the only grandkids you'll get to enjoy. You go on up and check on them. I'll be up in a minute. I'll grab us a nice bottle of wine and some fruit."

"Those are my grandkids. I mean, I know Perry and Gizelle aren't married yet, but they are still my grandkids. I love them like any grandmother would."

"I know and so do I. I love hearing them call me Poppy!" David exclaimed.

"Shhh. You may hear them say it tonight if you don't quiet down. I want them to sleep all night. They had a big dinner and hot baths with fresh, warm pajamas and have been sound asleep for a few hours. I'll check on them and then I'll be waiting for you."

"In something sexy, I hope?" David said, winking at her.

"Always."

After Marta walked up the steps, David walked around the house checking the locks and sent a text to the head of security that he was in for the night and as added protection, to have some of the guys work overtime. No one was ever going to get on his ranch on his watch.

He often worried about his children, but not like his wife did. He raised all of them to take care of themselves and those they loved. Perry had done just that and had made him proud. In fact, he meant to call him and decided to do that before he went upstairs, even though the hour was late. He pulled out his phone and dialed Perry's cell.

**

"Who was that?" Gizelle asked when Perry walked into the bedroom and got in bed after removing his pajama bottoms. Between the cozy heat of the house and the heat from the fireplace at the foot of the bed, she loved that he enjoyed sleeping naked. She never had before him and loved that he wanted to feel her body against his, skin to skin as they slept. When he got in bed and pulled her close, she snuggled up to him in the darkened room with the only light coming from the fireplace.

"That was my dad. He ran into Mr. Baxter who was on his way here to the ranch to thank us for getting a crew onboard to fix the house. He has insurance, but my dad decided to just level the entire house and have our team build a new one. The plans he's having drawn up include a lot of upgrades that weren't in the house when you were living there. Mr. Baxter also wanted to know if you were planning on moving back into the house once the construction is done. He said he loved you as a tenant and wanted to check with you first before he rented it out to someone else once everything is done. I didn't answer for you. I told my dad you would call Mr. Baxter in the morning."

"I need to let him know he is free to rent it when

it's done. You could have answered for me since you already knew the answer. I'm never leaving your side. If we're in bed, we're in it together, under the same roof. This is our home – right here with you."

Leaning up, Gizelle accepted the luscious kiss Perry gave her. She would never tire of getting them.

"We are one," he whispered in her ear.

"I need us to be one right now. I need you. I need to feel you," she said, turning so that Perry was on his back and she lay atop his body, naked skin to naked skin.

"Aren't your bruises sore?"

"Bruises or not, I still need you and making love with you soothes all pain – you should know that by now. Don't you want a hand in making me feel better? There's a part of me that's screaming out to you for attention and you want me to rest?"

When Perry chuckled softly, she made her point even clearer by sitting straight up and moving her hips around on his hardness which lay between them, flush against his stomach, long, hard and just as ready for her as she is it. Her body felt no pain, only desire. The anticipation of what was to come flooded her body with sizzling heat. Reaching down, she lifted slightly while taking him into her hand and guided his manhood to the place where she needed and wanted him the most, between her hot, wet folds. The moment she felt the head of him, the heat that radiated from his body seared through her as she slowly slid down, taking every delicious inch in.

"Baby!" Perry yelled and grabbed a hold of her hips. She loved the feel of his big, strong hands holding her, but the way she wanted to move, he wouldn't be able to hold on for long.

Leaning forward, she placed her hands flat on his chest as she began to move, slow at first and then faster and wilder. She looked down and saw lips that knew how to make every part of her body come alive and she knew she had to have a taste. Without stopping the precise of her hips going up and down and around in a circle in a way she knew pleased him greatly, she licked her lips and then used her tongue to caress his, moaning into his mouth as she did so. Her womanhood hummed as she flicked her tongue across his lips and then down across the thin hairs on his chest. The moment she blew on the wet trail she'd left there, she felt his hips piston up into her. The deep, low growl from Perry edged her on to give him more as she gripped him tight between her legs.

Without warning, an orgasm slammed into her so hard that she reared back and screamed out her pleasure to the space around them. She was thankful that Perry held onto her or she'd go flying to the floor. She felt numb, weightless as her climax, with one wave after another, cascaded through her.

Perry bucked and growled and tried his best to hold onto Gizelle's hips as she increased their pleasure and rode him into a heavenly bliss. Across the inside of his eyes, hot, white lights streaked, heightening the feeling of her gripping him tighter even more. He was a goner and he knew it, yet he wouldn't have it any other way.

Taking in huge gulps of air, Perry tried to gain control of his senses as his release began to subside and Gizelle collapsed onto his chest and into his arms.

"Pinch me so that I know I'm still alive," she said and then laughed along with Perry as he did just that.

"You and me both, sweetheart. I guess you were in need and any time you are, all you have to do is come and get it. I'll always want and need you," he said softly.

Gizelle wanted to reply, but instead, she tried to get even closer where she always wanted to be. Finally, she understood the way a man is supposed to love a woman. Perry's love was what she'd longed for and their love together was going to last them a lifetime and she was ready for it.

Epilogue
Three Months Later

"I can't believe a woman got you down the aisle. This is a big day in the Sullivan household," Shelton said patting Nick on the back.

"Your time is coming, too," Nick said as he looked over at Parker in her long, form-fitting white Vera Wang wedding dress, made exclusively for her. Never had she looked more beautiful than today, their wedding day.

He looked around the inside of the large, exclusive, luxuriously new event hall where his wedding to Parker and now their reception was being held. There were over three hundred guests in attendance, but he only had eyes for his gorgeous bride.

"Not a chance. Between you and Perry, I think there is something in the water that's making Sullivan men race to the altar and I'm steering clear of all water fountains around this place," Shelton laughed.

"At least I gave the family a chance to take part in

my big day, unlike someone who I will leave nameless who ran off and got married at the court house three months ago," Nick said, looking at Perry while not saying his name.

"I would have done this big wedding thing too, but Gizelle didn't want that and what my little lady wants, she gets. She's already been through one once and we decided all we wanted to do was be a family."

"I hear that and as long as you're happy, we're happy," Shelton said.

"Please explain that to mom. She's still giving me the evil eye to this day because she wasn't at our wedding. I told her after we got through Nick and Parker's wedding and reception that Gizelle and I would have a nice, big reception here on the ranch. That seemed to appease her, but still, I get a pinch on the arm every few days as a reminder that I robbed her of the chance to be at my wedding."

"I've never seen you happier," Nick said as his gaze followed Perry's gaze to Gizelle who was glowing in her long mint green bridesmaid's gown.

"I've never been this happy before and to top it off, the case with Clyde is over for us here and he got twenty years for the havoc he wreaked here. He's now being extradited for charges in two other states that will secure him behind bars for a lot of years. We thought we were going to have an uphill battle over getting him to give up his rights to the kids so that I could adopt them, but he already signed the papers saying he didn't want anything to do with any of them and I said good riddance," Perry said.

"That's great! There will be some Sullivan grandkids after all, even if not by birth," Nick said.

Perry didn't respond when he looked from one brother to the other with a silly grin on his face.

"What?" Shelton asked as he and Nick looked between each other.

"Oh, did I forget to mention Gizelle is two month's pregnant?"

"What!" Nick exclaimed while Shelton stood with his mouth gaping open.

"You heard me and if you tell another living soul before I tell mom later tonight, you'll never forget the beating I'm going to give each of you."

"Congratulations! I thought Parker and I would be first. We want kids right away now that we're an old married couple."

"Shut up. You've been married for an hour. That hardly counts as old. Yup, in seven months, the two of you will be uncles and yes, I'm adopting Carrie and Brody and we're changing their last names to Sullivan."

"When you tell that to mom, she'll forget about being angry over not being at your wedding. She had a company out to child-proof all of our houses since we all toss a coin when it comes to who they spend the night with. I love having them over and when they call me uncle Shelton, I melt. Even more of a reason to celebrate. Speaking of celebrating, has anyone seen Dayton after we took pictures?" Shelton asked.

"Not since that woman showed up as his date that he couldn't keep his eyes off of. I think he said she's from London or Paris or something like that. Did either of you get a chance to meet her?" Nick asked. "I was too busy, but I told him I wanted to meet her after the wedding. Isn't he leaving tomorrow to go back out on the racing circuit?"

"I know that her name is Kima, spelled with an "I" but sounds like two "E's". When he told me he was hanging around a lot longer at home than originally planned, I asked for more details and he brushed me off," Perry said.

"When he first arrived, I asked if he wanted me to set up some video conferencing meetings since he would be busy with races for the next six months or so and the response I got was cryptic. I wanted to make sure I included him in on every discussion about the new go-kart track and to get his ideas for the race track we need to get approval to build. Both have been the talk of the town and neither track has even been built yet. We've just received all of the paperwork to pull up and replant the trees on the property where the first track for families will go. I thought he was going to be out of the country. I wonder what's keeping him home? He's another one who couldn't wait to get off of the ranch like Nick," Shelton said.

"Hey, how did this turn to me. I'm rehabilitated

and loving my life on the ranch, well as much of it as I get to spend here after my days at the fire house."

"We're happy to have you back home on the ranch," Perry said.

"Hey guys! Can I steal my husband away?" Parker asked walking up to them.

"Husband? That has a nice ring to it," Perry said.

"Yeah, I like it," Nick joked.

"I'm going to see if I can find Dayton. He's acting strange," Shelton said.

"You do that and, in the meantime, I'm going in search of my own wife to get a few more dances in. We promised the kids a family night of pizza and movies," Perry said as he walked away making a beeline for Gizelle who stood smiling, laughing and glowing with Brielle and some other ladies she'd become good friends with over the past few months.

He thought back over where their lives had been earlier in the year and how good life was for them now that they were married and living as a real family. He never thought he could be this happy, but he was.

Before he could get far, he saw Buck walking toward him and he didn't look too happy. Perry met him before he reached the reception crowd.

"Hey, Buck. Is everything okay?"

"No, sir. There is a man at the gate demanding to be let in to see Dayton."

"What man? Wait one second." Perry looked around and spotted Shelton and called to him. Moving away from the crowd, Shelton met them as walked.

"What's up?" Shelton asked.

"Buck said there's a man at the gate demanding to see Dayton."

"Dayton? Why?"

"The story he gave me and my men is that he's from out of the country and he owns the circuit that Dayton has been racing in."

"In Canada? That's where he was last," Perry said.

"No, he's from someplace else, I forgot where. It seems, Dayton is under contract, but gave notice that he wasn't returning to do anymore racing and this man is demanding that Dayton return all the money he's been paid and not only that, he claims his daughter is missing and he believes she flew here to be with Dayton. He hasn't seen or heard from her in weeks."

"That must be the woman he brought to the wedding," Shelton said.

"Yeah, well whoever she is, if that's her, her daddy is piping mad and he's also claiming Dayton knocked his daughter up and he wants to know when Dayton is going to marry her."

"Pregnant?" Perry said.

"Pregnant!" Shelton exclaimed at the same time.

"Did she look pregnant to you?" Perry asked Shelton.

"No, but if she is, it looks like Gizelle won't have the only Sullivan grandchild this year. Let's get to the gate and check this out before we alert the family."

Perry followed in step behind Shelton.

"I have a feeling this wedding and reception won't be the most explosive situation today," Perry said.

"Seems that way," Shelton added as he walked even faster to the main gate. Life on the Sullivan ranch was getting more interesting by the day.

The minute they arrived, they could see Dayton in a heated exchange on the other side of the gate. Perry took off running first with Shelton right behind him. Tuxedos or not, they were ready to throw down if they needed to. There was a man screaming and pointing in Dayton's face and if he knew his brother, Perry knew that Dayton wasn't far from knocking the guy to the ground.

Just as Dayton reared back to let the older man have it, Perry grabbed him and spun him around, out of fighting range.

"Whoa, whoa! What the hell is going on here?" Shelton asked.

"Who are you?" the man asked, surprising them all with his aggression.

Perry was now ticked off.

"You're on our property and if you don't cool off, we'll have you thrown out into the street. Who are you?" Perry asked, taking the lead position between Dayton and the man.

"I'm Oscar Tillery and I'm here to collect what's mine!" he shouted.

"Really? You have something on this ranch that you think belongs to you?" Perry asked.

"I do. First there is my money that Dayton there owes me for backing out on a race that cost me a fortune when he didn't show up and second is my daughter, Kima McDonald. I know she's here. There isn't any other place she would go other than running behind Dayton and I want her here and right now!" Oscar demanded.

Perry turned to Dayton for an explanation.

"Perry, he's crazy. I'm not giving him any money for any race. I found out he bet on the race and had someone rig my car for it to crash. Yes, his daughter is here on the ranch with me and she's not going anywhere she doesn't want to be."

Perry saw fire the minute he heard that something life-threatening could have happened to Dayton if he'd been at that race.

He turned around to Oscar.

"I'm Perry Sullivan, Dayton's oldest brother and I would advise you to get off of our property and if your daughter wants to leave, she's not being held captive. How old is she Dayton?" he asked.

"She's twenty-six and trust me, she doesn't want to go with him."

"Kima can speak for herself. Get her out here now or I'll get the law to make you!" Oscar screamed.

Perry had to hold Dayton back to keep him from charging at the man.

"Perry, what's going on here?"

They all turned to see their father get out of one of the ranch trucks and rush over to them.

"Pop," Dayton said and then quieted.

"Perry, Shelton, Dayton? I said what's going on here? You look like you're about to brawl."

"This man, Oscar Tillery, says that Dayton owes him money and he says he wants his daughter who is on the ranch as Dayton's guest for the wedding. I got here and they were having a heated exchange. I don't know the whole story," Perry said.

"Dayton?" David said, turning to him.

"Pop, I swear I don't owe him anything and as far as Kima is concerned, she is here because she wants to be. She got as far away from her father as she could because he's a crook, a cheat and a liar and besides, she's carrying my baby and I'll shoot him if he tries to physically remove her from the ranch. I'm promising that on everything!" Dayton yelled.

"Perry, let the man on the ranch and let's figure out what's going on. You can't do this standing here. If there is a young lady on this ranch and this is her father, then we need to hear from her. If she says she doesn't want to leave, then she won't have to. She's an adult and has a right to decide where she wants to be," David explained.

"He's not taking my woman and child off of this ranch and I'm done with racing because the circuit is filled with weasels like him," Dayton shouted.

"Son, calm down."

"I can't, Pop. The only reason he wants to get his hands on Kima is because without her, he's dead broke. The money and the racing circuit I've been on all belong to Kima, not her father and he needs her in order to have access to anything. It's why he tried to rig my car to crash in the last race. If I had been behind the wheel of the car, I wouldn't be here today. I'd be dead!" he shouted.

No one knew what was coming next and what they saw was a shocker. Before anyone could respond or react to Dayton's words, David reared back and hit Oscar so hard, that he fell straight back to the tarred driveway and was knocked out cold.

Perry chuckled. He knew that the apple didn't fall far from the tree. No one threatens a Sullivan without payback and Oscar had just received his.

"Pop!" Dayton yelled.

"What? He tried to hurt my son and thought coming here to make demands was the answer? I want an explanation and I need it now because when your mother hears about what I just did, she's going to come after all of us and I need to be ready. Tell me what's going on Dayton and I want to hear it all," David said.

"It's like this. I fell in love with a woman who is richer than we are, she's carrying my baby and she's engaged to another man, a wedding her father arranged in order to get his hands on her money.

There are depths to this whole thing that I need to sit you all down and explain, but I mean it when I say, he's not taking my woman or my baby anywhere and Kima isn't going to marry another man unless it's over my cold, dead body!"

"Buck, have some guys pick this man up and bring him to medical. Looks like there is a lot of explaining to be had and it looks like the Sullivan family is about to get even bigger."

When everyone started walking away, Dayton didn't move. He cleared his throat to get their attention. With all eyes on him, he coughed and stepped closer to them.

"Dayton?" David asked.

"Well, there is something else that you need to know before he wakes up."

"That is?" Perry asked.

"If Kima doesn't marry the man she's scheduled to marry in six months, she'll lose her wealth; not just some of it, all of it. Her father is willing to do anything to make sure that wedding happens. Kima doesn't care about the money, but she cares about what her mother built for her to have before her death, which was under strange circumstances. One last thing – Kima told me that she believes it as her father who was responsible for her mother's death and if he gets anywhere near her, she may be next on his list in order to get his hands on her money. I can't lose her. You have to help me," Dayton said.

He watched his family look around at each other as he pleaded with them. He came back to the ranch because he knew that if anyone could help him and Kima, they could.

"Oh, this just keeps getting better. We'll get to the bottom of this. We'll need help with looking into all this to get us on the right track and if this guy is as dangerous as he sounds to be, he'll regret the day he ever came up against a Sullivan," David said.

Join me in the next chapter of the series, *"The Sullivans of Montana"* with *On the Right Track,* Dayton Sullivan and Kima McDonald's love story.

Dayton Sullivan is the youngest of the Sullivan boys and has found himself in a bit of a jam. As a professional race car driver, he has spent the last two years traveling the country and other parts of the world making a name for himself, staying at the top of every race he's competed in. His love for the race also fueled his love for Kima McDonald, the daughter of a man who could be responsible for the death of Kima's mother, the woman whose fortune Kima now holds in her hands that her father wants to get his own hands on.

Kima fell in love with Dayton the minute she saw him and is willing to give up everything to be with him. The obstacle that may keep her from having the man of her dreams could be the man she has been told she has to marry if she plans to keep the legacy of her mother alive.

Dayton and Kima run off to the Sullivan Ranch in Montana in order to escape the life she's being told she has to live. Kima believes she has seen first-hand the depths her father would go to protect what he believes is his and she wants no parts of it.

Keeping Kima safe is all that matters to Dayton, but what he didn't anticipate was the length her father would go to get his daughter back and to claim her riches as his own.

Can their love sustain them through the ups and downs they'll face or will Kima's father and those he is indebted to find a way to get Dayton back on the race track and Kima married to a man she doesn't love, but who holds all the cards when it comes to her future?

Find out in, "On the Right Track", book 3 in "The Sullivans of Montana".

Make sure you check out book 1 of "The Sullivans of Montana" – Home for Thanksgiving

Firefighter Nicholas Sullivan is going home for the holiday after he was sidelined due to an injury on the job. Guilt over a life lost has kept him away from his family's ranch in Montana and now he's forced to face his past demons and deal with a self-imposed life of regret.

Veterinarian Parker Wingate's first encounter with the handsome firefighter was less than pleasurable. She sympathized with his hurt, understood his pain and before long, felt his love.

Knowing the holiday season is ending soon, can Nick go from living in love for the moment to allowing himself to finally live in love forever?

Make sure you check out book 1, of "The Brothers of Chi-Town", I Can't Let Go – now available for download and in paperback.

Carter Garrison vowed to love, honor and cherish his wife, Sienna, forsaking all others, something he forgot to do during a weekend of fun, bad company and poor judgement.

Sienna Garrison never dreamed her college sweetheart, Carter, whom she pledged her life to, would break her heart and when he did, she moved out and moved on - or tried to.

What better occasion is there than a friend's wedding to stir up old feelings and memories of love, intense passion and nights of sensual titillation. Gazes from across a room after almost two years apart revealed depths of love that had never died.

Seeing Sienna again reminded Carter of what he'd lost and he vowed to never let go by doing whatever he could to get his wife back even if it included begging and pleading. Is Sienna ready to forgive and take a chance on life again with the only man she'd ever really loved?

When Carter brings on the charm and turns up the heat, no woman is immune, especially Sienna.

Don't forget to snag your copy of book 2, Swagger and Baggage, in "The Brothers of Chi-Town" series – now available

It's not a coincidence that casino owner, Torrence Allen, ran into his college sweetheart, Reese Michaels again; it's fate. As his memories unfold, he had tried everything to keep her in his life and his bed back then and failed at both. She wasn't ready for him then, but he hopes she is ready for him now.

Reese Michaels never thought she'd see Torrence again. Their split in college was dramatic and hurtful and still, no man had been able to win her heart. She considered herself the permanent third wheel to friends who had found love and marriage.

Their whirlwind affair, quickly turned into love just as it suddenly crashed and burned when a woman shows up to claim Torrence as hers. When it's also revealed that this woman isn't the only 'other woman', Reese finds herself left with a broken heart, shattered love and dreams of forever beyond her reach. How did she not know about the other part of Torrence's active and amorous life?

Torrence isn't ready to give up on having Reese in his life after his deceit. He finds himself in the fight of his life to finally have the love and commitment he wanted only with her. His swagger had always won women over, but it's his baggage that's causing his life to spiral out of control and he could once again find himself without the woman he has always loved.

Have you checked out book 3 of, "The Brothers of Chi-Town" series, "Claiming His Child"?

Business magnate Dexter Patterson refused to let anything keep him from checking off all of the boxes equating to achievement in life to prove that though he came from a rough childhood on the south side of Chicago, he still thrived and became a success. Looking around at those closest to him, Dexter found that he was still missing something...Love.

When aspiring model, Alyssa Kincaid met Dexter, she couldn't get enough of his sexual magnetism, fiery nights of passion, and secret rendezvous. She thought they were headed toward forever when a surprising call from him ended what they had causing her to leave Chicago, taking with her a secret.

Dexter thought that no woman could ever tame him, not even Alyssa who entranced him with her sexy body, smoky, sultry voice and untamed desire. Too little, too late, he realized he'd made a mistake by walking away and then she was gone.

Will Alyssa continue to curse kismet when Dexter suddenly reappears in her life or will she believe that his yearning for her isn't just because of their child, but because when she left Chicago, she took his heart with her?

Don't miss book 4 of, "The Brothers of Chi-Town," series, "Always Bet on Black."

Sexy, debonair, Delvin "DJ" "Black" Michaels, left Chicago as a man in search of a better life than the one he had where everyone knew him as "Black". Being fair-skinned, his nickname wasn't because of the color of his skin, but was due to his inclination to always wear the color black from head to toe.

Avalon Hart had lived her life on the edge, making due the best way she knew how even if it meant scheming men out of their hard-earned money. She learned how to survive from the streets and she was a woman who had a way with men that got her whatever she wanted, that was until she encountered DJ Michaels in Chicago, a man from her past who she had once easily swayed to her desires. She realized early that the man she encountered in New York had grown immune to her tricks, even the ones she learned how to do in bed that he loved so much.

DJ and Avalon are on a roller coaster ride to love and neither knew it. There was no telling who would end up on top, but one thing was for sure – the road to getting there was going to be filled with hot, sexy fun, a pair of handcuffs and a whole lot of sensuality that neither could resist!

Are you ready for the fire and attitude that comes with book 5 of, "The Brothers of Chi-Town" series? Come get some in "It Takes Two to Tangle"- available now.

Councilman Tucker Glass, a native of Chicago, has set his eyes on the biggest prize, that of Mayor of the city he has loved all of his life. At thirty-nine, his career spans back many years as a City Council member and then most recently, as City Council President. His resume reads like a ratings-topper novel full of accomplishments that make him more than qualified for the job, but what he wants to avoid is the drama that could block his path to the Mayor's mansion. He's always been a strait-laced politician, but his personal life could spawn a real-life reality show complete with hair pulling, tongue-lashing and accusatory finger pointing which would all occur in the first episode.

Tucker wasn't expecting his past to come back to haunt him just as he'd found the woman who was making his life complete. He would do anything to keep her in his life, but is he willing to give up his run for the Mayor's office to keep that love in-tact?

Nichelle Michaels didn't know that love could be so right until she met and fell in love with Tucker Glass, a man fourteen years older and wiser than her, but who showed her how a man should treat a woman, and that's after she spent the past year testing the water between how a man loves and how a woman loves. Now that she knows what she wants, a woman from Tucker's past could ruin her perfect love.

Tucker and Nichelle are in love, but is he willing to risk his chance at being Mayor because his ex-wife, or the woman he thought was his ex-wife, wants to now be First Lady of Chicago? Was he really ready to tangle with a woman who specialized in drama every day on television as the star on the nation's number one reality show?

Tucker may be ready for Chicago, but is Chicago ready for the drama that comes along with the popular politician?

Get the next exciting installment of "The Brothers of Chi-Town" with "Crashing into Love", book 6, available in paperback and download in 2021

Joey Kincaid was all set to finally have the life he wanted as a professional wrestler. Scouts were looking at him and thanks to a family friend, he was able to showcase his talent at monthly wrestling matches at the Montiel Avage Casino in Chicago. Along with his brother, Carlos, the two of them were unstoppable. Just when he thought that all if his dreams were about to come through, a car crash curtailed his dreams and he was left not knowing if would ever wrestle again.

Marlow Warren was offered the job of a lifetime as a physical therapist in New York City. After growing up in Chicago, she was ready to leave one big city to trade it in for another. As she was saying her final goodbye to the city that brought her one tragedy after another, one wrong mistake behind the wheel of her car could cost a man his life and it would be her fault. She couldn't leave Chicago after that.

Never had anyone sad that a car crash was the best day of their life. Joey could say it, but then Marlow's past showed up and his life was headed for another collision and this time, he wasn't fighting for his life, he was fighting for love.

Available Now – True Lies or True Love
by Cheryl Barton

FBI Agent, Quintin Bell was sent to work undercover at Tee King Investment Securities to get proof that Carlos King, owner and hedge-fund boss, was embezzling money from his own employees' retirement accounts. In a chance encounter, he noticed Carlos' daughter, Meadow and before he could keep his heart from getting lost in her beauty, he found himself at a crossroads between doing his job and following his heart.

Meadow King wasn't looking for love that day in the café, but there was no way she could resist the handsome, rugged looks of a stranger when the intoxicating vibe between them became undeniable and irresistible. Unbeknownst to Meadow, the man she's fallen in love with has a secret that could not only ruin the love that grew between them, but it could topple her entire world.

Quintin knows that love can be real and it can be true, but his lies are what create a façade of their love affair and could cause it to crash and burn just as it has begun to heat up with passion that neither of them had ever experienced before nor could they see themselves without ever again. Quintin is running out of time in trying to find a way to do his job and hold on to the woman he loves. His biggest hurdle will be if he does his job, can he convince Meadow that his lies may have been true, but his love is truer!

Book 3, "Heartbreaker" of "A Lovers" Heart Series

In book 3, of "A Lovers' Heart" steamy romance series, Cameron Lymon, the sexy, youngest brother of Hollywood heartthrob, Cade Weston and Navy SEAL, Calvin Lymon, with his Master's degree in Journalism and a minor in Communications and Sports Management in hand, landed his dream job in Denver, Colorado as the co-host for a new morning talk show. Women love to call him the "Heartbreaker" because of the bevy of beautiful ladies he's left in his wake, not interested in giving up being a bachelor for falling in love. He enjoys taking after his big brother's old lifestyle of being a playboy.

Dakota Kane sacrificed a personal life and fought hard in her career to be the lead personality on Denver's top television morning show, but she was about to risk it all for passionate, steamy encounters with her new, much younger co-host, who is ten years younger and fifty shades hotter than any man she'd ever encountered. All he had to do was smile at her and she was a goner.

Cameron didn't know what he was in for when what he thought would be casual, behind closed door romps with the ever-so-sexy Dakota began to turn into much more when his heart became as invested in her as much as his body had. As things turned serious, his heartbreaker status came back to haunt him and his relationship with Dakota was threatened by his past.

Cameron and Dakota have to decide if what they are beginning to feel for each other is worth the risk of their careers when their secret love affair becomes the topic of public opinion and ridicule.

Connect with Cheryl Barton

www.cherylbarton.net
www.crbarton.com
www.amazon.com/author/cherylbarton

Instagram: @cherylbartonbooks
Twitter: @cbartonbooks
Facebook: @cherylbartonbooks

About the Author

Cheryl Barton lives in Maryland and in her spare time she loves to read espionage, crime and romance novels, cook, watch Sci-fi movies, spend time with family and friends and enjoy Maryland steamed crabs. Cheryl is celebrating 30 years as a government employee and loves writing romance novels when she's not working. Cheryl is the author of 31 romance novels, 3 inspirational novels and is proud of 4 book compilation projects with several other incredible women called, "One Sister Away: Encouraging Words from One Sister to Another" – a series of books meant to encourage, empower and inspire other women. People often ask Cheryl which book is her favorite of all of those she's written. While she finds it hard to select one favorite, Cheryl still looks to her first novel, Bachelor Not for Sale, if she had to pick a favorite because it was her first novel and the one that inspired her to continue writing.

Cheryl was a 2019 Finalist for the Emma Award given by Romance Slam Jam and a 2018 Finalist for the Literary Trailblazer of the Year award by the Indie Author Legacy Award. Cheryl is a member of the Romance Writers of America – National Chapter, the Maryland Romance Writers and the Contemporary Romance Writers groups, the Black Writers' Guild of Maryland and the International Women Writers Guild.

Indulge in more romance and inspirational novels by visiting her website at www.cherylbarton.net and connect with Cheryl on Facebook, Twitter and Instagram as @cherylbartonbooks.